IN THE FOREST OF FORGETTING

IN THE FOREST OF FORGETTING

∾

THEODORA GOSS

O prime books

Second edition, September 2006.
ISBN 0-8095-5691-X

"The Rose in Twelve Petals," *Realms of Fantasy*, April 2002. ∾ "Professor Berkowitz Stands on the Threshold," *Polyphony 2*, April 2003. ∾ "The Rapid Advance of Sorrow," *Lady Churchill's Rosebud Wristlet 11*, November 2002. ∾ "Lily, With Clouds," *Alchemy 1*, December 2003. ∾ "Miss Emily Gray," *Alchemy 2*, August 2004. ∾ "In the Forest of Forgetting," *Realms of Fantasy*, October 2003. ∾ "Sleeping With Bears," *Strange Horizons*, November 2003. ∾ "Letters from Budapest," *Alchemy 3*, April 2006. ∾ "The Wings of Meister Wilhelm," *Polyphony 4*, September 2004. ∾ "Conrad," original to this volume. ∾ "A Statement in the Case," *Realms of Fantasy*, August 2005. ∾ "Death Comes for Ervina," *Polyphony 5*, November 2005. ∾ "The Belt," *Flytrap 4*, May 2005. ∾ "Phalaenopsis," original to this volume. ∾ "Pip and the Fairies," *Strange Horizons*, October 2005. ∾ "Lessons with Miss Gray," *Fantasy Magazine 2*, May 2006.

Published in the United States by Prime Books.

www.prime-books.com

For Kendrick

TABLE OF

CONTENTS

INTRODUCTION
BY TERRI WINDLING

I first encountered the stories of Theodora Goss in the pages of the 'zine *Lady Churchill's Rosebud Wristlet* (edited by Kelly Link and Gavin Grant), which provides a forum for writers working at the literary and experimental edges of the fantasy field. At that time, I was co-editing *The Year's Best Fantasy and Horror* annual anthologies for St. Martin's Press, a job which entailed reading many hundreds of magical and surrealist stories each year. In such a deluge of fiction, it takes an exceptional writer to stand out among all the rest—yet from her very first publications, Goss's stories caused me to sit up and take notice. Here was a fresh and original voice, combined with an elegance of craft and an artist's eye for imagery. Her fiction is rooted in the Romantic and Gothic traditions, Victorian fantasy and fairy tales, yet it is also thoroughly contemporary, fashioning the tropes of such genres into new, unfamiliar forms. It is this deft combination of the old and the new that gives Goss's work its resonance; her stories lull the reader with the familiarity of a myth or a fairy tale re-told and then turn a sharp corner to reveal unexpected streets and vistas beyond. She is a master at evoking liminal spaces, those mysterious places and moments that lie "in between": the borderlands between countries, between historical eras, between the everyday and numinous worlds, between the shadowed streets of Eastern Europe and the sun drenched roads of America.

Goss was born in Hungary, crossing the Iron Curtain while she was still a child; she lived in Italy, then Belgium, and eventually settled in the United States. "My childhood is a collection of disjointed memories," she writes of her early years. "I remember water-weeds clinging to my legs as I hung from the edge of our wooden platform in Lake Balaton. I remember dangling double cherries from my ears - for propriety's sake, the only earrings I was allowed to wear. I remember the taste of *Madár Tej*, a sugary cloud of whipped egg whites floating on a pale yellow lake of yolk and milk. And I remember listening, at night, long after I was already supposed to be asleep, to stories from a book of Hungarian fairy tales. Hungarian fairy tales are frightening and sad. Soldiers go off to war, maidens die despite their innocence, witches are relentlessly wicked. I remember a picture of a dragon, green like linden leaves, writhing while the soldier he had eaten chopped open his side with a cavalry saber and emerged from his bowels. Red stained his vivid hide. Dragons were easy to understand. It was harder to understand why no one could know that we would soon be leaving the country, why I could not practice the English words I was learning in front of my friends.

"My mother had worked for a year in the United States as a medical student, and she had always wanted to return. She no longer wanted to live in Hungary, where everything seemed lost—land to redistribution, families to diaspora, history to propaganda—and where the air itself tasted of defeat. After her divorce she began the long process of leaving a country with closed borders, bribing officials with liquor and their secretaries with candy, sending money to her sister, who had been allowed to leave the country when she fell in love with and married an Italian. And then, one day, we were gone, a mother and two children over the border, with two suitcases full of children's clothes, a perfectly acceptable tourist visa, and no intention of returning. My mother had twenty-five dollars and a medical degree to sustain us.

"We lived for a time with my aunt in Milan, where I refused to eat a dinner of frogs' legs after a day of catching frogs on the paths between the flooded rice fields—to play with, I had thought. The next morning, I saw the skeleton of a frog next to the road, picked clean by ants. Just as Hungarian fairy tales had taught me terror, and my carefully rationed mouthfuls of *Madár Tej* had taught me delight, that skeleton, so delicately perfect, taught me the beauty of form. We lived for a time in Brussels, where we were taught, in school, to brush our teeth twice a day—my first introduction to the hygienic West. On Sundays the Grand Place was filled with flowers—and with parrots, who brought the colors of the tropics to that staid city, where every pedestrian seemed to be a teacher or a banker. And then, at last, a visa—the medical degree having worked its magic—and the lights of New York City, seen from the scratched oval of an airplane window. I had never seen anything so confusing in my life."

Goss goes on to reflect on how these early experiences shaped the woman, and the writer, that she eventually became. "We are, all of us, creatures of place," she says. "Even the roaming tribes of the Mongolian steppes or African grasslands have their seasonal routes, their preferred grazing grounds and water holes. Their places are wider than ours, but they are formed by them just as we are by a house our family has lived in over the years, a hill we have rolled down, a tree we have seen from a bedroom window since childhood. The places we live determine who we are. That is why homelessness is experienced as a loss of self. I had spent my childhood moving from country to country, learning language after language. When we landed that day in New York City, all of my possible selves seemed to have been lost, as though a baggage carrier had mislaid them in the airport of some country we had passed through. I still think, sometimes, of landing in Iceland and finding my younger selves there, grown up and living happily on the side of a glacier."

Goss's sense of displacement began to ease when she discovered the local library and found echoes of her early experiences in the pages of classic fantasy books: tales of young heroes who travel through unknown worlds both wondrous and strange. "I had lost one country after another, but now I discovered new ones, which could never be conquered by foreign powers and which required no passport when crossing the border. I traveled into Narnia through Lantern Waste, then went south to Aslan's How. I stopped for a week in the Shire and proceeded through the dark passes of Mirkwood to the Lonely Mountain. At some point I took a boat and sailed out to the West Reach, where the dragon Yevaud still curls around the hills of Pendor, guarding his treasure. I watched the sun play on the eddies in the River with Mole and Water Rat, ventured into the mysterious third story of Thornfield Hall, and looked down on London, sweeping past below, from a nest in North Wind's hair. I lived for a time, very happily, in the valleys of Nangiyala, then went adventuring again in the strange kingdoms where Azhriaz ruled.

"I read through elementary school, under the Japanese cherry trees that grow everywhere around Washington D.C., where we had moved so that my mother could work at the National Institutes of Health. In late spring, when the blossoms fell, the asphalt was covered with piles of fragrant pink petals, like the rags of a ball gown. I read through high school, in the National Museum of Art, on a bench in front of my favorite painting—a mid-Victorian allegory of golden-haired Youth sailing down a placid river on a boat piled high with flowers, whose sentimentality exactly suited my taste. I read through college, on the golf-course grass of the University of Virginia, surrounded by Thomas Jefferson's neoclassical columns, while my mind searched through the library of Miskatonic University for forbidden tomes, or wandered down the streets of Portsmouth, where in the alcoves albino beasts conducted unholy rites."

After completing a J.D. at Harvard Law School and working for several years at law firms in New York and Boston, Goss gave in to her passion for literature and decided to leave the law behind. She returned to school to complete an M.A. in English literature at Boston University, where she is currently working on a Ph.D. focusing on the Victorian gothic. She also teaches undergraduate courses on fantasy, and incorporates fantastic stories and poems into courses on more canonical literature. Goss's scholarly expertise in the realms of romantic and gothic literature forms the ground on which she builds the elegant, mordant, carefully-crafted stories for which she has become known. As a writer who has crossed many borders in her life, she moves easily across the category borders erected by the publishing industry, creating works that could be alternately labeled as fantasy, horror, magical realism, surrealism, revisionist fairy tales and gothic romance, or that fall into the interstitial realm that lies in-between these genres. As a scholar and a critic, she champions "interstitial fiction," a term used to identify, study, and celebrate works that cross the borders between literary categories; she is currently compiling an anthology of such works with co-editor Delia Sherman. "As a student studying literature," Goss writes, "I was told there were borders indeed: national (English, American, colonial), temporal (Romantic, Victorian, Modern), generic (fantastic, realistic). Some countries (the novel) you could travel to readily. The drinking water was safe, no immunizations were required. For some countries (the gothic), there was a travel advisory. The hotels were not up to standard; the trains would not run on time. Some countries (the romance) one did not visit except as an anthropologist, to observe the strange behavior of its inhabitants. And there were border guards (although they were called professors), to examine your travel papers as carefully as a man in an olive uniform with a red star on his cap. They could not stop you from crossing the border, but they would tell you what had been left out of your luggage, what was superfluous. Why the journey was a terrible idea in the first place.

"My problem is not with borders," Goss explains, "although they are often badly drawn, so that villages within sight of each other, whose inhabitants have intermarried for generations, are assigned to different countries, or Jane Austen, who acknowledged the influence of Ann Radcliffe, is placed in a different tradition. My problem is with the guards who say, 'You cannot cross the border.' Because when borders are closed, those on either side experience immobility and claustrophobia, and those who cross them (illegally, by night) suffer incalculable loss."

In the stories that follow, Goss is our travel guide across borders both real and imaginary: borders of time, of gender, of genre, of landscape, of culture, and of expectation. She is a writer unafraid to explore countries that lie far beyond the marked map of the fantasy field. Her stories enchant me, surprise me, and move me, and I can't wait to see where she travels next.

Terri Windling

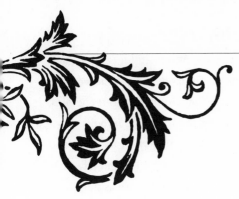

THE ROSE IN TWELVE PETALS

I ∾ THE WITCH

THIS ROSE HAS twelve petals. Let the first one fall: Madeleine taps the glass bottle, and out tumbles a bit of pink silk that clinks on the table—a chip of tinted glass—no, look closer, a crystallized rose petal. She lifts it into a saucer and crushes it with the back of a spoon until it is reduced to lumpy powder and a puff of fragrance.

She looks at the book again. "Petal of one rose crushed, dung of small bat soaked in vinegar." Not enough light comes through the cottage's small-paned windows, and besides she is growing near-sighted, although she is only thirty-two. She leans closer to the page. He should have given her spectacles rather than pearls. She wrinkles her forehead to focus her eyes, which makes her look prematurely old, as in a few years she no doubt will be. Bat dung has a dank, uncomfortable smell, like earth in caves that has never seen sunlight.

Can she trust it, this book? Two pounds ten shillings it cost her, including postage. She remembers the notice in *The Gentlewoman's Companion*: "Every lady her own magician. Confound your enemies, astonish your friends! As simple as a cookery manual." It looks magical enough, with *Compendium Magicarum* stamped on its spine and gilt pentagrams on its red leather cover. But the back pages advertise "a most miraculous lotion, that will make any lady's skin as smooth as an infant's bottom" and the collected works of Scott.

Not easy to spare ten shillings, not to mention two pounds, now that the King has cut off her income. Lather lucky, this cottage coming so cheap, although it has no proper plumbing, just a privy out back among the honeysuckle.

Madeleine crumbles a pair of dragonfly wings into the bowl, which is already half full: orris root; cat's bones found on the village dust heap; oak gall from a branch fallen into a fairy ring; madder, presumably for its color; crushed rose petal; bat dung.

And the magical words, are they quite correct? She knows a little Latin, learned from her brother. After her mother's death, when her father began spending days in his bedroom with a bottle of beer, she tended the shop, selling flour and printed cloth to the village women, scythes and tobacco to the men, sweets to children on their way to school. When her brother came home, he would sit at the counter beside her, saying his *amo, amas*. The silver cross he earned by taking a Hibernian bayonet in the throat is the only necklace she now wears.

She binds the mixture with water from a hollow stone and her own saliva. Not pleasant this, she was brought up not to spit, but she imagines she is spitting into the King's face, that first time when he came into the shop, and leaned on the counter, and smiled through his golden beard. "If I had known there was such a pretty shopkeeper in this village, I would have done my own shopping long ago."

She remembers: buttocks covered with golden hair among folds of white linen, like twin halves of a peach on a napkin. "Come here, Madeleine." The sounds of the palace, horses clopping, pageboys shouting to one another in the early morning air. "You'll never want for anything, haven't I told you that?" A string of pearls, each as large as her smallest fingernail, with a clasp of gold filigree. "Like it? That's Hibernian work, taken in the siege of London." Only later does she notice that between two pearls, the knotted silk is stained with blood.

She leaves the mixture under cheesecloth, to dry overnight.

Madeleine walks into the other room, the only other room of the cottage, and sits at the table that serves as her writing desk. She picks up a tin of throat lozenges. How it rattles. She knows, without opening it, that there are five pearls left, and that after next month's rent there will only be four.

Confound your enemies, she thinks, peering through the inadequate light, and the wrinkles on her forehead make her look prematurely old, as in a few years she certainly will be.

II ∾ THE QUEEN

PETALS FALL FROM the roses that hang over the stream, Empress Josephine and Gloire de Dijon, which dislike growing so close to the water. This corner of the garden has been planted to resemble a country landscape in miniature: artificial stream with ornamental fish, a pear tree that has never yet bloomed, bluebells that the gardener plants out every spring. This is the Queen's favorite part of the garden, although the roses dislike her as well, with her romantically diaphanous gowns, her lisping voice, her poetry.

Here she comes, reciting Tennyson.

She holds her arms out, allowing her sleeves to drift on the slight breeze, imagining she is Elaine the lovable, floating on a river down to Camelot. Hard, being a lily maid now her belly is swelling.

She remembers her belly reluctantly, not wanting to touch it, unwilling to acknowledge that it exists. Elaine the lily maid had no belly, surely, she thinks, forgetting that Galahad must have been born somehow. (Perhaps he rose out of the lake?) She imagines her belly as a sort of cavern, where something is growing in the darkness, something that is not hers, alien and unwelcome.

Only twelve months ago (fourteen, actually, but she is bad at numbers), she was Princess Elizabeth of Hibernia, dressed in pink satin, gossiping about the riding master with her friends, dancing with her brothers through the ruined arches of Westminster Cathedral, and eating too much cake at her seventeenth birthday party. Now, and she does not want to think about this so it remains at the edges of her mind, where unpleasant things, frogs and slugs, reside, she is a cavern with something growing inside her, something repugnant, something that is not hers, not the lily maid of Astolat's.

She reaches for a rose, an overblown Gloire de Dijon that, in a fit of temper, pierces her finger with its thorns. She cries out, sucks the blood from her finger, and flops down on the bank like a miserable child. The hem of her diaphanous dress begins to absorb the mud at the edge of the water.

III ∾ THE MAGICIAN

WOLFGANG MAGUS PLACES the rose he picked that morning in his buttonhole and looks at his reflection in the glass. He frowns, as his master Herr Doktor Ambrosius would have frowned, at the scarecrow in faded wool with a drooping gray mustache. A sad figure for a court magician.

"Gott in Himmel," he says to himself, a childhood habit he has kept from nostalgia, for Wolfgang Magus is a reluctant atheist. He knows it is not God's fault but the King's, who pays him so little. If the King were to pay him, say, another shilling per week—but no, that too he would send to his sister, dying of consumption at a spa in Berne. His mind turns, painfully, from the memory of her face, white and drained, which already haunts him like a ghost.

He picks up a volume of Goethe's poems that he has carefully tied with a bit of pink ribbon and sighs. What sort of present is this, for the Princess' christening?

He enters the chapel with shy, stooping movements. It is full, and noisy with court gossip. As he proceeds up the aisle, he is swept by a Duchess' train of peau de soie, poked by a Viscountess' aigrette. The sword of a Marquis smelling of Napoleon-water tangles in his legs, and he almost falls on a Baroness, who stares at him through her lorgnette. He sidles through the crush until he comes to a corner of the chapel wall, where he takes refuge.

The christening has begun, he supposes, for he can hear the Archbishop droning in bad Latin, although he can see nothing from his corner but taxidermed birds and heads slick with macassar oil. Ah, if the Archbishop could have learned from Herr Doktor Ambrosius! His mind wanders, as it often does, to a house in Berlin and a laboratory smelling of strong soap, filled with braziers and alembics, books whose covers have been half-eaten by moths, a stuffed basilisk. He remembers his bed in the attic, and his sister, who worked as the Herr Doktor's housemaid so he could learn to be a magician. He sees her face on her pillow at the spa in Berne and thinks of her expensive medications.

What has he missed? The crowd is moving forward, and presents are being given: a rocking horse with a red leather saddle, a silver tumbler, a cap embroidered by the nuns of Iona. He hides the volume of Goethe behind his back.

Suddenly, he sees a face he recognizes. One day she came and sat beside him in the garden, and asked him about his sister. Her brother had died, he remembers, not long before, and as he described his loneliness, her eyes glazed over with tears. Even he, who understands little about court politics, knew she was the King's mistress.

She disappears behind the scented Marquis, then appears again, close to the altar where the Queen, awkwardly holding a linen bundle, is receiving the Princess' presents. The King has seen her, and frowns through his golden beard. Wolfgang Magus, who knows nothing about the feelings of a king toward his former mistress, wonders why he is angry.

She lifts her hand in a gesture that reminds him of the Archbishop. What fragrance is this, so sweet, so dark, that makes the brain clear, that makes the nostrils water? He instinctively tabulates: orris-root, oak gall, rose petal, dung of bat with a hint of vinegar.

Conversations hush, until even the Baronets, clustered in a rustic clump at the back of the chapel, are silent.

She speaks: "This is the gift I give the Princess. On her seventeenth birthday she will prick her finger on the spindle of a spinning wheel and die."

Needless to describe the confusion that follows. Wolfgang Magus watches from its edge, chewing his mustache, worried, unhappy. How her eyes glazed, that day in the garden. Someone treads on his toes.

Then, unexpectedly, he is summoned. "Where is that blasted magician!" Gloved hands push him forward. He stands before the King, whose face has turned unattractively red. The Queen has fainted and a bottle of salts is waved under her nose. The Archbishop is holding the Princess, like a sack of barley he has accidentally caught.

"Is this magic, Magus, or just some bloody trick?"

6

Wolfgang Magus rubs his hands together. He has not stuttered since he was a child, but he answers, "Y–yes, your Majesty. Magic." Sweet, dark, utterly magic. He can smell its power.

"Then get rid of it. Un-magic it. Do whatever you bloody well have to. Make it not be!"

Wolfgang Magus already knows that he will not be able to do so, but he says, without realizing that he is chewing his mustache in front of the King, "O–of course, your Majesty."

IV ∾ THE KING

WHAT WOULD YOU do, if you were James IV of Britannia, pacing across your council chamber floor before your councilors: the Count of Edinburgh, whose estates are larger than yours and include hillsides of uncut wood for which the French Emperor, who needs to refurbish his navy after the disastrous Indian campaign, would pay handsomely; the Earl of York, who can trace descent, albeit in the female line, from the Tudors; and the Archbishop, who has preached against marital infidelity in his cathedral at Aberdeen? The banner over your head, embroidered with the twelve-petaled rose of Britannia, reminds you that your claim to the throne rests tenuously on a former James' dalliance. Edinburgh's thinning hair, York's hanging jowl, the seams, edged with gold thread, where the Archbishop's robe has been let out, warn you, young as you are, with a beard that shines like a tangle of golden wires in the afternoon light, of your gouty future.

Britannia's economy depends on the wool trade, and spun wool sells for twice as much as unspun. Your income depends on the wool tax. The Queen, whom you seldom think of as Elizabeth, is young. You calculate: three months before she recovers from the birth, nine months before she can deliver another child. You might have an heir by next autumn.

"Well?" Edinburgh leans back in his chair, and you wish you could strangle his wrinkled neck.

You say, "I see no reason to destroy a thousand spinning wheels for one madwoman." Madeleine, her face puffed with sleep, her neck covered with a line of red spots where she lay on the pearl necklace you gave her the night before, one black hair tickling your ear. Clever of her, to choose a spinning wheel. "I rely entirely on Wolfgang Magus," whom you believe is a fraud. "Gentlemen, your fairy tales will have taught you that magic must be met with magic. One cannot fight a spell by altering material conditions."

Guffaws from the Archbishop, who is amused to think that he once read fairy tales.

You are a selfish man, James IV, and this is essentially your fault, but you have spoken the truth. Which, I suppose, is why you are the King.

V ∾ THE QUEEN DOWAGER

WHAT IS THE girl doing? Playing at tug-of-war, evidently, and far too close to the stream. She'll tear her dress on the rosebushes. Careless, these young people, thinks the Queen Dowager. And who is she playing with? Young Lord Harry, who will one day be Count of Edinburgh. The Queen Dowager is proud of her keen eyesight and will not wear spectacles, although she is almost sixty-three.

What a pity the girl is so plain. The Queen Dowager jabs her needle into a black velvet slipper. Eyes like boiled gooseberries that always seem to be staring at you, and no discipline. Now in her day, thinks the Queen Dowager, remembering backboards and nuns who rapped your fingers with canes, in her day girls had discipline. Just look at the Queen: no discipline. Two miscarriages in ten years, and dead before her thirtieth birthday. Of course linen is so much cheaper now that the kingdoms are united. But if only her Jims (which is how she thinks of the King) could have married that nice German princess.

She jabs the needle again, pulls it out, jabs, knots. She holds up the slipper and then its pair, comparing the roses embroidered on each toe in stitches so even they seem to have been made by a machine. Quite perfect for her Jims, to keep his feet warm on the drafty palace floors.

A tearing sound, and a splash. The girl, of course, as the Queen Dowager could have warned you. Just look at her, with her skirt ripped up one side and her petticoat muddy to the knees.

"I do apologize, Madam. I assure you it's entirely my fault," says Lord Harry, bowing with the superfluous grace of a dancing master.

"It *is* all your fault," says the girl, trying to kick him.

"Alice!" says the Queen Dowager. Imagine the Queen wanting to name the girl Elaine. What a name, for a Princess of Britannia.

"But he took my book of poems and said he was going to throw it into the stream!"

"I'm perfectly sure he did no such thing. Go to your room at once. This is the sort of behavior I would expect from a chimney sweep."

"Then tell him to give my book back!"

Lord Harry bows again and holds out the battered volume. "It was always yours for the asking, your Highness."

Alice turns away, and you see what the Queen Dowager cannot, despite her keen vision: Alice's eyes, slightly prominent, with irises that are indeed the color of gooseberries, have turned red at the corners, and her nose has begun to drip.

VI ∾ THE SPINNING WHEEL

IT HAS NEVER wanted to be an assassin. It remembers the cottage on the Isles where it was first made: the warmth of the hearth and the feel of its maker's hands, worn smooth from rubbing and lanolin.

It remembers the first words it heard: "And why are you carving roses on it, then?"

"This one's for a lady. Look how slender it is. It won't take your upland ram's wool. Yearling it'll have to be, for this one."

At night it heard the waves crashing on the rocks, and it listened as their sound mingled with the snoring of its maker and his wife. By day it heard the crying of the sea birds. But it remembered, as in a dream, the songs of inland birds and sunlight on a stone wall. Then the fishermen would come, and one would say, "What's that you're making there, Enoch? Is it for a midget, then?"

Its maker would stroke it with the tips of his fingers and answer, "Silent, lads. This one's for a lady. It'll spin yarn so fine that a shawl of it will slip through a wedding ring."

It has never wanted to be an assassin, and as it sits in a cottage to the south, listening as Madeleine mutters to herself, it remembers the sounds of seabirds and tries to forget that it was made, not to spin yarn so fine that a shawl of it will slip through a wedding ring, but to kill the King's daughter.

VII ∾ THE PRINCESS

ALICE CLIMBS THE tower stairs. She could avoid this perhaps, disguise herself as a peasant woman and beg her way to the Highlands, like a heroine in Scott's novels. But she does not want to avoid this, so she is climbing up the tower stairs on the morning of her seventeenth birthday, still in her nightgown and clutching a battered copy of Goethe's poems whose binding is so torn that the book is tied with pink ribbon to keep the pages together. Her feet are bare, because opening the shoe closet might have woken the Baroness, who has slept in her room since she was a child. Barefoot, she has walked silently past the sleeping guards, who are supposed to guard her today with particular care. She has walked past the Queen Dowager's drawing room thinking: if anyone hears me, I will be in disgrace. She has spent a larger portion of her life in disgrace than out of it, and she remembers that she once thought of it as an imaginary country, Disgrace, with its own rivers and towns and trade routes. Would it be different if her mother were alive? She remembers a face creased from the folds of the pillow, and pale lips whispering to her about the lily maid of Astolat. It would, she supposes, have made no difference. She trips on a step and almost drops the book.

She has no reason to suppose, of course, that the Witch will be there, so early in the morning. But somehow, Alice hopes she will be.

She is, sitting on a low stool with a spinning wheel in front of her.

"Were you waiting for me?" asks Alice. It sounds silly—who else would the Witch be waiting for? But she can think of nothing else to say.

"I was." The Witch's voice is low and cadenced, and although she has wrinkles at the corners of her mouth and her hair has turned gray, she is still rather beautiful. She is not, exactly, what Alice expected.

"How did you know I was coming so early?"

The Witch smiles. "I've gotten rather good at magic. I sell fortunes for my living, you see. It's not much, just enough to buy bread and butter, and to rent a small cottage. But it amuses me, knowing things about people—their lives and their futures."

"Do you know anything—about me?" Alice looks down at the book. What idiotic questions to be asking. Surely a heroine from Scott's novels would think of better.

The Witch nods, and sunlight catches the silver cross suspended from a chain around her neck. She says, "I'm sorry."

Alice understands, and her face flushes. "You mean that you've been watching all along. That you've known what it's been like, being the cursed princess." She turns and walks to the tower window, so the Witch will not see how her hands are shaking. "You know the other girls wouldn't play with me or touch my toys, that the boys would spit over their shoulders, to break the curse they said. Even the chambermaids would make the sign of the cross when I wasn't looking." She can feel tears where they always begin, at the corners of her eyes, and she leans out the window to cool her face. Far below, a gardener is crossing the courtyard, carrying a pair of pruning shears. She says, "Why didn't you remove the curse, then?"

"Magic doesn't work that way." The Witch's voice is sad. Alice turns around and sees that her cheeks are wet with tears. Alice steps toward her, trips again, and drops the book, which falls under the spinning wheel.

The Witch picks it up and smiles as she examines the cover. "Of course, your Goethe. I always wondered what happened to Wolfgang Magus."

Alice thinks with relief: I'm not going to cry after all. "He went away, after his sister died. She had consumption, you know, for years and years. He was always sending her money for medicine. He wrote to me once after he left, from Berlin, to say that he had bought his old master's house. But I never heard from him again."

The Witch wipes her cheeks with the back of one hand. "I didn't know about his sister. I spoke to him once. He was a kind man."

Alice takes the book from her, then says, carefully, as though each word has to be placed in the correct order, "Do you think his spell will work? I mean, do you think I'll really sleep for a hundred years, rather than—you know?"

The Witch looks up, her cheeks still damp, but her face composed. "I can't answer that for you. You may simply be—preserved. In a pocket of time, as it were."

Alice tugs at the ribbon that binds the book together. "It doesn't matter, really. I don't think I care either way." She strokes the spinning wheel, which turns as she touches it. "How beautiful, as though it had been made just for me."

The Witch raises a hand, to stop her perhaps, or arrest time itself, but Alice places her finger on the spindle and presses until a drop of blood blossoms, as dark as the petal of a Cardinal de Richelieu, and runs into her palm.

Before she falls, she sees the Witch with her head bowed and her shoulders shaking. She thinks, for no reason she can remember, Elaine the fair, Elaine the lovable . . .

VIII ❧ THE GARDENER

LONG AFTER, WHEN the gardener has grown into an old man, he will tell his grandchildren about that day: skittish horses being harnessed by panicked grooms, nobles struggling with boxes while their valets carry armchairs and even bedsteads through the palace halls, the King in a pair of black velvet slippers shouting directions. The cooks leave the kettles whistling in the kitchen, the Queen Dowager leaves her jewels lying where she has dropped them while tripping over the hem of her nightgown. Everyone runs to escape the spreading lethargy that has already caught a canary in his cage, who makes soft noises as he settles into his feathers. The flowers are closing in the garden, and even the lobsters that the chef was planning to serve with melted butter for lunch have lain down in a corner of their tank.

In a few hours, the palace is left to the canary, and the lobsters, and the Princess lying on the floor of the tower.

He will say, "I was pruning a rosebush at the bottom of the tower that day. Look what I took away with me!" Then he will display a rose of the variety called Britannia, with its twelve petals half-open, still fresh and moist with dew. His granddaughter will say, "Oh, grandpa, you picked that in the garden just this morning!" His grandson, who is practical and wants to be an engineer, will say, "Grandpa, people can't sleep for a hundred years."

IX ∾ THE TOWER

LET US GET a historical perspective. When the tower was quite young, only a hovel really, a child knocked a stone out of its wall, and it gained an eye. With that eye it watched as the child's father, a chieftain, led his tribe against soldiers with metal breastplates and plumed helmets. Two lines met on the plain below: one regular, gleaming in the morning sun like the edge of a sword, the other ragged and blue like the crest of a wave. The wave washed over the sword, which splintered into a hundred pieces.

Time passed, and the tower gained a second story with a vertical eye as narrow as a staff. It watched a wooden structure grow beside it, in which men and cattle mingled indiscriminately. One morning it felt a prick, the point of an arrow. A bright flame blossomed from the beams of the wooden structure, men scattered, cattle screamed. One of its walls was singed, and it felt the wound as a distant heat. A castle rose, commanded by a man with eyebrows so blond that they were almost white, who caused the name Aelfric to be carved on the lintel of the tower. The castle's stone walls, pummelled with catapults, battered by rams, fell into fragments. From the hilltop a man watched, whose nose had been broken in childhood and remained perpetually crooked. When a palace rose from the broken rock, he caused the name D'Arblay to be carved on the lintel of the tower, beside a boar rampant.

Time passed, and a woman on a white horse rode through the village that had grown around the palace walls, followed by a retinue that stretched behind her like a scarf. At the palace gates, a Darbley grown rich on tobacco plantations in the New World presented her with the palace, in honor of her marriage to the Earl of Essex. The lintel of the tower was carved with the name Elizabeth I, and it gained a third story with a lead-paned window, through which it saw in facets like a fly. One morning it watched the Queen's son, who had been playing ball in the courtyard, fall to the ground with blood dripping from his nostrils. The windows of the palace were draped in black velvet, the Queen and her consort rode away with their retinue, and the village was deserted.

Time passed. Leaves turned red or gold, snow fell and melted into rivulets, young hawks took their first flight from the battlements. A rosebush grew at the foot of the tower: a hybrid, half wild rose, half Cuisse de Nymphe, with twelve petals and briary canes. One morning men rode up to the tower on horses whose hides were mottled with sweat. In its first story, where the chieftain's son had played, they talked of James III. Troops were coming from France, and the password was Britannia. As they left the tower, one of them plucked a flower from the rosebush. "Let this be our symbol," he said in the self-conscious voice of a man who thinks that his words will be recorded in history books. The tower thought it would be alone again, but by the time the leaves had turned, a procession rode up to the palace gates, waving banners embroidered with a twelve-petaled rose. Furniture arrived from France, fruit trees were planted, and the village streets were paved so that the hooves of cattle clopped on the stones.

It has stood a long time, that tower, watching the life around it shift and alter, like eddies in a stream. It looks down once again on a deserted village—but no, not entirely deserted. A woman still lives in a cottage at its edge. Her hair has turned white, but she works every day in her garden, gathering tomatoes and cutting back the mint. When the day is particularly warm, she brings out a spinning wheel and sits in the garden, spinning yarn so fine that a shawl of it will slip through a wedding ring. If the breezes come from the west, the tower can hear her humming, just above the humming that the wheel makes as it spins. Time passes, and she sits out in the garden less often, until one day it realizes that it has not seen her for many days, or perhaps years.

Sometimes at night it thinks it can hear the Princess breathing in her sleep.

X ∿ THE HOUND

IN A HUNDRED years, only one creature comes to the palace: a hound whose coat is matted with dust. Along his back the hair has come out in tufts, exposing a mass of sores. He lopes unevenly: on one of his forepaws, the inner toes have been crushed.

He has run from a city reduced to stone skeletons and drifting piles of ash, dodging tanks, mortar fire, the rifles of farmers desperate for food. For weeks now, he has been loping along the dusty roads. When rain comes, he has curled himself under a tree. Afterward, he has drunk from puddles, then loped along again with mud drying in the hollows of his paws. Sometimes he has left the road and tried to catch rabbits in the fields, but his damaged paw prevents him from running quickly enough. He has smelled them in their burrows beneath the summer grasses, beneath the poppies and cornflowers, tantalizing, inaccessible.

This morning he has smelled something different, pungent, like spoiled meat: the smell of enchantment. He has left the road and entered the forest, finding his way through a tangle of briars. He has come to the village, loped up its cobbled streets and through the gates of the palace. His claws click on its stone floor.

What does he smell? A fragrance, drifting, indistinct, remembered from when he was a pup: bacon. There, through that doorway. He lopes into the Great Hall, where breakfast waits in chafing dishes. The eggs are still firm, their yolks plump and yellow, their whites delicately fried. Sausages sit in their own grease. The toast is crisp.

He leaves a streak of egg yolk and sausage grease on the table-cloth, which has remained pristine for half a century, and falls asleep in the Queen Dowager's drawing room, in a square of sunlight that has not faded the baroque carpet.

He lives happily ever after. Someone has to. As summer passes, he wanders through the palace gardens, digging in the flower beds and trying to catch the sleeping fish that float in the ornamental pools. One day he urinates on the side of the tower, from which the dark smell emanates, to show his disapproval. When he is hungry he eats from the side of beef hanging in the larder, the sausage and eggs remaining on the breakfast table, or the mice sleeping beneath the harpsichord. In autumn, he chases the leaves falling red and yellow over the lawns and manages to pull a lobster from the kitchen tank, although his teeth can barely crack its hard shell. He never figures out how to extract the canary from its cage. When winter comes, the stone floor sends an ache through his damaged paw, and he sleeps in the King's bed, under velvet covers.

When summer comes again, he is too old to run about the garden. He lies in the Queen Dowager's drawing room and dreams of being a pup, of warm hands and a voice that whispered "What a beautiful dog," and that magical thing called a ball. He dies, his stomach still full with the last of the poached eggs. A proper fairy tale should, perhaps, end here.

XI ∾ THE PRINCE

HERE COMES THE Prince on a bulldozer. What did you expect? Things change in a hundred years.

Harry pulls back the break and wipes his forehead, which is glistening with sweat. He runs his fingers through blond hair that stands up like a shock of corn. It is just past noon, and the skin on his nose is already red and peeling.

Two acres, and he'll knock off for some beer and that liver and onion sandwich Madge made him this morning, whose grease, together with the juice of a large gherkin, is soaking its way through a brown paper wrapper and will soon stain the leather of his satchel. He leans back, looks at the tangle of briars that form the undergrowth in this part of the forest, and chews on the knuckle of his thumb.

Two acres in the middle of the forest, enough for some barley and a still. Hell of a good idea, he thinks, already imagining the bottles on their way to Amsterdam, already imagining his pals Mike and Steve watching football on a color telly. Linoleum on the kitchen floor, like Madge always wanted, and cigarettes from America. "Not that damn rationed stuff," he says out loud, then looks around startled. What kind of fool idiot talks to himself? He chews on the knuckle of his thumb again. Twenty pounds to make the Police Commissioner look the other way. Damn lucky Madge could lend them the money. The bulldozer starts up again with a roar and the smell of diesel.

You don't like where this is going. What sort of Prince is this, with his liver and onion sandwich, his gherkin and beer? Forgive me. I give you the only Prince I can find, a direct descendant of the Count of Edinburgh, himself descended from the Tudors, albeit in the female line. Of course, all such titles have been abolished. This is, after all, the Socialist Union of Britannia. If Harry knows he is a Prince, he certainly isn't telling Mike or Steve, who might sell him out for a pack of American cigarettes. Even Madge can't be trusted, though they've been sharing a flat in the commune's apartment building for three years. Hell, she made a big enough fuss about the distillery business.

The bulldozer's roar grows louder, then turns into a whine. The front wheel is stuck in a ditch. Harry climbs down and looks at the wheel. Damn, he'll have to get Mike and Steve. He kicks the wheel, kicks a tree trunk and almost gets his foot caught in a briar, kicks the wheel again.

Something flashes in the forest. Now what the hell is that? (You and I know it is sunlight flashing from the faceted upper window of the tower.) Harry opens his beer and swallows a mouthful of its warm bitterness. Some damn poacher, walking around on his land. (You and I remember that it belongs to the Socialist Union of Britannia.) He takes a bite of his liver and onion sandwich. Madge shouldn't frown so much, he thinks, remembering her in her housecoat, standing by the kitchen sink. She's getting wrinkles on her forehead. Should he fetch Mike and Steve? But the beer in his stomach, warm, bitter, tells him that he doesn't need Mike and Steve, because he can damn well handle any damn poacher himself. He bites into the gherkin.

Stay away, Prince Harry. Stay away from the forest full of briars. The Princess is not for you. You will never stumble up the tower stairs, smelling of beer; never leave a smear of mingled grease and sweat on her mouth; never take her away (thinking, Madge's rump is getting too damn broad) to fry your liver and onions and empty your ashtray of cigarette butts and iron your briefs.

At least, I hope not.

XII ❧ THE ROSE

LET US GO back to the beginning: petals fall. Unpruned for a hundred years, the rosebush has climbed to the top of the tower. A cane of it has found a chink in the tower window, and it has grown into the room where the Princess lies. It has formed a canopy over her, a network of canes now covered with blossoms, and their petals fall slowly in the still air. Her nightgown is covered with petals: this summer's, pink and fragrant, and those of summers past, like bits of torn parchment curling at the edges.

While everything in the palace has been suspended in a pool of time without ripples or eddies, it has responded to the seasons. Its roots go down to dark caverns which are the homes of moles and worms, and curl around a bronze helmet that is now little more than rust. More than two hundred years ago, it was rather carelessly chosen as the emblem of a nation. Almost a hundred years ago, Madeleine plucked a petal of it for her magic spell. Wolfgang Magus picked a blossom of it for his buttonhole, which fell in the chapel and was trampled under a succession of court heels and cavalry boots. A spindle was carved from its dead and hardened wood. Half a century ago, a dusty hound urinated on its roots. From its seeds, dispersed by birds who have eaten its orange hips, has grown the tangle of briars that surround the palace, which have already torn the Prince's work pants and left a gash on his right shoulder. If you listen, you can hear him cursing.

It can tell us how the story ends. Does the Prince emerge from the forest, his shirtsleeve stained with blood? The briars of the forest know. Does the Witch lie dead, or does she still sit by the small-paned window of her cottage, contemplating a solitary pearl that glows in the wrinkled palm of her hand like a miniature moon? The spinning wheel knows, and surely its wood will speak to the wood from which it was made. Is the Princess breathing? Perhaps she has been sleeping for a hundred years, and the petals that have settled under her nostrils flutter each time she exhales. Perhaps she has not been sleeping, perhaps she is an exquisitely preserved corpse, and the petals under her nostrils never quiver. The rose can tell us, but it will not. The wind sets its leaves stirring, and petals fall, and it whispers to us: you must find your own ending.

This is mine. The Prince trips over an oak log, falls into a fairy ring, and disappears. (He is forced to wash miniature clothes, and pinched when he complains.) Alice stretches and brushes the rose petals from her nightgown. She makes her way to the Great Hall and eats what is left in the breakfast dishes: porridge with brown sugar. She walks through the streets of the village, wondering at the silence, then hears a humming. Following it, she comes to a cottage at the village edge where Madeleine, her hair now completely white, sits and spins in her garden. Witches, you know, are extraordinarily long-lived. Alice says, "Good morning," and Madeleine asks, "Would you like some breakfast?" Alice says, "I've had some, thank you." Then the Witch spins while the Princess reads Goethe, and the spinning wheel produces yarn so fine that a shawl of it will slip through a wedding ring.

Will it come to pass? I do not know. I am waiting, like you, for the canary to lift its head from under its wing, for the Empress Josephine to open in the garden, for a sounds that will tell us someone, somewhere, is awake.

PROFESSOR BERKOWITZ
STANDS ON THE THRESHOLD

I ❧ THE SUN RISES IN AN ECSTASY OF BRIGHTNESS

WHEN THE SUN rose, Alistair Berkowitz realized that he was standing on a beach. His slippers were covered with sand, and cold water was seeping up the bottoms of his pajamas. He could smell the sea, and as the mist began to dissipate he could see it, a line of gray motion closer than he had imagined. He stood beside a tidal pool, which was probably responsible for the uncomfortable feeling of wet fabric around his ankles. In it, iridescent snails crawled over a rock. In the distance, he heard the scream of a gull. He shivered. The wind off the water was cold.

Then the sun shone on the water, creating a gold pathway, and he said without thinking,

the sun rises in an ecstasy of brightness,
like a lion shaking its mane, like a chrysanthemum
discovering itself

"Ah, you speak English."

Berkowitz turned so quickly that he lost a slipper and had to find it again in the sand. The man behind him was dressed in a suit of purple velvet. Dark hair hung over his eyes. It looked as though he had combed it with his fingers.

"Myself, I speak English also. My mother, when she was sober, told me my father was an English duke. When she was drunk, she told me he was a Russian sailor. Unfortunately I speak no Russian."

Berkowitz stared at him, then looked down at his slippers and shifted his feet. Why was he wearing pajamas? He rubbed his hands in an effort to warm them. "I'm assuming," he said, "that this is a dream. Sorry to imply that you're a figment of my imagination."

"Pas du tout," said the man in the purple suit, smiling. His teeth were crooked, which gave his smile the charm of imperfection. "Although as for that, perhaps you are a—how you say? Figment of my imagination. Perhaps I am lying with my head on the table of a café in Montmartre, and Céline is drawing a mustache over my mouth with charcoal, while that scoundrel Baudelaire is laughing into his absinthe. Perhaps all of this," he extended his arms in a gesture that took in the rocks behind them, and the sand stretching down to the water, and the sun that was rising and covering the gray sky with a wash of gold, "is all in my head. Including you, mon ami. Although why I should dream of an Englishman . . ."

"American," said Berkowitz. "I'm American. From Vermont." Then, putting his hands in his pajama pockets, he said, "I'm a professor. At a university."

"Ah," said the man in the purple suit. "If my father were an English duke, I might have travelled to the land of Edgar Poe. It is a difficult question. Did my mother lie when she was drunk, or when she was sober?"

"I mean," Berkowitz continued, annoyed at the interruption. It was what he habitually said when students interrupted his lectures with ringing cell phones. "I mean, I'm not an art historian. But Baudelaire. 'Le Visage Vert,' about the death of the painter Eugène Valentin, poisoned by his mistress Céline la Creole. At a café in Montmartre. It makes sense for a professor of comparative literature to dream of Eugène Valentin. Not the other way around."

Valentin looked up at the sky. "Citron, with blanc de chine and strips of gris payne. Ah, Céline. Did you love me enough to poison me?"

Berkowitz shifted his feet again, trying to knock sand off his slippers. A gull flew over them, its wings flashing black and silver in the sunlight. How much longer would he remain a professor of comparative literature? Next week was his tenure evaluation. The department chairman had never believed in his research, never recognized the importance of Marie de la Roche. No wonder he was talking to a man in a purple suit, on a beach, in pajamas.

"And is she a figment of your imagination as well?" asked Valentin.

A woman was walking toward them, along the edge of the water. Her skin had the sheen of metal, and she was entirely hairless, from her bald head to her bare genitals. She had no breasts. Berkowitz would have assumed she was a boy, except that she lacked the usual masculine accoutrements.

Berkowitz stared at her and rubbed the bridge of his nose.

"If I imagined a female form," Valentin added, "it would look like Venus, not Ganymede."

The woman stopped a few feet away from them and, without speaking, turned and looked at the water. The two men turned as well. Between the sky and the sea, both of which were rapidly beginning to turn blue, a black speck was moving toward them.

"What is it?" he asked Valentin. He really should get glasses.

Valentin brushed his hair back from his eyes. "A ship. At last, I believe something is beginning to happen."

II ∾ SEASHELLS, WHOSE CURVES ARE AS INTRICATE AS MADNESS

THE HARBOR WAS built of stone blocks, so large that Berkowitz wondered how they had been moved. Like those statues on Easter Island. He looked over the side of the ship, at the waves below. If he were in someone else's dream, he would disappear when the dreamer woke up. What did that remind him of? Humpty Dumpty, he thought, and realized that he had answered in Helen's voice. Once, they had gone to Nantucket together. He remembered her sitting on the beach under a straw hat, taking notes for her article on the feminist implications of the Oz books. He wondered how she liked Princeton, and tenure.

He stumbled as the ship pitched and rolled.

Valentin opened his eyes. "You have kicked my elbow." He had been asleep for the last hour, with his head on a coil of rope.

"Sorry," said Berkowitz. The metallic woman was sitting on the other side of the deck, legs crossed and eyes closed. She seemed to be meditating. About noon, Berkowitz had decided to call her Metallica.

Valentin sat up and combed his fingers through his hair. "Have you considered that perhaps we are dead? If, as you say, I am poisoned . . ."

Berkowitz looked around the deck and up at the sails. "This isn't exactly my idea of death."

"Ah," said Valentin. "Are they still dancing, les petits grotesques?"

They were not dancing, exactly. But they moved over the deck and among the rigging, women with the calves of soccer players below gossamer tunics, like the workings of an intricate machine.

Berkowitz said, "At first I thought they were wearing masks."

One had the head of a cat as blue as a robin's egg, with fins for ears. Another, the head of a parrot covered with scales, the green and yellow and orange of an angelfish. Another, a pig's head with the beak of a toucan. This one had taken Berkowitz's hand and said in a hoarse voice, as though just getting over the flu, "The Luminous Vessel. The Endless Sea." Then he had realized they were not wearing masks after all. Now, they seemed to be taking down the sails.

"You know," he said to Valentin, "I think we've arrived."

Metallica rose and walked to their part of the ship. She looked over the side, at the harbor and the water below.

Berkowitz whispered, "I wonder if she's a robot?"

"Look at their legs," said Valentin, rising. "So firm. I wonder . . ."

The path from the harbor was covered with stone chips. Berkowitz felt them through his slippers, edged and uncomfortable. They walked through a thicket of bushes with small white flowers.

Ahead of him, Valentin was trying to put his arm around Catwoman's waist. Berkowitz touched him on the shoulder. "Feathers," he said. "Not flowers. See, on the bushes. They're growing feathers."

"Yes?" said Valentin. "I have made a discovery also, mon ami." Catwoman took the opportunity to walk ahead. "She is a flirt, that one. But look, you see our silver-plated friend?" Ahead of them, Metallica and Pigwoman walked together. They were gesturing rapidly to one another.

"Are they playing a game?" asked Berkowitz.

"I think," said Valentin, "it is a conversation."

They emerged from the bushes. Ahead of them was a castle. At least, thought Berkowitz, it looks more like a castle than anything else.

It was built of the same stone blocks as the harbor, but on one side it seemed to have grown spines. On the other, metal beams extended like a spider's legs. Towers rose, narrowing as they spiraled upward. What did they remind him of? Something from under the sea—probably seashells. He suddenly understood why Marie de la Roche had compared seashells to madness. The castle glittered in the sunlight, as though carved from sugar.

They passed through a courtyard carpeted with moss and randomly studded with rocks, like a Zen landscape. They passed under a doorway shaped, thought Berkowitz, like the jawbone of a whale. He felt as though he were being swallowed.

The room they entered seemed to confirm that impression. It was large, with a ceiling ribbed like a whale's skeleton. Pale light filled the room, from windows with panes like layers of milk glass. Valentin's footsteps echoed. Berkowitz could even hear the shuffle of his slippers reverberating.

At the other end of the room, he saw robed figures, huddled together. They looked like professors in academic robes. In the moment it took for his eyes to adjust to the light, he imagined they were discussing his tenure evaluation. But when they turned, he clutched Valentin's arm. They were not wearing masks either. One had the head of a stag, its horns tipped with inquisitive eyes. Another was a boar, with bristles like butterfly wings. Another seemed to be a serpent with spotted fur. Their robes were a random patchwork of satin, burlap, and what looked like plastic bags, held together with gold thread and bits of straw.

They moved apart to reveal an ordinary kitchen chair, painted a chipped and fading green. On it was sitting a girl in a white dress, sewn at the sleeves and hem with bleached twigs, coral beads, pieces of bone. Her hair was held back by a gold net. She looked like she had been dressed for a school play.

Pigwoman curtsied. "The Endless Sea," she said. "The August Visitors."

The girl rose from her chair. "Bienvenu, Monsieur Valentin. Welcome, Professor Berkowitz." She turned toward Metallica and bowed. Metallica answered with a movement of her fingers.

"I understand you have been communicating in English," she continued. "I shall do the same. Aeiou, of course, requires no verbal interpretation."

The collection of vowels, Berkowitz assumed, was Metallica's name. He stared at the girl. What had Helen told him? "Look at Alice, and Ozma. Literature, at least imaginative literature, is ruled by adolescent girls." Then she had leaned across the library table, with her elbows on a biography of Verlaine, and asked him on their first date.

"Of course you have already learned one another's qualifications?" She looked at them, as though expecting confirmation. "No? Well then. Eugène Valentin, perhaps most celebrated for your *Narcisse à l'Enfer*. Although *L'Orchidée Noire*, your painting of the dancer Céline la Creole, is equally magnificent, Monsieur. Professor Alistair Berkowitz, translator of the fragmentary poems of Marie de la Roche. I am, of course, addressing you chronologically. Aeiou, follower of Vasarana, the goddess of wisdom, once temple singer for the goddess." She turned to Valentin and Berkowitz. "Her name, as you may have guessed, is a chanted prayer. I have not pronounced it correctly. Her vocal chords were surgically removed during incarceration, to prevent her from spreading the teachings of her sect. Professor, I believe you have heard of American Sign Language? She has asked me to tell you that she wishes you the blessings of wisdom."

She looked at them, as though waiting for a response.

They looked at each other. Valentin shrugged. Then, simultaneously, Valentin said, "We are pleased to make her acquaintance," and

Berkowitz blurted, "I don't understand. Who are you? Where are we? What kind of dream is this, anyway?"

She raised her eyebrows. "I am the Questioner. Haven't you discussed this at all among yourselves? Surely you must have realized that you have come to the Threshold."

III ∾ THE SEA IS AS DEEP AS DEATH, AND AS FILLED WITH WHISPERS

VALENTIN AND BERKOWITZ stared at the mossy courtyard.

"This garden was planted to represent the known world," said the Questioner. "The mosses, of course, represent the Endless Sea, with darker varieties for the depths, lighter for the relative shallows. And there," she pointed to a central area where rocks were clustered, "are the Inner Islands. That gray one is your island."

"I still don't understand," Berkowitz whispered to Valentin.

Valentin looked back at the doorway, where Pigwoman stood as though on guard. "I wonder if she is so firm everywhere, mon ami?" he whispered.

Berkowitz edged away from him. Did he have to share his dream with a lecherous Frenchman?

"Around the Inner Islands lies the Endless Sea," said the Questioner, "unnavigable except in the Luminous Vessel. Anyone sailing to the Outer Islands must stop here, at the Threshold."

She turned to them and smiled as though she had explained everything.

"I still don't understand," he said.

The Questioner frowned. She looked, thought Berkowitz, as though she were trying to solve an algebra problem. "Professor Berkowitz, I have tried to suit my explanation to your understanding. But you are a man of the space age. Perhaps if I call those central rocks the Inner Planets, and the mosses an Endless Space, and tell you that you can only reach the Outer Planets in the Luminous Rocketship. To a tribesmen I might speak of the Inner Huts. Aeiou, who needs no explanation, understands them as representations of Inner Consciousness. The result is the same. Tomorrow I will ask you the Question, and based on your answer you will either return to the Inner Islands, or proceed onward."

"But I still don't . . ." said Berkowitz.

"Excellent," said Valentin. "Look, mon ami. We are from there." He pointed to the central cluster of rocks. "But we have qualifications, as she said. You have your book, I have my paintings, and our companion of the vowels has evidently been singing. If we answer her question correctly, we will be allowed to go on."

"But to where?" asked Berkowitz, with exasperation. He was coming to the uncomfortable conviction that, rather than dreaming, he was probably going mad. Perhaps he was at that moment being strapped into a straitjacket.

"Out, out!" said Valentin. "Have you never wanted to go out and away?"

He suddenly remembered a story he had told Helen, when they had been together for almost a year. One morning in high school, the captain of the wrestling team had locked him into the boy's bathroom, shouting, "Man, if my name were Alistair, I would have drowned myself at birth!" He had wanted, more than anything, to go out and away. Away from the small town in New Jersey, away from his father, a small town lawyer who could not understand why he had wanted to study something as useless as literature. Helen had smiled at him across the scrambled eggs and said, "Lucky for me you had a lousy childhood."

Perhaps that was why he had become interested in Marie de la Roche. She had wanted to go out and away. Away from her parents' olive trees, away from the convent. He imagined her, on her cliff beside the sea, in a hut made of driftwood lashed together with rope. Each morning she climbed down its nearly perpendicular face to gather seaweed and whatever the sea had left in tidal pools: crabs, mussels, snails. Fishermen claimed her broth could revive drowned men. Each afternoon she sat on her cliff and wrote, on driftwood with sharp rocks, on scraps of her habit with cuttlefish ink, and sent the fragments flying. Fishermen believed they brought a good catch. He thought of the year he had spent studying her fragments, now in a case at the Musée National. How many had been lost, buried by sand or floating out to sea? She had found her way out, through madness and suicide. Fishermen had built a church in her honor, and in certain parts of Brittany she was still considered a saint. Was that what had fascinated him, her willingness to toss everything—her poems, herself—over a cliff?

Valentin and the Questioner were staring at him. How long had he been standing there, lost in thought?

"Perhaps," said the Questioner, "if I showed you the Repository?"

It looked like a museum. Where the walls were not covered with shelves, they were covered with tapestries, paintings, photographs. Metal staircases twisted upward to balconies, containing more shelves. They were filled with books and scrolls, disappearing upward into the shadows of the ceiling. Toward the center of the room were glass cases filled with manuscripts, small statues, things he did not recognize. One looked like a collection of sea sponges. They passed a sculpture that looked suspiciously like the *Nike of Samothrace*, and the skeleton of a rhinoceros painted blue. "Not bad, that," said Valentin, examining it with admiration.

"By those who have come to the Threshold," said the Questioner. "I believe my collection is fairly complete." At the end of the room was a fireplace. Over it hung Van Gogh's *Irises*. She walked to a long table that looked like it belonged in a public school library. "Ah," she said, "the collected works of Keats. I wondered where I had left it." She opened a box on the table, which began to play music, low and melancholy, that Berkowitz faintly recognized. "Lady Day," she said. "And of course Elihu's *Lamia*." She tapped her index finger on one of the glass cases. A green glow levitated and stretched elegant tendrils toward her, like an art nouveau octopus. "So simple, yet so satisfying."

"My *Narcisse*, is it here?" asked Valentin.

"I will show it to you," said the Questioner. "But I believe Professor Berkowitz would like to see this." She opened a glass case and took out a scrap of fabric. "When Marie de a Roche leaped into the sea, she held this in her hand. It was the last piece of her habit. She gave it to me, when she passed through the Threshold."

Berkowitz took the linen, which looked fresh although worn, as though it had never touched sea water. He recognized her angled writing. Mentally, he translated into rough iambs and anapests:

the sea is as deep as death, and as filled with whispers
of the past

She had been here. She had walked through the Threshold. He wondered what sort of question he would be asked, and whether he would pass the test.

IV ∽ MY MIND CRAWLS, LIKE A SNAIL, AROUND ONE THOUGHT

BERKOWITZ DRANK THROUGH a course of tangerine fish and fish-shaped tangerines, through a course of translucent jellies. The liquid in his glass was the color of amber, and shards of gold leaf floated in it. It tasted like peaches and burned his throat going down. Every once in a while he had to peel gold leaf from his teeth.

He looked down the table and felt a throbbing start in his left temple. A woman with what looked like a flamingo on her head winked at him. The flamingo winked as well. Too much fur, too many wings, and not a single nose was the correct shape or size. The Abominable Snowman jogged his elbow.

He stared at his soup, which tasted like celery.

The Questioner leaned over to him and said, "Aeiou is a neighbor of yours. She comes from Connecticut."

"Oh," said Berkowitz. She smiled encouragingly, as though waiting for him to respond with something clever. He said, "Connecticut isn't really that close to Vermont." He tried to laugh and knocked over his bowl, which looked like a sea urchin. Soup spilled over the table.

She turned to Stagman, who was sitting on her other side.

Damn, thought Berkowitz. I've already failed. Who made up the rules of this game anyway?

The Questioner rose. "I believe it's time for a quadrille. Are the musicians ready?"

They evidently were, because the music began.

The Questioner led with Stagman. Valentin, who was learning the steps as he went along, capered behind Pigwoman.

Berkowitz drank, and despised them all. He despised the musicians, playing citoles, lyres, pipes that curled like the necks of swans, and what looked like the lid of a trash can. He despised the dancers, gliding or shuffling or hopping in complicated figures he could not understand. He despised Aeiou, weaving through them in a dance of her own, and Valentin, who kept treading on Pigwoman's toes. He despised himself, which had never been difficult for him. The department would never give him tenure. The chairman had told him that Marie de la Roche was marginal. Hell, how much more marginal could you get than an insane nun living on a cliff? He should have written a book on Baudelaire. He should have stayed in New Jersey and become a lawyer. By the time he began to despise Marie de la Roche, on her damn rock, with her damn poetry, the room was beginning to look distinctly lopsided.

"Enough," said the Questioner. The music, which had been drifting from a waltz to cacophony, ceased. Valentin stopped abruptly and would have fallen, except that his arm was wrapped around Pigwoman's waist. "It is time for your questions."

Already? thought Berkowitz. I didn't even have a chance to study.

"Tomorrow morning, as you know, I will ask each of you the Question that will determine whether you step through the Threshold." There she went again with her "as you know." As though they knew anything. "Tonight, however, you may each ask me a question of your own."

Stagman brought her green chair, and she sat in the middle of the room. Light flickered from candles and oil lamps and fluorescent bulbs. That explained why the room was beginning to blur. Berkowitz pinched the bridge of his nose. Helen had been right—he should get glasses.

Valentin, who had been trying to kiss Pigwoman's neck, stumbled and kissed the air. He must be drunk, thought Berkowitz.

"Aeiou will begin," said the Questioner. Aeiou gestured. The pain spread to Berkowitz's right temple. God, he needed an aspirin.

She smiled and nodded. "Your songs will be sung for a thousand years, until the factories and prisons of the Imperium return to dust, and pomegranates grow on Manhattan Island."

Aeiou bowed her head, and metallic tears ran down her cheeks. The audience clapped.

Damn, thought Berkowitz. This must be part of the test. The Questioner looked at him. Not me, he thought. Not yet. I need time to think.

"Monsieur Valentin," she said. "What would you like to ask me?"

Valentin looked down at the floor, then said, "Did she poison me? Céline."

The Questioner looked amused. "Yes, in the absinthe. If you choose not to return, she will wear black orchids in your memory." The audience clapped. The Abominable Snowman giggled, and Catwoman nudged whoever was standing beside her.

What a stupid question, thought Berkowitz. That won't get him any brownie points. He tried to think of something profound.

The Questioner said, "And finally, Professor Berkowitz."

Profound. What was the most profound question he could think of? He needed a hundred aspirins. She was leaning toward him, waiting for his question. Berkowitz said, "Is there a God?"

She leaned back in her chair. She seemed disappointed, or perhaps just tired. "Yes," she said. "Once, she would visit our island. We would work in the garden together, tying back the roses. But she has grown old, and sleeps a great deal now. I do not know what will happen when—but that wasn't your question."

There was a moment of silence. Then the audience clapped, without enthusiasm. A thousand aspirins, that's what he needed. Berkowitz took another drink and despised the universe.

Later, lying in bed and trying to keep the room from spinning, he thought about the test. Clearly, he had already failed. All the failures of his life gathered around him. Failing to make the soccer team because he couldn't kick worth a damn. Failing calculus. Failing to get into Yale. Failing with Helen, who had waited for him in the kitchen, under a lightbulb he had forgotten to replace, with the letter from Princeton in her hand. "Tell me," she had said. "How am I supposed to compete with a dead nun?" Failing his tenure evaluation, because he already knew he would fail.

Marie de la Roche had not failed. She had succeeded at going mad, at committing suicide, at becoming a saint. She had stepped through the Threshold.

The question. His mind crawled around it like a snail.

Valentin would get through, because the Questioner liked him. Look at the way she had answered him tonight. She didn't like Berkowitz. The question. His mind crawled around and around it, in the darkness.

V ∾ FAITH, LIKE A SEAGULL HANGING IN MID-AIR

BERKOWITZ WOKE WITH the sun shining on his face and a headache that made him long for swift decapitation. Seeing no sign of breakfast, he walked to the moss garden. Valentin was standing with his hands in his pockets, staring at the central rocks.

"Sleep well?" asked Berkowitz. His voice sounded unnaturally loud, and his tongue was a piece of lead covered with felt.

"No," said Valentin. "That is, I did not sleep. She was very firm, the petit cochon." He smiled to himself.

"What do you think the question will be?" asked Berkowitz. He had no desire to learn the details of Pigwoman's anatomy.

Valentin shrugged and touched a rock with the tip of his shoe. "A little gray stone. Just what one would expect, no?"

Stagman walked into the courtyard. He looked at Valentin and said, "The Ambiguous Threshold."

"My turn," said Valentin. "The one of the vowels has already gone."

"Good luck," said Berkowitz.

"Mon ami," said Valentin, "I suspect luck has nothing to do with it."

When Valentin had gone, Berkowitz walked around the garden, looking at the Outer Islands. Rocks, no different than the ones in the central cluster. Rocks scattered across a carpet of moss.

He looked down at his pajamas. They were badly wrinkled, and one sleeve was spotted with soup. Didn't that prove this was a dream? Showing up for an exam in pajamas. One of the classic scenarios. Lucky he wasn't naked. He wondered if Marie de la Roche had been.

"The Ambiguous Threshold." Stagman was waiting for him. Berkowitz felt a sudden impulse to shake him by the shoulders and beg him to say something, anything, else—to get one real answer in this place. His stomach gave a queasy rumble. They could at least have fed him breakfast.

Instead, he followed Stagman into the garden. They passed between rosebushes that seemed to whisper as he walked by. Berkowitz looked closely and realized, with distaste, that the petals on the roses were pink tongues. They passed a fountain, in which waterlilies croaked like frogs. In alcoves on either side of the path, ornamental cherries were weeping on the heads of stone nymphs that were evidently turning into foxes, owls, rabbits—or all of them at once. He brushed against a poppy, which fluttered sepals that looked like lashes.

Beyond the fountain was a hedge of Featherbushes, with an opening cut into it, like an arch. Berkowitz followed Stagman through the archway.

The hedge grew in a circle, its only opening the one they had passed through. Grass grew over the ground, so soft under his slippers that Berkowitz wanted to take them off and walk barefoot. He had often gone barefoot as a child, but he could not remember what it felt like, walking on grass. The grass was spotted with daisies that were, for once, actually daisies.

At the center of the circle was a stone arch, shaped like the arch in the hedge, but built of the same blocks as the harbor and the castle. Its top and sides were irregular, and broken blocks lay scattered on the grass beside it, as though it were the final remnant of some monumental architecture. Sitting on one of those blocks was the Questioner.

"Good morning, Professor," she said. Today she was wearing a blue dress decorated with bits of glass. Her hair hung in two braids tied with blue ribbons.

"Good morning," said Berkowitz, trying to put as much irony into his voice as he could with a felted tongue. The silence in the circle made him uncomfortable. Even the sound of the fountain was muted.

The Questioner rose and asked, "Are you ready for the Question?"

"I guess," he said. He looked at Stagman, waiting with his hands folded together, like the Dalai Lama. This had to be a dream.

"Would you like to step through the Threshold?"

"What," said Berkowitz, "you mean now?"

"That is the Question, Professor. The only Question there is. Would you like to step through the Threshold?"

Berkowitz stared at her, and then at the arch. "You mean that thing?" Through it he could see the hedge, and grass spotted with daisies.

The Questioner sighed. "That thing is the Threshold. Everything you see around you, including myself, is what you might call an emanation of it. If you step through it, you will proceed to the Outer Islands."

"So that's the whole test?"

"There is no test," said the Questioner. "There is only the Question. Would you like to step through the Threshold?"

"What if I don't?" asked Berkowitz.

"You will, of course, return to the Inner Islands."

"You mean I'll be back at the university?"

"Yes," said the Questioner. "You will return to your life, as though you had never left it. You will forget that you once stood on the Threshold, or you will think of it as a dream whose details you can never quite remember."

"And if I do?"

The Questioner tugged at one of her braids. For the first time, she looked like an impatient child. "You will, of course, proceed to the Outer Islands." She added, slowly and with emphasis, "As I have previously explained."

"What about the university?"

"You will appear to have died. Probably of a heart attack. Your diet, Professor, is particularly conducive." She gave him a lopsided smile, which looked almost sympathetic. "Unless you would prefer suicide?"

"Died?" said Berkowitz. "No one said anything about dying. If I go back to the Inner Islands, whatever they are, will I ever come here again?"

"No one gets more than one chance to stand on the Threshold."

"Why?" asked Berkowitz. "Look, here are the things I want to know. What exactly are the Outer Islands? What will I be if I go there? Will I be me or something else, like a chicken man with daisies growing out of my head?"

"Enough," said the Questioner. She was no longer smiling. "I am a questioner, not an answerer. When Marie de la Roche stepped through the Threshold, she said,

la foi, une mouette suspendue
au milieu de l'air

Professor Berkowitz, will you step through the Threshold?"

Berkowitz looked at her, standing beside the archway. He looked at the arch itself, and through it at the hedge. A breeze ruffled the feathers on the bushes.

He thought of returning to the house they had rented, without Helen. Without the smell of her vegetarian lasagna, without her voice, which would suddenly, even while reading the newspaper, begin reciting "Jabberwocky." To his bookshelves, now relatively bare. He thought of gray rocks scattered across a moss courtyard. Of the collected works of Keats, a woman with a flamingo on her head, roses whispering as he walked by. Of the university, and his students with their ringing cell phones. Perhaps Helen would call. He did not think so.

Then he looked at Stagman, who was rubbing the side of one furred cheek. This was a dream, and next week was his tenure evaluation.

"No," he said. The Questioner nodded with finality. He looked at her for an excruciating moment, then put his hands over his eyes. He waited to wake up.

THE RAPID
ADVANCE OF SORROW

I SIT IN one of the cafés in Szent Endre, writing this letter to you, István, not knowing if I will be alive tomorrow, not knowing if this café will be here, with its circular green chairs and cups of espresso. By the Danube, children are playing, their knees bare below school uniforms. Widows are knitting shapeless sweaters. A cat sleeps beside a geranium in the café window.

If you see her, will you tell me? I still remember how she appeared at the University, just off the train from Debrecen, a country girl with badly-cut hair and clothes sewn by her mother. That year, I was smoking French cigarettes and reading forbidden literature. "Have you read D. H. Lawrence?" I asked her. "He is the only modern writer who convincingly expresses the desires of the human body." She blushed and turned away. She probably still had her Young Pioneers badge, hidden among her underwear.

"Ilona is a beautiful name," I said. "It is the most beautiful name in our language." I saw her smile, although she was trying to avoid me.

Her face was plump from country sausage and egg bread, and dimples formed at the corners of her mouth, two on each side.

She had dimples on her buttocks, as I found out later. I remember them, like craters on two moons, above the tops of her stockings.

∾

SORROW: A FEELING of grief or melancholy. A mythical city generally located in northern Siberia, said to have been visited by Marco Polo. From Sorrow, he took back to Italy the secret of making ice.

∾

THAT AUTUMN, INTELLECTUAL apathy was in fashion. I berated her for reading her textbooks, preparing for her examinations. "Don't you know the grades are predetermined?" I said. "The peasants receive ones, the bourgeoisie receive twos, the aristocrats, if they have been admitted under a special dispensation, always receive threes."

She persisted, telling me that she had discovered art, that she wanted to become cultured.

"You are a peasant," I said, slapping her rump. She looked at me with tears in her eyes.

∾

THE PRINCIPAL EXPORT of Sorrow is the fur of the arctic fox, which is manufactured into cloaks, hats, the cuffs on gloves and boots. These foxes, which live on the tundra in family groups, are hunted with falcons. The falcons of Sorrow, relatives of the kestrel, are trained to obey a series of commands blown on whistles carved of human bone.

∾

SHE BEGAN GOING to museums. She spent hours at the Vár-muzeum, in the galleries of art. Afterward, she would go to cafés, drink espressos, smoke cigarettes. Her weight dropped, and she became as lean as a wolfhound. She developed a look of perpetual hunger.

When winter came and ice floated on the Danube, I started to worry. Snow had been falling for days, and Budapest was trapped in a white silence. The air was cleaner than it had been for months, because the Trabants could not make it through the snow. It was very cold.

She entered the apartment carrying her textbooks. She was wearing a hat of white fur that I had never seen before. She threw it on the sofa.

"Communism is irrelevant," she said, lighting a cigarette.

"Where have you been?" I asked. "I made a paprikás. I stood in line for two hours to buy the chicken."

"There is to be a new manifesto." Ash dropped on the carpet. "It will not resemble the old manifesto. We are no longer interested in political and economic movements. All movements from now on will be purely aesthetic. Our actions will be beautiful and irrelevant."

"The paprikás has congealed," I said.

She looked at me for the first time since she had entered the apartment and shrugged. "You are not a poet."

∾

THE POETRY OF Sorrow may confuse anyone not accustomed to its intricacies. In Sorrow, poems are constructed on the principle of the maze. Once the reader enters the poem, he must find his way out by observing a series of clues. Readers failing to solve a poem have been known to go mad. Those who can appreciate its beauties say that the poetry of Sorrow is impersonal and ecstatic, and that it invariably speaks of death.

SHE BEGAN BRINGING home white flowers: crocuses, hyacinths, narcissi. I did not know where she found them, in the city, in winter. I eventually realized they were the emblems of her organization, worn at what passed for rallies, silent meetings where communication occurred with the touch of a hand, a glance from the corner of an eye. Such meetings took place in secret all over the city. Students would sit in the pews of the Mátyás Church, saying nothing, planning insurrection.

At this time we no longer made love. Her skin had grown cold, and when I touched it for too long, my fingers began to ache.

We seldom spoke. Her language had become impossibly complex, referential. I could no longer understand her subtle intricacies.

She painted the word ENTROPY on the wall of the apartment. The wall was white, the paint was white. I saw it only because soot had stained the wall to a dull gray, against which the word appeared like a ghost.

One morning I saw that her hair on the pillow had turned white. I called her name, desperate with panic. She looked at me and I saw that her eyes were the color of milk, like the eyes of the blind.

IT IS INSUFFICIENT to point out that the inhabitants of Sorrow are pale. Their skin has a particular translucence, like a layer of nacre. Their nails and hair are iridescent, as though unable to capture and hold light. Their eyes are, at best, disconcerting. Travelers who have stared at them too long have reported hallucinations, like mountaineers who have stared at fields of ice.

∞

I EXPECTED TANKS. Tanks are required for all sensible invasions. But spring came, and the insurrection did nothing discernible.

Then flowers appeared in the public gardens: crocuses, hyacinths, narcissi, all white. The black branches of the trees began to sprout leaves of a delicate pallor. White pigeons strutted in the public squares, and soon they outnumbered the ordinary gray ones. Shops began to close: first the stores selling Russian electronics, then clothing stores with sweaters from Bulgaria, then pharmacies. Only stores selling food remained open, although the potatoes looked waxen and the pork acquired a peculiar transparency.

I had stopped going to classes. It was depressing, watching a classroom full of students, with their white hair and milky eyes, saying nothing. Many professors joined the insurrection, and they would stand at the front of the lecture hall, the word ENTROPY written on the board behind them, communicating in silent gestures.

She rarely came to the apartment, but once she brought me poppy seed strudel in a paper bag. She said, "Péter, you should eat." She rested her fingertips on the back of my hand. They were like ice. "You have not joined us," she said. "Those who have not joined us will be eliminated."

I caught her by the wrist. "Why?" I asked.

She said, "Beauty demands symmetry, uniformity."

My fingers began to ache with cold. I released her wrist. I could see her veins flowing through them, like strands of aquamarine.

∾

SORROW IS RULED by the absolute will of its Empress, who is chosen for her position at the age of three and reigns until the age of thirteen. The Empress is chosen by the Brotherhood of the Cowl, a quasi-religious sect whose members hide their faces under hoods of white wool to maintain their anonymity. By tradition, the Empress never speaks in public. She delivers her commands in private audiences with the Brotherhood. The consistency of these commands, from one Empress to another, has been taken to prove the sanctity of the Imperial line. After their reigns, all Empresses retire to the Abbey of St. Alba, where they live in seclusion for the remainder of their lives, studying astronomy, mathematics, and the seven-stringed zither. During the history of Sorrow, remarkable observations, theorems, and musical arrangements have emerged from this Abbey.

∾

NO TANKS CAME, but one day, when the sun shone with a vague luminescence through the clouds that perpetually covered the city, the Empress of Sorrow rode along Váci Street on a white elephant. She was surrounded by courtiers, some in cloaks of white fox, some in jesters' uniforms sewn from white patches, some, principally unmarried women, in transparent gauze through which one could see their hairless flesh. The eyes of the elephant were outlined with henna, its feet were stained with henna. In its trunk it carried a silver bell, whose ringing was the only sound as the procession made its way to the Danube and across Erzsébet Bridge.

Crowds of people had come to greet the Empress: students waving white crocuses and hyacinths and narcissi, mothers holding the hands of children who failed to clap when the elephant strode by, nuns in ashen gray. Cowled figures moved among the crowd. I watched one standing ahead of me and recognized the set of her shoulders, narrower than they had been, still slightly crooked.

I sidled up to her and whispered, "Ilona."

She turned. The cowl was drawn down and I could not see her face, but her mouth was visible, too thin now for dimples.

"Péter," she said, in a voice like snow falling. "We have done what is necessary."

She touched my cheek with her fingers. A shudder went through me, as though I had been touched by something electric.

❧

TRAVELLERS HAVE ATTEMPTED to characterize the city of Sorrow. Some have said it is a place of confusion, with impossible pinnacles rising to stars that cannot be seen from any observatory. Some have called it a place of beauty, where the winds, playing through the high buildings, produce a celestial music. Some have called it a place of death, and have said that the city, examined from above, exhibits the contours of a skull.

Some have said that the city of Sorrow does not exist. Some have insisted that it exists everywhere: that we are perpetually surrounded by its streets, which are covered by a thin layer of ice; by its gardens, in which albino peacocks wander; by its inhabitants, who pass us without attention or interest.

❧

I BELIEVE NEITHER of these theories. I believe that Sorrow is an insurrection waged by a small cabal, with its signs and secrets; that it is run on purely aesthetic principles; that its goal is entropy, a perpetual stillness of the soul. But I could be mistaken. My conclusions could be tainted by the confusion that spreads with the rapid advance of Sorrow.

So I have left Budapest, carrying only the mark of three fingertips on my left cheek. I sit here every morning, in a café in Szent Endre, not knowing how long I have to live, not knowing how long I can remain here, on a circular green chair drinking espresso.

Soon, the knees of the children will become as smooth and fragile as glass. The widows' knitting needles will click like bone, and geranium leaves will fall beside the blanched cat. The coffee will fade to the color of milk. I do not know what will happen to the chair. I do not know if I will be eliminated, or given another chance to join the faction of silence. But I am sending you this letter, István, so you can remember me when the snows come.

LILY, WITH CLOUDS

ELEANOR TOLLIVER'S HEELS clicked on the sidewalk—click click, click click, like a cantering horse, if a horse could canter in size 7½ shoes. It was odd, this lopsided step, in a woman whose lavender suit had been bought last week at Lord and Taylor. Really, she admitted to herself as she clicked down Elm Street, she should not have bought the narrows. The left shoe, in particular, pressed against her corn and produced the cantering gait we have noticed. And this was fitting because Eleanor, in spite of her lavender suit and matching handbag, looked like nothing so much as a horse.

The Eliots had always been horsy. The men had ridden hard, shot straight, and drunk whiskey. Their women had ruled the social world of Ashton, North Carolina. Any of them could show you the foundations of a house destroyed in what they still privately referred to as The War. If you looked carefully, you could see the stump of a column among the lilac bushes. When a daughter of the house, in the irresponsible twenties, had run off with a black chauffeur, her name in the family Bible had been scratched over with ink. The Eliots were rich and respectable. On Sundays, they took up the first two pews of the Methodist church.

Eleanor had been a quintessential Eliot. Although her face had the approximate dimensions of a shoe box, its length fitted her particular type of beauty, which was angular and expensive. Charles Tolliver had felt himself lucky to catch the oldest Eliot girl, when he was only a junior partner at her father's law office. The youngest, now, he wouldn't have touched with a ten foot pole, in spite of her father's money.

Poor Lily, thought Eleanor, clicking past the hardware store that was going out of business now a Walmart had opened fifteen miles down the interstate. She had been an inadequate Eliot, an unsatisfying sister. Instead of being angular, she had been round, with startled brown eyes and a figure that Eleanor in her less generous moments described as chubby. Instead of Sweet Briar, which had matriculated three generations of Eliot women, she had gone to an art school in New York. There, she had met and presumably married an artist. Presumably was the word Eleanor used to her friends. After all, no one had been invited to her wedding with András Horvath, and although Lily wrote a letter about it afterward, since when was Lily to be trusted? Look at how she had burned Eleanor's school uniform by leaving a hot iron on it, in ninth grade. The artist had died in an airplane crash. He had been flying alone and probably, Eleanor told her friends, drunk. Afterward, Eleanor had assumed Lily would move back to Ashton. But she had stayed in New York.

This thought brought Eleanor to a gate that was half off its hinges, which anyway were attached to a fence that was half fallen over from the masses of honeysuckle climbing over it. Just like Lily, to come back not to Eleanor's house, where she and Charles had lived since her father's death, but to this shack with its peeling paint and its gutters hanging down from the roof. Everyone would think Eleanor had refused to take her sister in. How perfectly unfair. She would have put Lily in the guest bedroom, which had lavender-scented liners in all of the drawers. Lily could have shared a bathroom with Jane.

Eleanor smiled at this reminder of her evolutionary success. Jane had the sandy Eliot hair, the angular Eliot features. Everyone said she would grow up to be as attractive as her mother. On her last report card from Saint Catherine's, Sister Michael had written, "Jane is a bright girl, who could accomplish a great deal if she would only apply herself." Catholics were so good at educating girls.

As if she had unconsciously internalized her clicking, Eleanor repeated its pattern on the door: knock knock, knock knock. After an impatient moment, which she spent inspecting her fingernails, manicured a week ago and painted in Chanel Pink Fantasy, someone opened the door.

Someone might have been a housekeeper or a hospital nurse, but she held out her hand and, in a voice Eleanor would later describe to everyone as "New York, you know, though I'm sure she's a very nice woman," invited Eleanor into the house. "I'm Sarah Goldstein. Lily probably wrote about me."

Eleanor refrained from mentioning that Lily had rarely written, and that even her last postcard, with a picture of the Statue of Liberty on it, has said only, "Dying of cancer. Coming home June 7, 2:30 p.m. Charlotte. Could you send Charles to pick me up? Lots of baggage. Love, Lil." Charles had talked about her baggage all through dinner. "You know what she had?" He spooned more mashed potatoes onto his plate. In the last two years, his waist had expanded. If he didn't stop eating so much, he would have hips like a woman. But he refused to exercise, except for golf. "Cardboard boxes. Hell of a lot of cardboard boxes. I think I sprained my back carrying them to the car." Eleanor had said "Charles," because you didn't say "Hell" at the dinner table. Jane had looked superior, because everyone nowadays said "Hell." Even Sister Michael had said it once, when her chalk broke on the blackboard.

"Let me make sure she's awake," said Sarah. She stepped around the cardboard boxes on the living room floor and opened a door on the far wall. She said something Eleanor couldn't hear, then closed the door again. "She needs a minute to get herself together. She's still tired from travelling." She gestured around at the boxes. "We had some time getting these through airport security. You'd think we were carrying automatic weapons. Would you like some tea?" Eleanor said that would be fine. Charles hadn't mentioned that Lily was travelling with someone. But Charles never noticed unattractive women, she thought, looking at Sarah's bottom, retreating through what was presumable the kitchen door. Why did anyone wear puce?

Eleanor walked around the living room, her shoes sounding hollow on the wooden floor. No furniture, just boxes. Lily would have to come live with her. Jane could probably lend Lily her television, at least while she was in school. Eleanor looked out the window, at the overgrown honeysuckle. Charles kept the grass in their yard trimmed short enough that he could practice golf swings. On Jane's seventh birthday, they had installed a pool so she could have friends over for swimming parties. In summer, there were always young people in swimsuits lying on the deck chairs, smelling like coconuts. Jane was one of the most popular girls in school.

Eleanor looked at the boxes again. The tape on one had been torn off and balled into a sticky brown tangle on the floor. She reached down to open it, more out of boredom than curiosity, when Sarah walked back into the room. "I've put the water on. It took me a while, figuring out the stove. Lily hated leaving that apartment. She said she had spent the happiest years of her life there. I don't mind that, but I do miss the dishwasher. We had everything there—and a toaster just for bagels. But don't mind me, I'm a little homesick for New York. I think she's ready to see you now. Go on in. I'll bring the tea when it's ready."

Lily had changed. She was lying in a double bed, the only piece of furniture Eleanor had seen so far in the house, with a blanket pulled over her breasts. Her cheeks, which had always been round and slightly red from rosacea, were yellow and sagged toward the pillow. She seemed to have melted, all but her small, sharp nose. Even her hands, lying on the blanket, looked like puddles of flesh. And she was bald.

"Ellie," she said. Her voice sounded like an echo, as though she were speaking from the bottom of a well. "Do you have a cigarette? Sarah won't let me have one." From the living room, Eleanor could hear the sound of ripping tape. "She thinks they make my throat worse, but they help me, Ellie. I can't think without them." On Lily's bedside table were orange plastic bottles, with varying levels of pills. Eleanor counted them twice, and got two different numbers.

So this was Lily. The same old Lily, who couldn't take care of herself, who made wrong decisions. The same old Lily, but wrinkled and unattractive—and dying.

There was no chair. Eleanor sat down on the side of the bed, which sagged under her. "I think Sarah's quite right. Look where smoking has gotten you."

"Sarah's always right." Lily shook her head from side to side, fretfully. "I was so mad when I found out András had been sleeping with her, almost from the day we got married. But he said she was the best manager he ever had. She found him galleries, you know. Really good galleries. And when she moved in, she managed the apartment for us. She's a wonderful manager." Lily's voice faded. She lay with one cheek on the pillow, her eyes closed, like a piece of parchment that had been folded many times, then smoothed out again.

Eleanor sat up straighter and put her handbag on her lap. So this was her sister's marriage to the great artist. Poor, stupid Lily. "I don't understand why you're staying here with that woman, instead of coming home to your family." Eleanor spoke calmly, as though to a horse that wouldn't jump over a hedge. One always had to be calm around Lily when she was unreasonable. Like when she had refused to come downstairs at Eleanor's debutante ball. "A woman your husband—well. If this were my house, I'd turn her out at once."

Lily opened her eyes and put one hand on Eleanor's knee. "Ellie, it wasn't like that. I was mad at first, but then I realized it didn't matter. I invited her to move in with us. She had such a small apartment in Brooklyn, and we had that huge loft. She cleaned and paid the bills. She would have cooked, but I wanted to do it. They liked my cooking, you know. They never minded when I burned anything."

Ellie put her manicured hand on Lily's. It felt cold and flabby. "Did he continue sleeping with her, after she moved in?" It was best to know these things, distasteful as they were.

Lily pulled her hand out from under her sister's, as though it had grown too hot. "But he painted me. He slept with her, but he painted me. He never painted her, not once. Such wonderful paintings. Oh Ellie, you have to see the paintings."

"Chamomile tea," said Sarah, opening the door. "Am I interrupting?"

"Sarah, you have to show Ellie the paintings." Lily tossed her head again, from side to side.

"Calm down, you," said Sarah, "or you'll lose the benefits of your beauty sleep. I put a little honey in it," she said to Eleanor, handing her a pottery mug decorated with yellow bees.

"See, isn't she a good manager?" said Lily. "I don't know what I would have done without her after András died. I had run out of money, you know. She sold his paintings to all the right galleries, and paid for my treatments." She raised her hand, then dropped it again over the edge of the bed. Sarah took it, put it back on the blanket, and stroked it for a moment. Lily closed her eyes. Without those spots of brown, she looked curiously colorless, as though already a corpse.

"I think we'd better leave her," Sarah said in a low voice. "She's worn out. Maybe she'll have more energy tomorrow."

Eleanor followed her out of the room, wondering what András Horvath had seen in this woman, with her puce bottom and her gray hair, which looked like it had been cropped by a barber. Artists, she thought, had peculiar tastes in women.

In the living room, Sarah said, "I'm glad you came to see Lily today. I don't think she'll hold on much longer. You'll want to bring your husband, and Lily said you had a daughter?"

Ellie nodded and tapped her fingernails on the mug. What did you say to your sister's husband's mistress? "Maybe I'll bring Jane. My daughter, Jane." Of course she wouldn't bring Jane. And Charles never liked being around sick people. He hadn't visited his own mother in the nursing home before she died.

Sarah looked at her for a moment, then looked toward the window, where the honeysuckle was growing over the fence. "Lily wanted you to see the paintings." She leaned down and opened one of the cardboard boxes. Many more of them were untaped, now. Out of it, she pulled an unframed canvas.

It was a painting of Lily. But Lily as she had never appeared in real life. Lily elongated and white as a sheet of paper. Lily with for-get-me-nots for eyes. In the painting behind it, Lily had horns: short, curving spirals like seashells. Behind that, Lily held a pomegranate in her left hand. Lily, her head covered with butterflies. A lily that was also, improbably, Lily. Lily blue like the sky, with clouds moving over her breasts. Endless Lilies, all different, all—Eleanor caught herself before she said the word—beautiful.

Sarah pointed to the painting with the clouds. "He painted all sorts of things, of course, but before his death he only painted Lily. He did a larger one of those, with the sun as her left eye. I gave it to the Guggenheim."

"Gave it? You gave it?" Lily had said something about spending all her money. What, Eleanor suddenly wondered, were András Horvath's paintings worth?

Sarah looked at her, and continued to look at her until Eleanor shuffled her feet. "András left his paintings to me. Just like he left Lily to me. He knew I would manage everything." She put down the paintings she had been holding. "András could see things. He once told me his great-grandfather had married a witch or a woman who lived in a tree or something like that. Back in his own country." She smiled, and shrugged. "Hell, I don't know. But you can see it in the paintings. If he painted a rock, it looked like a snake, and every time you looked at that rock afterward, it would look like a snake to you, because he was right. It was a snake, even though it was also a rock. Then maybe every rock would start looking like a snake, or a flower, or a piece of bread. Sometimes I wonder if that's how he died. There he was, flying a plane. What if he saw something—really saw it? He wouldn't have cared that he was about to crash. It's frightening, if you think about it too hard. Maybe art always is." Sarah turned to the window again. "He saw people, too. He saw me so well. One day he said, 'I'll never paint you, Sarah. I don't need to paint you, because you're exactly yourself.' But he saw Lily better than he saw anyone else in the world."

Click click, went the heels of Eleanor's shoes on the sidewalk. She clicked homeward because Charles would need his dinner. She would make mashed potatoes. What did she care about his weight? Men always looked more dignified with a little extra padding. She would make mashed potatoes and peas, and she would ask Jane about school, and Jane would look superior, and maybe afterward they would all play monopoly.

Was it already five-thirty? Eleanor looked up at the sky, and there was Lily, with clouds moving over her breasts. Her left eye was the sun. She tried to imagine Lily with her yellow skin sagging, her bald head sinking into the pillow. But Lily's head was covered with butterflies, and she was holding a pomegranate in her left hand.

Click click went her heels, faster and faster, and finally in spite of her corn Ellie began to canter in earnest through a world that was Lily, endlessly Lily, her handbag swinging like an irregular pendulum and her hair, which had been permed only last week, shedding hairpins behind her.

MISS EMILY GRAY

I ❧ A LANE IN ALBION

IT WAS APRIL in Albion. To the south, in the civilized counties, farmers were already putting their lambs out to pasture, and lakeshores were covered with the daffodils beloved of the Poet. The daffodils were plucked by tourists, who photographed the lambs, or each other with bunches of daffodils, or the cottage of the Poet, who had not been particularly revered until after his death. But this was the north of Albion, where sea winds blew from one side of the island to the other, so that even in the pastures a farmer could smell salt, and in that place April was not the month of lambs or daffodils or tourists, but of rain.

In the north of Albion, it was raining. It was not raining steadily. The night before had wrung most of the water out of the sky, and morning was now scattering its last drops, like the final sobs after a fit of weeping. The wind blew the drops of water here and there, into a web that a spider had, earlier that morning, carefully arranged between two slats of a fence, and over the leaves, dried by the previous autumn, that still hung from the branches of an oak tree. The branches of the oak, which had stood on that spot since William the Conqueror had added words like mutton and testament to the language, stretched over the fence and the lane that ran beside it. The lane was still sodden from the night's rains, and covered by a low gray mist.

Along this lane came a sudden gust of wind, detaching an oak leaf from its branch, detaching the spiderweb from its fence, sweeping them along with puffs of mist so that they tumbled together, like something one might find under a bureau: a tattered collection of gray fluff, brown paper, and string. As this collection tumbled down the lane, it began to extend upward like a whirlwind, and then to solidify. Soon, where there had been a leaf and a spiderweb speckled with rain, there was now a plain but neat gray dress with white collar and cuffs, and brown hair pulled back in a neat but very plain bun, and a small white nose, and a pair of serious but very clear gray eyes. Beneath the dress, held up by small white hands so that its hem would not touch the sodden lane, were a pair of plain brown boots. And as they stepped carefully among the puddles, sending the mist swirling before them, they gathered not a single speck of mud.

II ∾ GENEVIEVE IN A MOOD

WHEN GENEVIEVE WAS in a "mood," she went to the nursery, to sulk among the rocking horses and decapitated dolls. That was where Nanny finally found her, sitting on a settee with broken springs, reading *Pilgrim's Progress*.

"There you are, Miss Genevieve," she said. She puffed and patted a hand against her ample bosom. She had been climbing up and down stairs for the last half hour, and she was a short, stout woman, with an untidy bun of hair held together by hairpins that dropped out at intervals, leaving a trail behind her.

"Evidently," said Genevieve. Nanny was the only person with authority who would not send her to her room for using "that" tone of voice. Therefore, she used it with Nanny as often as possible.

"Supper's almost over. Didn't you hear the bell? Sir Edward is having a fit. One of these days he'll fall down dead from apoplexy, and you'll be to blame."

Genevieve had no doubt he would. She could imagine her father's face growing red and redder, until it looked like a slice of rare roast beef. He would shout, "Where have you been, young lady?" followed by "Don't use that tone of voice with me!" followed by "Up to your room, Miss!" Then she would have brown bread and water for supper. Genevieve rather liked brown bread, and liked even better imagining herself as a prisoner, a modern Mary, Queen of Scots.

"And what will Miss Gray think?"

"I don't care," said Genevieve. "I didn't ask for a bloody governess."

"Genevieve!" said Nanny. She did not believe in girls cursing, riding bicycles, or—heaven forbid—smoking cigarettes.

"Do you know who's going away to school? Amelia Thwaite. You know, Farmer Thwaite's daughter. Who used to milk our cows. Whose grandfather was our butler. She's going to Paris, to study art!" Genevieve shut *Pilgrim's Progress* with a bang and tossed it on the settee, where it landed in a cloud of dust.

"I know, my dear," said Nanny, smoothing her skirt, which Genevieve and occasionally Roland had spotted with tears when their father had refused them something they particularly wanted: in Roland's case, a brown pony and riding crop that Farmer Thwaite was selling at what seemed a ridiculously low price. "Sir Edward doesn't believe in girls going away to school, and I quite agree with him. Now come down and make your apologies to Miss Gray. How do you think she feels, just arrived from—well, wherever she arrived from—without a pupil to greet her?"

Genevieve did not much care, but the habit of obedience was strong, particularly to Nanny's comfortable voice, so she rose from the settee, kicking aside *Pilgrim's Progress*. This, although unintentional, sufficiently expressed her attitude toward the book, which Old Thwaite had read to her and Roland every Sunday afternoon, after church, while her father slept on the sofa with a handkerchief over his face. When she read the book herself, which was not often, she imagined him snoring. More often, when she was in a "mood," she would simply hold it open on her lap at the picture of Christian in the Slough of Despont, imagining interesting ways to keep him from reaching the Celestial City, which she believed must be the most boring place in the universe.

As she clattered down the stairs after Nanny, speculating that her father would not shout or send her to her room in front of the new governess, she began to imagine a marsh with green weeds that looked like solid ground. From it would rise seven women, nude and strategically covered with mud, with names like Desire and Foolishness. They would twine their arms around Christian and drag him downward into the muddy depths, where they would subject him to unspeakable pleasures. She did not think he would escape their clutches.

III ∾ THE BOOK IN THE CHIMNEY

IT WAS NOT what she was, exactly. She was not anything, exactly. Genevieve could see her now, through the library window, sitting in a garden chair, embroidering something. Once, Genevieve had crept up behind her and seen that she was embroidering on white linen with white thread so fine that the pattern was barely perceptible.

Her gray dress was always neat, her white face was always solemn. Her irregular verbs, as far as Genevieve could judge, were always correct. She knew the principle exports of Byzantium. When Genevieve did particularly well on her botany or geography, she smiled a placid smile.

It was not, then, anything in particular, except that her hands were so small, and moved so quickly over the piano keys, like jumping spiders. She preferred to play Chopin.

No, it was something more mysterious, something missing. Genevieve reached into the back of the fireplace and carefully pulled out a loose brick. Behind it was an opening just large enough for a cigar box filled with dead beetles, which was what Roland had kept there, or a book, which was what she had kept there since Roland had left for Harrow and then the university. No fire had been lit in the library since her mother's death, when Genevieve was still young enough to be carried around in Nanny's arms. Her mother, who had liked books, had left her *Pilgrim's Progress* and a copy of *Clarissa* in one volume, which Genevieve read every night until she fell asleep. She never remembered what she had read the night before, so she always started again at the beginning. She had never made it past the first letter.

Out of the opening behind the brick, she pulled a book with a red leather cover, faded and sooty from its hiding place. On the cover, in gold lettering, Genevieve could still read the words *Practical Divination*. On the first page was written,

PRACTICAL DIVINATION FOR THE ADEPT OR AMATEUR
BY THE RIGHT REVEREND ALICE WIDDICOMB

ENDORSED BY THE THEOSOPHICAL SOCIETY

She brought the book to the library table, where she had set the basin and a bottle of ink. She was out of black ink, so it would have to be purple. Her father would shout at her when he discovered that she was out of ink again, but this time she could blame it on Miss Gray and irregular verbs.

She poured purple ink into the basin, then blew on it and repeated the words the Right Reverend Alice Widdicomb recommended, which sounded so much like a nonsense rhyme that she always wondered if they were strictly necessary. But she repeated them anyway. Then she stared at the purple ink until her eyes crossed, and said to the basin, as solemnly as thought she were purchasing a railway ticket, "Miss Gray, please."

First, the purple ink showed her Miss Gray sitting in the garden, looking faintly violet. Sir Edward came up from behind and leaned over her shoulder, admiring her violet embroidery. Then it showed a lane covered with purple mud, by a field whose fence needed considerable repair, over which grew a purple oak tree. Rain came down from the lavender sky. Genevieve waited, but the scene remained the same.

"Perfectly useless," she said with disgust. It was probably the purple ink. Magic was like Bach. If you didn't play the right notes in the right order, it never came out right. She turned to the back of the book, where she had tucked in a piece of paper covered with spidery handwriting. On one side it said "To Biddy, from Alice. A Sovereign Remedy for the Catarrh." On the other side was "A Spell to Make Come True Your Heart's Desire." That had not worked either, although Genevieve had gathered the ingredients carefully, even clipping the whiskers from the taxidermed fox in the front hall. She read it over again, wondering where she had made a mistake. Perhaps it needed to be a live fox?

In the basin, Miss Gray was once again working on her violet embroidery. Genevieve frowned, rubbing a streak of purple ink across her cheek. What was it, exactly? She would have to find out another way.

IV ∾ A WEDDING ON THE LAWN

HOW, AND THIS was the important question, had she done it? The tulle, floating behind her over the clipped lawn like foam. The satin, like spilled milk. The orange flowers brought from London.

Roland was drunk, which was only to be expected. He was standing beside the tea table, itself set beside the yew hedge, looking glum. Genevieve found it in her heart to sympathize.

"Oh, what a day," said Nanny, who was serving tea. She was upholstered in brown. A lace shawl that looked as thought it had been yellowing in the attic was pinned to her bodice by a brooch handpainted, entirely unnecessarily, thought Genevieve, with daffodils. Genevieve was "helping."

"The Romans," said Roland.

Genevieve waited for him to say something further, but he merely took another mouthful of punch.

"To think," said Nanny. "Like the woman who nursed a serpent, until it bit her bosom so that she died. My mother told me that story, and never did she say a truer word. And she so plain and respectable."

Miss Gray, the plain and respectable, was now walking around the garden in satin and tulle, on Sir Edward's arm, nodding placidly to the farmers and gentry. In spite of her finery, she looked as neat and ordinary as a pin.

"The Romans," said Roland, "had a special room where they could go to vomit. It was called the vomitorium." He lurched forward and almost fell on the tea table.

"Take him away, won't you, Nanny," said Genevieve. "Lay him down before he gives his best imitation of a Roman." That would get rid of them both, leaving her to ponder the mystery that was Miss Gray, holding orange blossoms.

When Nanny had taken Roland into the library—she could hear through the window that he had developed a case of hiccups—Genevieve circled behind the hedge, to an overgrown holly that she had once discovered in a game of hide and seek with Roland. From the outside, the tree looked like a mass of leaves edged with needles that would prick anyone who ventured too close. If you pushed your way carefully inside, however, you found that the inner branches were sparse and bare. It was the perfect place to hide. And if you pushed a branch aside just slightly, you could see through the outer leaves without being seen. Roland had never found her, and in a fit of anger had decapitated her dolls. But she had never liked dolls anyway.

Miss Gray was listening to Farmer Thwaite, who was addressing her as Lady Trefusis. She was nodding and giving him one of her placid smiles. Sir Edward was looking particularly satisfied, which turned his face particularly red.

The old fool, thought Genevieve. She wondered what Miss Gray had up those capacious sleeves, which were in the latest fashion. Was it money she wanted?

That did not, to Genevieve's disappointment, seem to fit the Miss Gray who knew the parts of the flower and the principle rivers of Cathay.

Security? thought Genevieve. People often married for security. Nanny had said so, and in this at least she was willing to concede that Nanny might be right. The security of never again having to teach irregular verbs.

Genevieve pushed the holly leaves farther to one side. Miss Gray turned her head, with yards of tulle floating behind it. She looked directly at Genevieve, as though she could see through the holly leaves, and—she winked.

I must have imagined it, thought Genevieve a moment later. Miss Gray was smiling placidly at Amelia Thwaite, who looked like she had stepped out of a French fashion magazine.

She couldn't have seen me, thought Genevieve. And then, I wonder if she will expect me to call her mother?

V ∾ A MEETING BY MOONLIGHT

GENEVIEVE WAS ON page four of *Clarissa* when she heard the voices.

First voice: "Angel, darling, you can't mean it."

Second voice: Inaudible murmur.

First voice, which obviously and unfortunately belonged to Roland: "If you only knew how I felt. Put your hand on my heart. Can you feel it? Beating and burning for you."

How embarrassing, having one's brother under one's bedroom window, mouthing banalities to a kitchenmaid.

Second voice, presumable the maid: Inaudible murmur.

Roland: "But you can't, you just can't. I would die without you. Don't you see what you've done to me? Emily, my own. Let me kiss this white neck, these little hands. Tell me you don't love him, tell me you'll run away with me. Tell me anything, but don't tell me to leave you. I can't do it any more than a moth can leave a flame." A convincing sob.

How was she supposed to read *Clarissa*? At this rate, she would never finish the first letter. Of course, she had never finished it on any other night, but it was the principle that mattered.

Genevieve put *Clarissa* down on the coverlet, open in a way that would eventually crack the spine, and picked up the pitcher, still full of tepid water, from her nightstand. She walked to the window. It was lucky that Nanny insisted on fresh air. She leaned out over the sill.

Below, she could see the top of Roland's head. Beside him, her neck and shoulders white in the moonlight, stood Emily the kitchenmaid.

Except, thought Genevieve suddenly, that none of the maids was named Emily. The woman with the white shoulders looked up.

This time it was unmistakable. Miss Gray had winked at her. Genevieve lay on her bed for a long time, with *Clarissa* at an uncomfortable angle beneath her, staring at the ceiling.

VI ∾ THE BURIAL OF THE DEAD

"I AM THE resurrection and the life, saith the Lord."

"He was so handsome," whispered Amelia Thwaite to the farmer's daughter standing beside her, whose attention was absorbed in studying the pattern of the clocks on Amelia's stockings. "I let him kiss me once, before he went to Oxford. He asked me not to fall in love with anyone else while he was away, and I wouldn't promise, and he must have been so angry because when I saw him again this summer, he would barely speak to me. And I'm just sick with guilt. Because I really did think, in my heart, that I could love only him, and now I will never, ever have the chance to tell him so."

"Blessed are the dead who die in the Lord; even so saith the Spirit, for they rest from their labors."

"There's something behind it," whispered Farmer Thwaite to the farmer standing beside him, who had been up the night before with a sick ewe and was trying, with some success, not to fall asleep. "You mark my words." His neighbor marked them with a stifled yawn. "A gun doesn't go off, not just like that, not by itself. They say he was drunk, but he must of been pointing it at the old man for a reason. A strict enough landlord he was, and I'm not sorry to be rid of him, I tell you. The question is, whether our Ladyship will hold the reigns as tightly. She's a pretty little thing in black satin, like a cat that's got into the pantry and is sitting looking at you, all innocent with the cream on its chin. But there's something behind it, you mark my words." His neighbor dutifully marked them.

"Why art thou so full of heaviness, O my soul? and why art thou so disquiet within me?"

It was inexplicable. Genevieve could hear the rustle of dresses, the shuffle of boots, the drone of the minister filling the chapel. Each window with its stained-glass saint was dedicated to a Trefusis. A Trefusis lay under each stone knight in his stone armor, each stone lady folding her hands over stone drapery. A plaque beside the altar commemorated Sir Roland Trefusis, who had come across the channel with William the Conqueror—some ungenerously whispered, as his cook.

"We must believe it was an accident," Mr. Herbert had said. "In that moment of confusion, he must have turned the pistol toward himself, examining it, unable to imagine how it could have gone off in his hands. And we have evidence, gentlemen," this to the constable and the magistrate of the county, "that the young man was intoxicated. What is the use, I put it to you, of calling it suicide under these circumstances? You have a son yourself," to the magistrate. "Would you want any earthly power denying him the right to rest in sacred ground?"

Nanny sniffed loudly into her handkerchief, which had a broad black border. "If it wasn't for that woman, that wicked, wicked woman, your dear father and that dear, dear boy would still be alive. I don't know how she done it, but she done it somehow, and if the good Lord don't smite her like he smote the witch of Endor, I'll become a Mahometan."

"By his last will and testament, signed and witnessed two weeks before the unfortunate—accident," Mr. Herbert had said, "your father left you to the guardianship of your stepmother, Lady Emily Trefusis. You will, of course, come into your own money when you reach the age of majority—or marry, with your guardian's permission. I don't suppose, Genevieve, that you've discussed any of this with your stepmother?"

Miss Gray turned, as though she had heard Nanny's angry whisper. For a moment she looked at Genevieve and then, inexplicably, she smiled, as though the two of them shared an amusing secret.

"There is a river, the streams whereof make glad the city of God, the holy place of the tabernacle of the Most High."

"I am quite certain it was an accident," the minister had said, patting Genevieve's hand. His palm was damp. "I knew young Roland when he was a boy. Oh, he would steal eggs from under a chicken for mischief, but there was no malice in his heart. Be comforted, my dear. They are in the Celestial City, singing hymns with the angels of the Lord."

Genevieve wondered. She was inclined, herself, to believe that Roland at least was most likely in Hell. It seemed, remembering Old Thwaite's Sunday lessons, an appropriate penalty for patricide.

She sniffed. She could not help it, fiercely as she was trying to hold whatever it was inside her so that it would not come out, like a wail. Because, as often as she thought of Mary, Queen of Scots, who had gone to her execution without hesitation or tears, she had to admit that she was very much afraid.

"For so thou didst ordain when thou createdst me, saying, dust thou art, and unto dust shalt thou return. All we go down to the dust; yet even at the grave we make our song: Alleluia."

It must, of course, be explicable. But she had hidden and watched and followed, and she was no closer to an explanation than that day on which, in a bowl of purple ink, she had watched violet clouds floating against a lavender sky.

For a moment she leaned her head against Nanny's arm, but found no comfort there. She would have, she realized, to confront the spider in its web. She would have to talk with Miss Gray.

VII ∾ A CONVERSATION WITH MISS GRAY

". . . AND THIS PRAYER I make,
Knowing that Nature never did betray
The heart that loved her; 'tis her privilege,
Through all the years of this our life, to lead
From joy to joy: for she can so inform
The mind that is within us, so impress
With quietness and beauty, and so feed
With lofty thoughts, that neither evil tongues,
Rash judgements, nor the sneers of selfish men,
Nor greetings where no kindness is, nor all
The dreary intercourse of daily life,
Shall e'er prevail against us, or disturb
Our cheerful faith, that all which we behold
Is full of blessings."

Miss Gray shut her book. "Hello, Genevieve. Can you tell me what I have been reading?"

"Wordsworth," said Genevieve. Miss Gray always read Wordsworth.

She was sitting on a stone bench beside the yew hedge, dressed in black with a white collar and cuffs, looking plain but very neat. The holly was now covered with red berries.

"In these lines, the Poet is telling us that if we pray to Nature, our great mother, she will answer us, not by transporting us to a literal heaven, but by making a heaven for us here upon earth, in our minds and hearts. I'm afraid, my dear, that you don't read enough poetry."

Genevieve stood, not knowing what to say. It had rained the night before, and she could feel a dampness around her ankles, where her stockings had brushed again wet grass.

"Have you been studying your irregular verbs?"

Genevieve said, in a voice that to her dismay sounded hoarse and uncertain, "This won't do, you know. Talking about irregular verbs. We must have it out sometime." How, if Miss Gray said whatever do you mean Genevieve, would she respond? Her hands trembled, and she clasped them in front of her.

But Miss Gray said only, "I do apologize. I assumed it was perfectly clear."

Genevieve spread her hands in a silent question.

"I was sent to make come true your heart's desire."

"That's impossible," said Genevieve, and "I don't understand."

Miss Gray smiled placidly, mysteriously, like a respectable Mona Lisa. "You wanted to go to school, like Amelia Thwaite, and wear fine clothes, and be rid of your father."

"You're lying," said Genevieve. "It's not true," and "I didn't mean it." Then she fell on her knees, in the wet grass. Her head fell forward, until it almost, but not quite, touched Miss Gray's unwrinkled lap.

"Hush, my dear," said Miss Gray, stroking Genevieve's hair and brushing away the tears that were beginning to fall on her dress. "You will go to school in Paris, and we will go together to Worth's, to find you an appropriate wardrobe. And we will go to the galleries and the Academy of Art . . ."

There was sobbing now, and tears soaking through to her knees, but she continued to stroke Genevieve's hair and said, in the soothing voice of a hospital nurse, "And my dear, although you have suffered a great loss, I hope you will someday come to think of me as your mother."

In the north of Albion, rain once again began to fall, which was no surprise, since it was autumn.

IN THE FOREST
OF FORGETTING

SHE STOOD AT the edge of the forest. She knew it was the edge because behind her the path disappeared into undergrowth. She could see rhododendrons, covered with flowers like cotton candy. There were bushes without flowers, which she could not name: *shrubus lea-fiana*. Ahead of her, the path was shadowed by oaks, poplars, maples with leaves like Canadian flags. In the shadow of the trees, the air was cool and smelled of toothpaste.

"Welcome," said the Witch. She was standing beneath an oak tree whose branches were covered with green acorns. The Witch was wearing a white coat. Around her neck was a silver chain, with a silver disk hanging from it. Just what a Witch should look like, she thought. It was comforting when things looked as they should. The forest, for instance.

"Where am I?" she asked.

"In the Forest of Forgetting," said the Witch. "Hence the forgetting. Let me check your heart."

"Why am I here?"

The Witch placed the silver disk on her chest. It felt cold against her bare skin. "Heart normal. You're here because you have lumps."

She looked down at her chest, where the silver disk had been placed. There they were, the only lumps she could see, above the slight bulge of her stomach.

"What's wrong with them?" They were small and a bit crooked, but they looked all right.

The Witch put her hands in her pockets. "Your lumps have metastasized. They must be removed."

"Well," she said. And again, "Well." Even in the stillness under the trees, which made her feel calm and a bit sleepy, this seemed unnecessarily repetitive. "How—"

"With this," said the Witch, pulling a silver wand from one pocket. It looked harmless enough. The Witch muttered something under her breath and waved her wand.

Before she had time to close her eyes or prepare herself for whatever might happen, two moths rose from her chest, white with flecks of gray on their wings. They fluttered along the path, looping and twisting around one another, as though making invisible macrame.

She looked down at her chest. The lumps were gone.

"That went quite well," said the Witch, replacing the wand in her pocket.

The moths fluttered upward, spiraling into the treetops until she could no longer see them. The clouds overhead were white and fluffy, like sheep. No, she thought. Like pillows, like unrolled toilet paper left in heaps on the floor. She liked creating unusual similes.

"Don't go too far into the forest," said the Witch. "You'll have to come back, eventually." The Witch began walking toward the rhododendrons and nameless bushes.

"Wait," she said. Something had been bothering her. She had almost forgotten it, watching the moths rise upward. "What is my name?"

The Witch turned back for a moment. Her silver disk winked in the shifting light under the trees. "Your name is Patient."

She looked down at the path: her feet were bare, and her toenails needed clipping. That didn't sound right at all. She wasn't particularly patient, was in fact generally impatient. She looked up, wanting to ask the Witch if she was certain, but the Witch was gone.

There was nothing to do but go farther into the forest. It was silent, except for the occasional rustle high among the treetops.

WHEN SHE HEARD laughter, she looked up. In the branches of a laurel, spiders had woven their webs, like a giant game of cat's cradle. They were brown, and about the size of her hand.

"What sort of web? What web? What web?" The words came down to her in clacking sing-song, as though she were being questioned by a collection of sewing machines. One spider spun itself down from a branch and hung by its thread in front of her. "What web?" It went into paroxysms of laughter, shaking on its thread like a brown yo-yo.

She looked around her, trying to see what the spiders were laughing about, and saw that the path behind her was littered with brown string. She knelt down, picked up a handful, and suddenly realized what she was holding

"Not a web," she said to the spiders. "My hair. See?" She put her hand on her head. It was bare. Her arms and legs were bare. Even the place under her belly was bare. "It's fallen out. I won't have to buy shampoo or disposable razors." She said this to show it was probably for the best. Perhaps they believed her, because their laughter stopped and the dangling spider rose again to his branch. But she sat on the path and cried, wiping her eyes with a handful of hair.

When she was finished, she blew her nose on an oak leaf and went on. It was no use, she told herself, crying over spilt hair. Perhaps she would grow a winter coat. Perhaps it would come in white, like an arctic hare's.

❧

SHE WAS SO focused on planning for winter, when her coat would come in and she would live on acorns, that she almost tripped over the coffin.

"Be careful," said the first Apprentice. He was dressed in a blue coat, and wore a blue showercap on his head. Around his neck was a silver chain, with a silver disk hanging from it.

"You'll trip over the Queen," said the second Apprentice, who was dressed just like him.

"If you tripped, she would blame us," said the third Apprentice. Her showercap was pushed back to show her bangs.

"Who?" she asked. "The Queen?" The Queen looked incapable of blaming anybody.

"The Witch. We're her Apprentices," said the Apprentices together. "Obviously," muttered the third Apprentice. She wondered if they had practiced beforehand.

"Let us check your heart," said the first Apprentice. All three came together and put their silver disks on her chest.

"Heart normal."

"Too slow."

"Too fast."

They glared at each other and began arguing among themselves.

She looked down at the Queen. The glass of the coffin was perfectly clear. Through it she could see the Queen's robe, a deep blue, and her blue turban. Her face was a little blue as well.

"She died of lumps," said the Apprentices.

"They metastasized."

"The Witch could not remove them in time."

"Magic is much more advanced, nowadays."

She put her hands on the coffin and, not knowing what else to do, tapped her fingers on the glass. Her cuticles were ragged. What would the Queen think?

"She left you gifts," said the Apprentices.

"A dress." It was made of paper, and tied in back. She could not reach the strings, so the first Apprentice tied it for her. She had never liked floral patterns, she thought, looking down at herself. But it would have to do until her winter coat came in.

"A mirror." The second Apprentice held it for her. She realized, with surprise, that she had no eyebrows. She should have expected that. It made her look surprised, which seemed appropriate.

The third Apprentice smiled and said, "You look a little like her, only not so blue."

She did, indeed, look a little like the Queen. "Thank you," she said. The Queen approved of politeness. "Did she, by any chance, leave me a name?" She did not want to seem ungrateful, but this was, after all, important to her. You needed a name, if someone was going to, for example, ask you to lunch. She had not eaten since breakfast, and she was beginning to feel hungry.

"Your name is Daughter," they said. "Now it's time to turn back."

"Why?" Surely she was too old for a name like Daughter.

They looked at each other, then muttered among themselves. "Because," they said decisively.

She frowned, wondering what it looked like without eyebrows, wondering if she should look in the mirror again to find out. Instead, she turned and walked farther along the path, deeper into the forest.

"Wait!" they shouted behind her.

"You're going too far!"

"Your heart can't take it!"

"Do you want to end up like the Queen?"

Eventually, it was silent again.

THE FOREST BEGAN to grow darker. Maples and poplars were replaced by pines. Needles prickled her feet as she walked on the path. She tried to eat a pinecone, but it left her hands sticky and tasted like gasoline. Not that she had tasted gasoline, but she imagined it would taste exactly like that. If she could wash her hands in the river—

"No one may cross the river," said the Knight.

"I don't want to cross. I just want to wash my hands and have a drink."

"No," said the Knight. Above the knees, he was dressed in a suit of armor. Below, he wore a pair of galoshes. "Ouyay aymay otnay ink-dray oray ashway. Onay Oneway." He lifted his visor. His mustache looked like it had been cut with nail clippers. It was turning gray.

"Why?" It was the question she had been asking since she entered the forest.

The Knight looked puzzled. "I don't know. I think it's a rule or something." He had a nice voice. The Witch and her Apprentices had sounded like subway conductors. And the Queen hadn't spoken at all. "I think you're supposed to go back."

"That's just it," she said. "Who is you? I mean, who is me?" She sounded impatient, and she realized that she must be: hungry, tired, impatient. No one in this forest answered questions directly. Would anyone tell her what she wanted to know?

"Well," he said. He tugged at his mustache, although his armored hands were clumsy. "You like blackberry pie. You overwater houseplants, feed stray cats on the back porch, sleep through your alarm clock." He began counting on his fingers. It must help him remember, she thought. "You write stories for children: *A Camembert Moon*, *Priscilla's Flying Pig*, *The Train to Nowhereton*. You complain about your knees, and you hate wearing glasses. Once, you went on a diet where you ate nothing but cucumbers for a week. You can't mend socks, play tennis, or sing. You hate scrubbing toilets." He reached ten and looked at her, fingers outspread. "How am I doing?"

"Well," she said. She did like blackberry pie, although she didn't need glasses. Her eyesight was perfectly clear. She could see, for instance, that the Knight had wrinkles under his eyes. They made him look rather handsome. "But what is my name?"

"I think," said the Knight, looking at his fingers as though trying to remember. "I think your name is Wife."

It was a nice name, whispery, like "wish" and "whinny" and "willow." It was the nicest name she had heard so far. But it wasn't quite right.

"I'm sorry," she said, because the Knight was looking at her with an anxious smile. She stepped into the river.

"Wait!" said the Knight.

The river was cold and clear and shallow. Although there were stepping stones, she walked on the muddy bottom, letting the water curl around her ankles, then around her knees. In the middle of the river, she bent down to wash her hands and frightened a brown fish under a rock. Once her hands were no longer sticky, she drank from them and splashed water on her face, scattering drops of water on her paper dress.

"Won't you reconsider?" shouted the Knight. He was standing in the water, up to the buckles of his galoshes. She wondered if he would follow her into the river, but he did not. Perhaps, she thought, he was afraid that his armor would rust. Instead, he stood near the riverbank, arms held out like an airplane. He was standing there each time she turned back to look. Finally, the path bent and she could no longer see him.

ONCE, A FAMILY of squirrels scrambled down from an oak tree and asked for her autograph. The squirrel children had copies of *A Camembert Moon*. When she told them she had no pen, they brought her berries. She signed each one "With regards, Author." She wondered where they kept books, whether there were shelves in the oak tree. When she had signed copies for Jumpy, Squirmy, Tailless, Nuthunter, and Squawk, they shared their dinner with her: an acorn mash that would have made a good meal, if she had been a squirrel. She was still hungry, although less hungry than before.

FINALLY, THE TREES grew farther apart. She saw undergrowth, including a bush with berries. They looked like the berries the squirrels had used for ink. She wondered if they were safe to eat, and thought of trying a few. Surely if they were poisonous she would feel sick or throw up. A few would not kill her. But she was too nervous to try.

The trees ended at the edge of a meadow filled with Queen Anne's lace, poppies, cornflowers. And beyond the meadow—

"Are you going to the mountains?" asked the Princess. She wore pajamas with feet and a necklace of paperclips.

Was she? They were blue with pines, and probably farther away than they appeared.

"Look at what I have," said the Princess. She was holding a wicker cage. In it were two moths, white with gray markings on their wings.

"I wondered where they had gone," she said. She was sorry, now, to have lost them. They were pretty, like sheets of newspaper turned into kites.

"I'll give them water in the teacups my dolls use. Do you know my dolls?"

"No," she said. It was an important question: was she going to the mountains?

"Their names are Octavia, because she only has eight toes, and Puddle. Because you know." The Princess raised her hand to her mouth, as though speaking through a trumpet. "She's just a baby."

"Do you like making dresses for your dolls?" she asked the Princess.

"Yes," said the Princess. "I make them from leaves and toilet paper."

"If you help me untie it," she said, "you can have my dress." It had been itching for some time, and anyway she would not need it in the mountains. When the strings were untied, she slipped the dress off and handed it to the Princess.

Someone was moving in the meadow, someone in a blue coat, with a blue shower cap on his head. He was holding an enormous butterfly net. And another someone, and another.

"We'll catch her!" shouted the Apprentices, jumping and turning as though chasing enormous butterflies.

"She shouldn't have crossed the river!"

"Her heart can't take the strain!"

"But we'll catch her here, never worry!"

Had she made her final decision? Was she going to the mountains? The Apprentices began stalking away from each other, like detectives.

"You're good at names, aren't you?" she said to the Princess.

The Princess nodded. "I once named seventeen caterpillars. They were named one, two, three, four, five, and so on, up to seventeen."

"What would you name me?" Every few minutes, one Apprentice would run up to another, shouting "Boo!" and making the other jump. The mountains looked mysterious and inviting.

The Princess considered. "I think I would name you Mother."

"An excellent name." But not her name, not quite. She would find her name in the mountains. It would be unexpected and inevitable, a name she could never have imagined, like Rumpelstiltskin. In the mountains she would learn about berries. Her winter coat would come in.

She leaned down and kissed the Princess, then put one hand on the wicker cage. "Goodbye," she said. "Take good care of them. I think they once belonged to the Queen."

She stepped into the sunlight. It was warm on her body. Bees circled around her, visiting the Queen Anne's lace. The Apprentices were stalking away from each other, butterfly nets raised and fluttering in the breeze. She hoped they would not notice her.

She held out her hands so they brushed the tops of the grasses, and started across the meadow.

SLEEPING WITH BEARS

I ∾ THE INVITATION

Dr. and Mrs. Elwood Barlow
request the honor of your presence
at the marriage of their daughter Rosalie
to Mr. T. C. Ursus
on Saturday the thirteenth of June
at one o'clock
in the First Methodist Church

Reception to follow in the Church Hall

II ∽ THE BRIDE

THEY ARE WEALTHY, these bears. Their friends come to the wedding in fur coats.

Rosie is wearing Mom's dress, let out at the waist. When Mom married, she was Miss Buckingham County. She shows us the tape measure. "That's what I was, twenty-two inches around the waist: can you imagine?" My sister, after years of jazzercize and Jane Fonda, is considerably thicker. When, I wonder, were women's waists replaced by abdominals? When cheerleaders started competing for state championships, I guess. Rosie was a cheerleader. Her senior year, our squad was fourth in state. That year she wore the class ring of the student council president, who was also the captain of the football team. She was in the homecoming court. She was furious when Lisa Callahan was elected queen.

After she graduated from Sweet Briar and began working as a legal secretary, she met a lawyer who was making sixty thousand a year. They started talking about having children, buying a Mercedes.

So I don't understand why she decided to marry a bear.

III ∽ THE GROOM

OF COURSE HE comes from old money. *Ursus Americanus* has been in Virginia since before John Smith founded the Jamestown Colony. The family has gone down in the social scale. It doesn't own as much land as it used to, and what it does own is in the mountains, no good for livestock, no good for tobacco. No good for anything but timber. But there sure is a lot of timber.

Anyway, that's how Southern families are. Look at the Carters or Randolphs. If you haven't degenerated, you're not really old. If you want to join the First Families of Richmond, you'd better be able to produce an insane uncle, an aunt who lives on whiskey, to prove you're qualified.

We don't come from that kind of family. Mom is the daughter of a Baptist preacher from Arvonia. There was no whiskey in her house. She didn't even see a movie until she was seventeen. Dad was a step up, the son of the town's doctor. Grandpa Barlow didn't believe in evolution. I don't think he ever got over learning, in medical school, that men don't have a missing rib. Mom and Dad met in third grade. They went to the sock hop and held hands in church, while sharing a hymnal. You can see their pictures in the Arvonia High School yearbook. Dad lists his future career as astronaut, Mom as homemaker. They were voted Most Likely to Get Married. They look clean, as though they just stepped out of a television show from the 1950s.

So maybe that's it, maybe Rosie's still mad that we didn't belong to the Richmond Country Club, that Dad didn't send her to Saint Gertrude's, where the daughters of the First Families learn geometry and which fork to use with the fish. That he didn't think of giving her a debutante ball. Mom's friends would have looked at her and said, with raised eyebrows, "My, isn't Rosie the society lady?"

And when I see them, the bears sitting on the groom's side of the church, I have to admit that they are aristocratic, like the Bear Kings of Norway, who sat on thrones carved from ice and ruled the Arctic tundra. (Nevertheless, they look perfectly comfortable in the heat, even in their fur coats.)

IV ∽ THE PROCESSION

"WHAT DO YOU call him in private?" I ask Rosie. I've never dared call him anything other than Mr. Ursus. When a man—or bear—is six feet tall and over two hundred pounds, he commands respect.

"Catcher," she says. "That's his middle name, or maybe part of his first name. Trout Catcher. That's what his family calls him."

"How much do you really know about bears?" I ask. "Like, do you know what to cook him for dinner?"

"For goodness' sake, Blanche," she says. "Put the brush down, you're tangling my hair. Some of his relatives eat garbage, all right? I'll figure it out as I go along."

I wonder. In the library, I found a book about bears. *Ursus Americanus* eats acorns, melons, honey (including the bees), and gut piles left by hunters. I don't know what Rosie's going to do with gut piles.

I help her with the veil, which comes down to her fingernails, manicured yesterday and painted bubble gum pink. I wonder if bears like bubble gum? I hold her train as she walks along the gravel path from the minister's house, where she's been applying a final coat of mascara, to the church. I'm careful not to let her skirt trail on the gravel.

Mom's and Dad's friends are standing, the women in dresses from Lord and Taylor, the men in linen suits. The bears are standing, black and brown and the toffee color called gold. "Black bear" is a misnomer, really. They look like a forest of tree trunks, without leaves.

The organist plays the wedding march. This is Rosie's choice. She has no originality. Which again makes me wonder: why is she marrying a bear?

V ∾ THE CEREMONY

OR PERHAPS I should ask, why is he marrying her?

When she first brought him home, Mom hid in the bathroom. Dad had to tell her repeatedly that bears don't eat people. That they're really quite gentle, except when their cubs are threatened. That they're probably more afraid of you than you are of them.

Still, Mom sat at the edge of her chair, moving the roast beef around on her plate, not reassured to see Catcher eating only peas and carrots, mashed potatoes.

"What do you do, Mr. Ursus?" asked Dad.

He managed the family property. Conservation land, most of it, in trust for future generations. You could call him a sort of glorified forest ranger. He laughed, or perhaps growled, showing incisors of a startling whiteness.

"Your children will never need dental work," said Dad.

Rosie was mortified. They hadn't gotten to that stage yet. I don't think she'd even kissed him good night.

She'll kiss him now, certainly, and I wait to see how it will happen: whether she will be swallowed by that enormous and powerful jaw. But he kisses her on the cheek. I can see his whiskers tickling her ear. I suppose the devouring will begin later.

VI ∾ THE PHOTOGRAPHS

DON'T GET ME wrong, I don't think he's going to eat her. Bears don't eat people, remember?

But I know the facts of life. When Mom married at eighteen, Grandma told her, "Just close your eyes and pray for children." When I was fifteen, Mom taught me what happens between men and women. Though I have to admit, she never said anything about bears.

When our photographs are taken, I stand next to the best man—or bear, Catcher's younger brother. He looks at me and grins, unless he's just showing his teeth. He's not as tall as his brother and only a few inches taller than me, so maybe he's not fully grown. Bears take five years to grow to maturity. I wonder where he goes to school, then decide he probably doesn't go anywhere. Bears probably home school. Otherwise, they'd have to go through several grades in a year, to make it come out right. I wonder how old I am in bear years, and if he's older than me.

VII ∾ THE RECEPTION

BEFORE SHE MET with the caterer, Mom asked me, "For goodness' sake, what do bears eat?"

There are ham biscuits for the people and honey biscuits for the bears, melon soup for everybody. Trout with sauce and *au naturale*, as they say in French class. Raspberries. She didn't take my suggestion to serve the honey biscuits with dead bees. I'm sure the bears would have appreciated that.

The bears drink mead, which is made from honey. I try some. It feels like fire going down my throat, and burns like fire in my stomach. Like a fire on the altar of the Bear Goddess. Her name is Callisto. Once, by accident when she was hunting in the forest, she killed her son, Arcas. So she put him in a cave for the winter, and when spring came again, he emerged healed. That's why bears sleep through the winter.

This isn't what it says in *Bullfinch's Mythology*. But Catcher says Bullfinch got it all wrong. He says Bullfinch is a bunch of bull—. You know what I mean. He doesn't curse often, but when he does, Mom clutches the hem of her dress, as though trying to hold it against a wind that will lift it over her knees.

VIII ∾ THE DANCING

DAD DOESN'T REMEMBER how to dance, so he and Rosie sway back and forth, like teenagers at prom. The bears know how to dance, of course. They begin a Virginia Reel, whirling down the line in each other's arms, then go into figures I don't recognize. To punctuate the rhythm, they growl and stamp their feet.

Frog Biter asks me to dance. I guess he was checking me out, too, when the photographs were taken. I'm worried about following the bear dances, but he swings me out in a waltz. I never knew anyone could be so strong.

Yeah, he tells me. And I'm only four and a half. Wait until I'm fully grown. I'll be taller than Catcher.

Hearing this makes something burn in the pit of my stomach, which may be the mead.

IX ∾ THE CAKE

CATCHER CUTS THE cake, which is shaped like a beehive.

"What a charming couple they make," says Mrs. Ashby.

"I'm surprised she wore white," says Mrs. Coates. "I heard her relationship with the lawyer was pretty hot and heavy."

He feeds a slice to Rosie, then licks frosting from the corner of her mouth. His tongue is the color of raspberry ice cream.

"Do you think their children will be black?" asks Mrs. Mason, the minister's wife. She walks with a cane and must be over eighty.

"There are bears in the ladies' room," says Mrs. Partlow. "Do you know they go just like a man?"

"I think he's sexy, with all that fur," says Alison Coates. She's in my French class.

"I don't know how she caught him," says Mrs. Sutton. "All that real estate, and I never thought she was pretty in the first place."

She feeds him a slice. Her hand disappears into the darkness between his teeth.

X ∾ THE HONEYMOON

BITER PROMISES TO stop whenever I want to.

When Rosie left on her honeymoon, everyone threw rose petals. They stuck to Catcher's fur. I could see her brushing them off through the limousine window.

It's nothing like when Eddie Tyler felt me up under the bleachers. His fur smells like rain, his mouth tastes like honey. I run my tongue over his incisors, and he laughs—or growls, I don't know which. And suddenly we're rolling around in the vestry, my fingers gripping his fur, trying to pull out brown tufts. It doesn't hurt him a bit.

I want to sleep with you, I say, and I mean through the winter, with the snow above us and branches covered with ice, creaking in the wind. While the deer are starving, searching for grasses under the snow, we'll lie next to each other, living off our fat, sharing body heat. I'll even cook him deer guts.

But he takes it another way, and that's all right too. His curved claws are good at climbing trees, and unbuttoning dresses. And I finally understand why my sister is marrying a bear. Maybe if Eddie Tyler had been a bear, I would have let him get to third base.

XI ∾ THE ANNOUNCEMENT

OUR JUNE BRIDES include Miss Rosalie Barlow, who was married in the First Methodist Church to Mr. T. C. Ursus. The new Mrs. Ursus has a B.A. from Sweet Briar College. Mr. Ursus manages his family's extensive property in the Blue Ridge Mountains. The maid of honor was Miss Blanche Barlow, the bride's sister. The best man was the groom's brother, Mr. F. B. Ursus. The bride carried white lilies and wore her mother's wedding dress of *peau de soie* decorated with seed pearls. The bride's mother, Mrs. Elwood Barlow, is the former Miss Buckingham County, 1965.

LETTERS FROM BUDAPEST

THE SUN HAD set over the mountains, leaving János Pál in a late autumn darkness that faded the gilding on the eighteenth-century chairs and turned obscure Italian masters into patches of ocher and sienna. He rose from his desk, where he had been balancing accounts, and walked to the shop door. The glass, on which was painted (backwards, from his perspective) Pál Arts and Antiquities, provided a view of the river, flowing slowly between banks that kept it from flooding the village each spring. Higher up the mountain, he thought, the river fell in cataracts and rushed down rocky slopes. Farther down it joined the Beszterc, flowing to Galati and eventually the Black Sea. They had camped at the meeting of the rivers when he was a boy—he and his brother István, with their father.

He sighed and opened the door, making the bell ring. He stepped out to see how far ice had covered the edges of the river, but something in front of the door crunched under his foot. It was an envelope, overstuffed and dirty from lying on the ground. He stooped to pick it up, cursing the Postal Department under his breath. But when he saw the handwriting, he breathed in sharply, although it only said,

PÁL JÁNOS

PÁL ARTS AND ANTIQUITIES

ERDÉLYORSZÁG

With a trembling hand, he pushed open the door, then stumbled to the back of the shop, knocking over and hastily righting a chair from the time of Napoleon, with armrests carved to resemble swans. He sat at his desk, put his elbows on his book of accounts, and stared at the envelope, as though afraid to open it. There was no return address, and it was missing a stamp. Slowly, methodically, he reached into a drawer, pulled out a paper knife, and slit the envelope. The pages were crumpled and closely-written. He flipped the switch on a lamp by his elbow, but it failed to come on. Electricity might not be available until later in the evening. He pulled a candle out of the drawer and tried to decide whether to pull out his pipe, stuffed into a back corner beside a box labeled Finest Yenidje Tobacco. He started to shut the drawer, then opened it and pulled the pipe out. He lit the candle, stuck it into a wooden holder, lit his pipe, and then looked at the letter again. In the flickering light, with smoke curling around his mustache, he began to read.

∾

MY DEAR JÁNOS,

I've tried to begin this letter three times now. The wastebasket is almost full, but I can't afford more paper, so this had better be the last time. At first, I tried to write how sorry I am that I left the University without telling you. I know you wanted me to stay in Szent Imre, to help you run the shop. It was generous of you, writing to the Director himself about my application. But I thought about how angry you must be to hear that I left, and I didn't know how to continue. Then I tried to write that I'm at a hotel in Budapest, nearly out of money. But I thought about Mother's bureau, how you sold it so I could afford brushes and paint. János, I'm so sorry. Once I explain, you'll understand why I couldn't have done anything else. I have an hour until Antoine arrives. That should be enough to explain almost everything. He promises that he'll take this letter to you himself, so I don't need to worry about what I write. The Postal Department will never see it.

The morning I left for the University, you warned me about Kolozsvár. "It isn't like Prague or Budapest," you told me, "but it's big enough for a boy from the mountains, like you, István, to get lost in. Keep your mind on your classes, stay away from bad companions, and wear a warm hat once winter comes. You don't want to catch a cold there, with no one to make you cabbage soup." I remember laughing at your advice, kissing you on both cheeks, then lifting my rucksack to my shoulder and climbing into the train, feeling like a man for the first time.

You were right about Kolozsvár. When I saw it for the first time from the train window, with apartment buildings and automobiles everywhere, I almost wished I were back in Szent Imre, fishing by the river and sketching the willow trees. Do you remember how I used to draw them, as though women were stepping out of them, like in old fairy tales? You never liked those pictures. I suppose you found them too strange. I wonder what you would think—but I'm getting ahead of myself. I found my way to the University and the School of Art, a modern building built from concrete the color of dried mud. The Director's secretary looked exactly like the Russian teacher at my high school in Szent Imre, with dyed hair and too much rouge. She sent me to a dormitory that had holes in the floor as large as soccer balls. I went back to her with the chocolates you had given me, and she moved me to another dormitory. This one had no holes, but only one water heater. After the first week I gave up on hot showers. My roommate was a boy named Petru, from Temesvár, who was in his second year. We took turns standing in line for books and bread. The food in the Art School cafeteria was even worse than your cooking!

The semester began well enough. I was busy with Art History, and Life Drawing, and Social Representation. Petru went drinking, and sometimes gambling, with other students, but I never joined him. I had a couple of dates with a figure model named Anna, who was studying to be an economist. She modeled to make money so she could afford black market clothes. We went to a café, and she told me her father would kill her if he found out she was posing naked for art students. Petru and I got along well. He was good, better than me—probably the best painter in school. But he didn't care about art. When he had won enough money from gambling, he bought a motor-cycle. He spent most of his time skipping classes and taking girls out to inns in the country, where no one cared what they did.

When the leaves started falling in the park across from the Art School, our professors started talking about the art exhibit at the end of the semester. We were each supposed to submit a painting, and the best paintings would be chosen by the Party Art Committee for a student display in the National Museum.

One day, while Petru was putting on his goggles for yet another motorcycle trip, I asked him, "So, are you working on anything for the exhibit?"

He laughed. In his goggles, he looked like a frog. "Don't you know what the exhibit is about, village boy?" He held out a pack of cigarettes. "Lucky Strikes. American. A friend of mind buys them in Galati on the black market."

I shook my head. "What do you mean about the exhibit?"

He sat down on his bed. "They tell us the exhibit is about art, and that the Committee's job is to pick out the best paintings submitted. Right?"

I nodded.

"Goat piss. The Committee's job is to pick out paintings that don't threaten the Party's standards on Social Representation. You think I'm going to paint another picture of village girls picking melons? I'd rather spend my time getting drunk. You want to see real art? Take a look at this."

He pulled a magazine out from under his mattress. On its cover was a naked girl and the English word *Playboy*.

"No, thank you," I said. I would have looked at it another time, but I was angry, and didn't want to take anything from him.

"Don't be an idiot." He flipped open the cover. Under it was another cover. Even upside down, I could tell it was a painting. Sprawled across it in snaking letters was the title *Les Fantaisistes*.

"Here." He thrust it toward me. "I have to go screw a ballerina. If you ever need a girl, István, you just tell me. Or maybe you prefer boys!" He laughed and walked out of the room on his long frog-legs, banging the door behind him.

I sat on my bed and opened *Les Fantaisistes*. In spite of the French title, it was in English. You remember I always did well in my English classes. But I didn't need to read the writing to understand. This was what our professors had warned us about when they told us not to develop a decadent style. I saw a painting of a woman sitting on a rock by the sea shore. Her legs, down from the knees, were the tails of fish. Her head was covered with scales, and there were gills on her neck. She stared at me with eyes as flat and silver as the eyes of fish in the market. I turned the page and saw a painting of a man with the head of a bull. He stood in the corridor of a maze, his arms and legs tangled with gold thread. His mouth was open, and I could almost hear him bellow. There was a charcoal sketch of a city filled with towers. Their roofs were covered with swallows's nests, and there were swallows in the sky, but the towers had no doors. It reminded me of a painting I told you I had seen once, in Father's office. I think it had towers too, without doors. But you told me Father had never sold modern paintings. The paintings in *Les Fantaisistes* meant nothing. They existed only for the pleasure of the artist. They were like riddles without answers.

For the exhibit, I had been planning to paint an orchard in our village, with the village girls gathering apples. But I didn't want to paint that any more. I didn't want the people who saw my picture to go back to their apartments hoping we would have a good apple harvest, or thinking about the village girls' legs. I wanted to paint a picture that would make them stare and whisper to each other, "What are we supposed to think?"

That night, while Petru sat on his bed smoking Lucky Strikes, I told him, "That's how I'm going to paint from now on."

He blew smoke in my direction. "You're joking, right?"

"Why should I be joking? Why shouldn't I paint something real, something important?"

He leaned back against the wall. "You should let me find you a ballerina. They're astonishingly flexible. Now that's an art worth practicing." If he hadn't been so much taller than me, I think I would have punched him.

The next day, I began my *Leda*.

That's not quite accurate. The next day, I went to the Art School library. Most of the shelves were empty, and for the first time I wondered what they had once contained. But I needed ideas, and I didn't know where else to begin. I walked through the R's and took down a book on the Renaissance. On the first page was a picture of

Leonardo's flying machine. The writing beneath described what a great mechanic Leonardo had been, what a friend of the people. I flipped through the book out of habit, not thinking I would find anything useful. And then I saw *Leda and the Swan*. You know it, János: a plump girl with her arms around the swan, smiling slightly. It was all wrong. Whoever had painted it after a sketch by Leonardo must have made a mistake. Leonardo would never have painted something so calm, so passionless, as though Leda and the Swan were friends from school.

It was at that moment, I think, that I began to see my *Leda*, a *Leda* for the modern age. In the next few weeks, I spent all my time working on the painting. I asked Anna to pose for me. She agreed, although she said the temperature in my room gave her goosebumps. It was getting cold, and the heating had never come on. But that was what I wanted: pale skin, almost blue at the tips of the fingers and under the eyes. I spent hours in the park, sketching the swans that still swam on the pond. For background, I relied on a sketch I had made of the hills above Szent Imre.

One day, Petru said, "Show me your painting. If I'm going to live in the stink of turpentine, I might as well know what for."

I pulled off the cloth I used to cover the canvas. It was a white madness: the wings of the swan and the body of the girl intertwined, until even I could not tell where one began and the other ended. In the lower right hand corner was the girl's pale face, her eyes wide with terror, her mouth parted in unexpected ecstasy. Her dark hair spread along the frozen ground, and above the sky was gray with the promise of snow.

Petru stared at the painting, then said, "It will be the best thing submitted to the exhibit, but the Committee will never allow it to be shown."

"Why? If it's as good as you say—"

"Because it has no social value. And because it will make them all want to go home and masturbate." With the stub of his cigarette, he lit another. "Make your life easier, István. Submit something else."

"No," I said. "This is the best thing I've ever done."

He shrugged. "Go to the Devil in your own way, then. I've certainly chosen mine."

On the day of the exhibit, I was told to hang my *Leda* between a painting of a village girl gathering melons and the Brassó soccer team in their uniforms. The student who had painted the soccer team looked at my painting with raised eyebrows, but everyone was silent as the Committee members walked around the room, examining the paintings. They looked at the soccer team, then at my *Leda*, expressionless. They passed on to the melon gatherer, but the Chairman stayed behind a moment, looking at the painting, and then at me. The Committee members gathered in one corner of the room with the Director and whispered among themselves. Then the Director announced the paintings that would be displayed in the National Museum. The melon gatherer was among them. So was the soccer team. My *Leda* was not.

Petru had told me to expect this. But somehow, I had thought, they would choose my painting, in spite of the standards. They were an Art Committee, after all. They should have seen that my *Leda* was better than any other painting in the room. My stomach felt empty, as thought I hadn't eaten all day, but it was an emptiness that could not be filled with food.

"István." The Director stood next to me. "Chairman Molnár would like to see you after the judging is over. Go to the Café Bánffy. Listen carefully to what he tells you. You don't want to disappoint your brother, do you?"

I waited in the café for half an hour before the Chairman arrived. I sent the waiter away twice, too nervous to eat or drink. When the Chairman arrived, he sat down across from me at the table and ordered a vodka.

"István Pál," he said. "How old were you when your father died?"

I looked at him, startled. "Eleven," I said.

He nodded. "I was sorry to hear about the automobile accident. He should have remarried after your mother's cancer. Women are practical. They keep you from—" he leaned over, slapped my shoulder, and chuckled, "—from driving too fast, eh?"

His vodka arrived, and he held the glass up in one hand, allowing the light to shine through it. "Today you did something stupid. You know that, don't you?"

I said nothing. What was I supposed to say?

"I have something I would like to show you." He drank his vodka in one mouthful. "Come, we will take my car."

I had never been inside a Mercedes before. It was more comfortable than my bed in the dormitory. I could almost have fallen asleep on the leather seats. We drove through Kolozsvár, and then through the countryside. Finally we came to a house that was almost as large as the School of Art, standing in the middle of a lawn so smooth it looked like a green canvas. So this is how Party members live, I thought.

I followed him into the living room, whose walls were covered with paintings: farmers in front of their tractors, factories in fields of wheat, troops of Young Pioneers wearing red kerchiefs around their necks. Portraits of sports stars and Party members. The Chairman offered me a vodka and a Cuban cigar. I shook my head. The palms of my hands were sweating. I was in much more trouble than I had thought. At any moment, the Secret Police would come through the door and take me to prison.

Instead, he led me into his office. "Sit there, István," he said, pointing to a leather chair in front of his desk. I wondered how many cowhides a Party member was worth, and whether the higher up you were, the more you were given. The most important members, I thought, must live in leather houses.

He walked behind the desk, to what looked like a cabinet with folding doors. He folded the doors back. "This is what I wanted to show you." It was not a cabinet. Behind the doors was a painting.

I saw a man with his back to the viewer, naked except for a helmet on his head and sandals on his feet. He seemed to be in a cave, or a crevice surrounded by rocks. He stood with his weight on one foot as though he had taken a step forward and then stopped. In one hand he held a short sword, in the other a circular shield. The shield reflected what stood behind him: the face of a woman. It must once have been beautiful, but it was now as pale and hard as stone. Around her head coiled thin green snakes, some already hissing at their reflection in the shield. The painting was remarkable. Not because of its technique, although its realism was so exact that I could see, on the hand holding the sword, a scar that ran up the back of the hand to the wrist. Not because of its color, although the gray-brown of the rocks, and the gray pallor of the man's body, and the gray-green of the snakes with their red mouths had the intensity of colors in a dream. But because he stood there, his weight on one foot, expressing everything: that he was hungry, that he had traveled for months to experience this moment, that he wanted it to last, wanted to understand the mysteries that lay behind Medusa's eyes.

"Good, isn't it?" said the Chairman. "Almost makes me want to pinch that cheek." He gestured toward the man's buttocks. "Not the sort of thing the people should see, of course. Unhealthy. But it's good, you have to agree it's good."

"It's the best thing I've ever seen."

He nodded. "I knew you would appreciate it. The Party Art Committee—what a joke. They know as much about art as a sausage."

"Who painted it?" I asked. Whoever had painted it would understand my *Leda*.

"A Hungarian." He took a sip of his vodka. "Támora Von Graff."

I shook my head. "Von Graff isn't a Hungarian name."

"Her mother married a German. He was an industrialist, she was a countess with a castle in the Carpathians. The castle was taken in '46. That's how we deal with Germans in Erdélyország. The Art Committee sent me to examine the paintings and decide whether they should be sent to the National Museum." He gestured toward the painting with his cigar. "Most of them were harmless. But this one. It's good all right, but not exactly—suitable."

"What happened to Támora Von Graff?"

"Devil if I know. She studied painting in Paris, before the war. She's probably still there, an old woman selling paintings to tourists and feeding stray cats." He walked around the desk and put his hand on my shoulder. I hadn't eaten lunch, and the smell of cigar smoke was nauseating. "Be careful, István. No more swans screwing good Erdélyi girls, all right? Especially not the daughter of the Director of High Schools." I had assumed Anna's father was a doctor or lawyer. "Next time, paint a busty village woman bending over her melons!" He laughed, and almost spilled vodka on the leather chair.

That night, I looked through *Les Fantaisistes*, searching for Támora Von Graff. She would have been in Paris at about the right time, and she was painting in the same style. But none of the pictures were hers, and I couldn't find her in the list of artists at the back of the book. Frustrated, I started flipping randomly through the pages. And suddenly, I saw her name in a paragraph about the Fantaisiste Antoine LeMaître, the painter of the Minotaur in the maze. It ended, "In his late twenties, LeMaître disappeared. Friends claimed he had left Paris with his mistress, the Hungarian Countess Támora Von Graff. It is unfortunate that the art world lost such a talented painter just when he was reaching the height of his powers."

When Petru came in, I asked him, "What do you know about Támora Von Graff?"

"So you're not in prison yet." He sat down on his bed. "You know, they took away your *Leda*. I bet it ends up in some Party member's house. They're supposed to have secret rooms filled with decadent art."

I walked over to my desk. The sketches for my *Leda* were still lying in the drawer. I realized that my fists were clenched and my fingernails were cutting into the palms of my hands. "I asked about Támora von Graff."

"Why do you want to know?" He leaned back against the wall and pulled out a *Playboy* magazine, minus its cover, from under his pillow. "Look at Miss September. Do you think girls really have breasts like that in America?"

"I'm curious."

He looked at me for a moment. "She had a studio in Prague for a while. She might have gone to Budapest after that. Who told you about Támora Von Graff?"

"Does it matter?"

He shook his *Playboy* at me. "Be careful, István. Unless you want to catch gonorrhea from prison guards."

That night, I took my sketches to Anna's apartment. I didn't want to leave them in the dormitory. She put them at the bottom of a box of spring clothes. "Stay for a drink, István," she said. "I have some Tokay. A seamstress gave my father three bottles, so her son would do better in school." I pulled on my coat and told her I wouldn't be able to see her for a while.

The next day, I left for Budapest. My ticket was cheap enough, but paying the conductor not to ask for my travel papers took more money than I had expected. There were two people in the train compartment with me, an old man who looked like a mechanic, with stained hands, and a student with a rucksack reading a Fodor's guide. As we approached the border, the old man began to make himself a sandwich, taking bread out of a paper bag, spreading lard on it, then pickles. I had bought coffee at the train station for breakfast, and I must have looked hungry, because he gave me the end of his loaf.

"Look at these foreigners," he said, waving his knife toward the student. "He probably thinks this is the land of ghosts and vampires!"

The student looked up from his reading. "Excuse me?" he said in English.

"The grandfather is talking about your guidebook," I answered.

"Hey, you speak American!" he said. "That's great. Are you going to Budapest? Maybe you can show me around the city."

The old man snorted. "What is he, Frenchie, Italian?"

"American," I said.

"Damn all Americans. If it wasn't for the Treaty of Trianon, I tell you . . ."

And he did, until we reached Budapest. I shrugged at the American and stared out the window, at fields of sunflowers. The flowers were already dry, and their heads hung stiff and brown.

I can hear dishes clattering in the café below. It's time to meet Antoine. I'll finish writing later. János, I'm finally going to meet her.

JÁNOS PÁL LET the paper drop to the desk and put his head in his hands. He stayed like that for several minutes, until the candle, which had burned level with the top of its holder, began to flicker. He raised his head and stared at it, as though it might contain some extraordinary meaning. Then he took another candle, his last but one, out of the drawer, lit it from the flame, and stuck it on the already-melted wax. He reached into the drawer again, pulled out the tobacco box, and opened the lid. In it were photographs. A man with a fishing pole beside a young boy holding a fish, both smiling into the camera. The same man with his mouth open, as though in the middle of a conversation, beside a painting of a train that ran across the sky, its tracks laid along clouds. This photograph was torn and taped together in one corner, as though someone had decided to destroy it and then changed his mind. Two boys sitting next to each other on a riverbank, the younger putting out his tongue and pretending to punch the older. János sighed and passed his hand over his mustache, then relit his pipe, which had gone out some time ago, and picked up the next sheet of paper.

JÁNOS, I'VE SPOKEN with her. Finally, after weeks of searching through art galleries, of sneers from old men in tweed coats and young women in black turtleneck sweaters. Once, I thought a man in a gallery on Váci Street gave me a strange look, but he said he'd never heard of Támora Von Graff. Finally, I started asking the artists who sit on the Fisherman's Bastion, sketching tourists for deutschmarks or dollars. I thought of joining them and making some extra money. But I remembered my *Leda*, and the thought of sketching fat Germans or Americans in Mickey Mouse t-shirts made me sick.

My money began to run out, and I knew I could no longer afford even this hotel, with its stained mattress and its ring of mold around the shower stall. I restricted myself to poppy seed rolls for breakfast and paprikás for lunch, with coffee to fill in the gaps. But my wallet kept getting thinner, until I had just enough money to pay for the train back to Kolozsvár.

Why am I dwelling on this? Everything is different now. Yesterday morning I was sitting in the café, feeling sick from hunger. The only other man in the café was sitting behind his newspaper, and I noticed without interest that the Soviet Party Chairman was meeting with the American President again. Then I noticed something else: his hand. It had a scar across the back, running up to the wrist.

If I hadn't been searching through art galleries for a month, if I hadn't been sleeping in a room where I could hear mice behind the walls, if I hadn't been so hungry, I would never have said to him, "Excuse me, do you know Támora Von Graff?"

He lowered the newspaper. He was older than I had expected, with cropped white hair and wrinkles under his eyes, but I recognized him even though she had painted Perseus from behind. "Támora is a good friend of mine. Are you an admirer?" He held out his hand, fingertips gray from newspaper ink. "My name is Antoine LeMaître."

Trying not to stammer, I told him I was an art student in Kolozsvár, where I had seen one of her paintings. I mentioned *Les Fantaisistes*.

"Really? Then perhaps you've seen one of my paintings as well." His mouth twisted into a pained smile. "They are not so well known, nowadays. But you must meet Támora. She collects young artists, like you."

He could not introduce me to her right way. "Támora enjoys her—seclusion," he said. But he promised to meet me the next day and introduce me to her if she would allow it. That was when I told him about my money problems, and about you. "Write to this brother of yours," he said. "Fortunately, I'm going to Erdélyország next week. I can take the letter for you. In the meantime, don't worry about money. Buy yourself a good meal, István. Now that we've met, I know everything will work out."

After he left, I bought myself a glass of wine and two pieces of sour cherry strudel. Finally, I thought, I have something to celebrate.

This morning, as we agreed, I went down to the café. I was too nervous to eat. I sat, drinking coffee and looking at yesterday's paper, probably the same one Antoine had left. The American President had a fish on his tie, and pollution was getting worse in the Danube.

I felt a hand on my shoulder. "Are you ready?" It was Antoine. "She's agree to meet you."

"Today?" I asked.

"Today. Now."

I followed Antoine through the narrow streets of Buda, wondering how he remembered his way among the twists and turns. If he suddenly disappears, I thought, I'll never find my way back to the hotel.

Finally, we turned into the courtyard of an apartment building, with a dry fountain at its center. I suppose the courtyard had originally been for carriages, so they could drive around the fountain and drop off their passengers. Now the bottom of the fountain was covered with dead leaves. We walked up to a wooden door, twice as tall as Antoine. "This used to belong to the Von Graffs," he said. "They would stay here when they came to Budapest." He opened the door, and we walked into a hallway that smelled like stale bread.

I followed him up the central staircase. Our footsteps echoed from the walls. They were painted ocher, but the paint was peeling and marked with water stains. At every landing, we passed closed doors. On one landing I smelled tobacco smoke, and I thought of your pipe, János.

"Who lives here?" I asked.

"Old people, who come out only to buy bread and vodka. Sometimes I hear the grandmothers, muttering to their cats. One more, now."

When we reached the fifth floor, Antoine pulled out a key. Here there was only one door. He unlocked it, and I entered the apartment of Támora Von Graff.

It was dim, the light from outside filtering through lace curtains too long for the windows. Their bottoms pooled on the floor. Wallpaper, gray with soot, had peeled from the walls, leaving bare patches of plaster. But the ceiling was still covered with molding, and although the room was mostly bare, the furniture would have made you choke on the stem of your pipe. I saw a pair of French chairs you could have sold for a hundred American dollars. But as I said, there wasn't much, and the upholstery was frayed and ragged. From the ceiling hung a chandelier, without lightbulbs. On the far side of the room was a double door, with panes of frosted glass.

"Támora!" said Antoine. "Come meet your visitor."

One of the glass doors opened, and she walked in. I had been right, she was Medusa, although of course considerably older. Her hair was gray, and twisted up around her head in a sort of braid. But her face was not hard or cold. She was smiling and holding out a hand with a paintbrush in it. She looked down at the paintbrush and laughed.

"Forgive me, Mr. Pál." Her voice was low, and reminded me of Mother's voice, telling me stories when I couldn't sleep. "You see I've been working. Would you like to see my latest painting?"

"Please call me István," I said, wondering why I sounded so hoarse. Anna had been pretty enough, and Támora Von Graff was not pretty at all. She had a thin, curved nose that looked like the beak of a hawk, and pale lips. But her eyes. You will laugh at me, János. I tell you, they were Medusa's eyes. They knew everything.

Antoine put a hand on my shoulder. "Oh, yes," I said, with a cough in my throat. "I would, very much."

"Come, then." Taking my arm, she led me through the glass door and into her studio. This room looked like the other, with the same dim light, the same peeling wallpaper, but the only pieces of furniture were a table covered with paints and sheets of paper, and a long divan. By the windows stood an easel.

She led me to the painting resting on it. "I finished it this morning," she said. "What do you think?"

I could not answer. Although it still shone with fresh paint, it was even more magnificent than her Medusa. Beneath a tree lay a man and a woman, completely naked except where her dark hair covered them both. The ground was bare, the branches of the tree were bare, and a gray sky stretched above everything. The woman's hair covered her face as well, except for her closed eyelids. But the man's face was turned to the viewer, and his eyes were open, wide open. His mouth was open also, perhaps in astonishment or because he wanted to cry out, and on his face was a look of absolute despair, as though he had just seen death.

"Do you like it?" she asked. "It's based on a poem by the Englishman John Keats. Oh what can ail thee, knight at arms, alone and palely loitering?" She smiled at me, and her fingers tightened on my arm. "That is the question I attempted to answer. And Sergei was kind enough to pose for the knight."

I turned around. Sergei must have entered the room while I was looking at the painting. He was not as old as Antoine, but he looked older than the knight in the painting. He put his hands in his pockets and scowled at me.

"You must forgive Sergei," said Támora. "He's jealous that I have such a young and fascinating visitor. But soon we will all get along, like a family." She pulled me toward the table. "István, let me offer you a glass of wine."

On the table, among the paints and brushes, was a decanter of wine—and the sketches for my *Leda*.

I stood and stared, not knowing what to say.

"Do you like these sketches?" she asked. "Sergei bought them on a recent trip to Erdélyország. The artist has an astonishing talent."

"But they're mine," I said. "I drew them." Why had Anna sold them? She must have been angry with me, when I left without telling her. "Look." I picked up a piece of charcoal on the table, turned one of the sketches over, and drew a swan on the back. It was identical to the swan on the front. I added water, and a overhanging tree like the one in Támora's painting.

She took the sketch and held it up in the dim light. "Remarkable! We were destined to meet, István. I had lost faith in the younger generation of artists. They had seemed to me lacking in technical skill, and passionless. But you! You must let me see the painting created from these sketches."

Then, while Antoine sat on the edge of the table, refilling our wine glasses, I told her about my *Leda*. I don't know if it was the wine or her sympathy, but I'm ashamed to admit that by the end of my story I was crying, with a case of the hiccups. The room was silent, and I realized that both Sergei and Antoine had left. Támora and I were alone.

She led me to the divan, sat beside me, and put her arms around me. I leaned my head on her shoulder. It was like putting my head on Mother's shoulder, late at night. I felt as though I could stay there forever and be perfectly content.

"How difficult it must have been for you, István," she whispered. "But all that is over now. You must stay in Budapest, with us. Now that we've found you, we never want to let you go." I felt her lips on my forehead, and her hair tickled my ear.

"János would miss me," I whispered. Her perfume reminded me of the incense in old churches.

"Don't you think János would want you to do what is best for your art?" She stroked my cheek. "It must have been difficult for him, getting you into art school."

"What do you mean?" I asked. Because of the wine, or perhaps her perfume, I was getting sleepy.

"Don't you know about your father, István?"

"He sold furniture in a town called Szent Imre." I added, as an afterthought, "Sometimes we would go fishing on the weekends."

"Not just furniture, István. Your father sold paintings. Paintings came into Erdélyország, from Italy and France. And paintings by Erdélyi artists went out of the country. But sometimes, behind those paintings, there were other paintings, by artists the Party did not approve of. Sometimes letters, about artistic methods and ideas. Did you believe your father died accidentally?"

János, is it true? Why didn't you tell me? That painting I remembered in Father's office, of the towers without doors. Why did you tell me I had imagined it? I understand now why you discouraged me from going to art school. It must have reminded you of Father's death, when I applied. Forgive me for being so ungrateful, for running away. But you should have told me. That was why you had to sell Mother's bureau, wasn't it? To pay the Director. He wouldn't have wanted to admit the son of a traitor.

You must understand why I have to stay in Budapest. I want to be with Támora, and learn everything she has to teach me. She seemed to sit for hours with her arms around me, describing how it would be, living and working with her, and Antoine—and Sergei. We would drink wine in cafés, and paint for days at a time, and live for art. She leaned down to kiss me on the cheek, like a mother, and I turned my head so she would have to kiss me on the lips. I had no intention of being her child.

But just then Sergei came into the room. "Isn't it late for the boy to be out?" János, he acts as though Támora belongs to him, but I'll show him whom she really prefers.

Támora said, "Sergei is right. Tonight you should return to the hotel. Tomorrow Antoine can help you carry your things here."

I would have liked Antoine to walk me to the hotel, but it was Sergei who showed me the way back. The light was fading, and the street lamps were coming on beside the Danube. I watched their reflections in the water. Sergei was silent, walking with his hands in his pockets. Once, he stopped beneath a street lamp, looked toward the river, and said, "I was an artist, in Leningrad. Sergei Vasilev. Have you heard of me, boy?"

"No," I said. If I had heard of him, I would still have said no.

"They destroyed my paintings. I had to draw comic books. Red-nosed Ruski, the Circus Clown. That was me." From his pocket, he took out a pack of cigarettes. He lit one and tossed the match into the river. "She doesn't like smoke. Says it gets into the curtains. Want one? They're Gauloises."

I shook my head and said, "You should be glad, then. To be here, with her. Painting together."

He laughed and started walking again. The tip of his cigarette glowed in the darkness, like a miniature street lamp. "Boy, I haven't painted for years. And neither has your friend Antoine."

I shook my head again, but he was ahead and couldn't see me. Certainly an artist who drew comic books could lost his desire to paint. But an artist like Antoine, who had painted the Minotaur. An artist like that never stops painting. I followed him back through the narrow streets, to my hotel.

So here I am, sitting at this table, with an empty coffee cup beside my elbow. Without coffee, I don't think I could have finished this letter. János, if you'll forgive me for running away, I'll forgive you for not telling me about Father. Brothers should forgive each other, and be friends. Out of my window, I can see the moon over the rooftops. It is a crescent, as though the night itself were smiling at me. I think—I put down my pen for a moment, not knowing how to write this. I think I'm in love. Am I in love with Támora, or Antoine, or the painting on the easel? Perhaps I'm in love with all three of them—certainly not with Sergei! I'm going to lie in the moonlight, imagining the feel of her lips on mine. Goodnight, my dear János.

THE CANDLE FLAME, which had been burning steadily, flickered for a moment, and János felt a chill on the back of his neck. He looked up, but the shop was dark and silent. He picked up the photograph of the two boys on the riverbank and rubbed his thumb over it, as though to wipe away an inadvertent mark. Then he put the photographs back in the tobacco box and pushed the box into its corner of the drawer, next to a pile of receipts. He looked down again at the paper in front of him. Anyone standing in the darkness of the shop, beyond the candlelight, would have seen that János, who was only thirty-one, looked old. The candlelight emphasized the sagging skin under his eyes and the furrows that extended from one side of his forehead to the other, making it resemble a plowed field. János closed his eyes for a moment and held the bridge of his nose between thumb and index finger. When he opened his eyes and picked up the final sheet of paper, his fingertips left wet marks that blurred the ink. It began,

JÁNOS, PLEASE HELP me. I'm sitting in a doorway close to the Erzsébet Bridge. Everything I own, except the money in my pockets, is in the apartment of an artist named Támora Von Graff. As soon as I finish this letter, I'll find a post office and mail it to you. Then I'll try to find an American student I met on the train from Kolozsvár. He gave me his address, and if he's still in Budapest I may be able to stay with him for a few days. Please send money to the postal box number on the envelope. I'll check the post office as often as I can, but I have to be careful. I don't have time to explain why.

The painting was dry. I brushed against it accidentally, while I was waiting for her in the studio. Nothing came away but a layer of linseed oil. For the first time, I looked at it closely and noticed the crackling underneath. It had been varnished long ago, and the reds were already faded. Why didn't I realize, the first time I saw it? And why didn't I realize that the woman with the closed eyelids was—her, always her? I suppose I didn't want to realize it because I was in love—with her, or something she represented, I don't know. Perhaps I'm still in love with her. But if I stayed, I would become like Antoine or Sergei. She would paint something even more magnificent than her Medusa. That's what she told me, and I suppose I should be flattered. But I would never paint again. She smiled when she saw that I understood, and I imagined the snakes twisting around her head, their red mouths grinning.

Why am I writing things you won't understand? I should rewrite this letter, but this is the only paper I have. I begged it from one of the students sketching on the Fisherman's Bastion. Please send money soon. Even now, sitting here not knowing how to finish, I can imagine her eyes

THAT WAS ALL. János put this paper on top of the pile and stared at it, as though it were a riddle he could not comprehend.

A voice spoke from the darkness. "You are a methodical man, Mr. Pál." A woman stepped into the candlelight. Her hair was gray, but she might once have been beautiful, with her hawk's nose and black eyes. She was not beautiful now.

"The bell—" said János, then stopped, as though uncertain how to continue.

She smiled, and the candlelight, which darkened the hollows under her cheekbones and at the sides of her temples, gave her face the contours of a skull. "We didn't want to disturb your reading."

"We?" János' fingers fumbled with his pipe, which had already grown cold.

"You must have heard of Antoine and Sergei." Two men stepped into the candlelight. "And I have a new friend, Mr. Petru Iliscu." János saw another standing behind them, his face still obscured by the darkness. "He knew István well."

The pipe rattled against the desk. János put his other hand over the one holding the pipe, to stop it from shaking. "What have you done with my brother?" It came out too shrill. As though frightened by his own voice, he added, in a whisper, "Anna Kovács died in the hospital—"

She walked toward him until she stood on the other side of the desk. She leaned forward for a moment and touched the pile of papers, with a sort of caress. "When I heard that a young man had been asking about me in the art galleries of Budapest, I sent Sergei to—investigate. He can be so impulsive. But the girl is not important. István—I will miss István. You understand, Mr. Pál, those who refuse to join us are capable of betraying us. Would you like to see him? Come, Petru. Show Mr. Pál my latest work of art."

The man in the darkness stepped forward and lifted a painting he had been holding in his right hand. It still smelled of linseed oil, although the vibrancy of its reds was already fading to the color of dried blood. János' head fell in his hands, and he let out a choked sob.

"I think it's the best of all my paintings. I call it *La Vampiresse*. I would like to keep it near me, but one cannot live by art alone, particularly with a growing household. Mr. Pál, I would like you to help me sell this painting. I believe I know a potential buyer, a Chairman Molnár."

János raised his head. "Do you think I would—"

"Yes, Mr. Pál. I think you would do a great deal. It was you, after all, who denounced your father to the Secret Police."

The man she had identified as Antoine said, "Did you really think we wouldn't find out, we Fantaisistes? After his death, who would agree to sell our paintings?"

In the candlelight, János' cheeks were slick with tears. "It was for István. The police were already suspicious. If I had said nothing, all of us would have been imprisoned. He was only eleven years old—"

The candle flame guttered, and the darkness closed around her. She smiled again, but this time he could see only her nose and the line of her mouth.

"Good night, Mr. Pál. Remember that I expect a good price. I intend to finish another painting soon. And I'm thinking of moving back to Kolozsvár, where the opportunities are so plentiful. I expect we will be doing business for some time to come."

The flame flickered and went out. The papers in front of him rustled in a chill draft. Then, just once, the bell on the shop door rang, and János Pál was left alone in the darkness.

THE WINGS OF
MEISTER WILHELM

MY MOTHER WANTED me to play the piano. She had grown up in
Boston, among the brownstones and the cobbled streets, in the hush
of rooms where dust settled slowly, in the sunlight filtering through
lace curtains, over the leaves of spider-plants and aspidistras. She had
learned to play the piano sitting on a mahogany stool with a rotating
top, her back straight, hair braided into decorous loops, knees covered by layers of summer gauze. Her fingers had moved with elegant
patience over the keys. A lady, she told me, always looked graceful on
a piano stool.

I did try. But my knees, covered mostly by scars from wading in
the river by the Beauforts' and then falling into the blackberry bushes,
sprawled and banged—into the bench, into the piano, into Mr. Henry,
the Episcopal Church organist, who drew in the corners of his mouth
when he saw me, forming a pink oval of distaste. No matter how often
my mother brushed my hair, I ran my fingers through it so that I
looked like an animated mop, and to her dismay I never sat up straight,

stooping over the keys until I resembled, she said, "that dreadful creature from Victor Hugo—the hunchback of Notre Dame."

I suppose she took my failure as a sign of her own. When she married my father, the son of a North Carolina tobacco farmer, she left Boston and the house by the Common that the Winslows had inhabited since the Revolution. She arrived as a bride in Ashton expecting to be welcomed into a red brick mansion fronted by white columns and shaded by magnolias, perhaps a bit singed from the war her grandfather the General had won for the Union. Instead, she found herself in a house with only a front parlor, its white paint flaking, flanked by a set of ragged tulip poplars. My father rode off every morning to the tobacco fields that lay around the foundations of the red brick mansion, its remaining bricks still blackened from the fires of the Union army and covered through the summer with twining purple vetch.

A MONTH AFTER my first piano lesson with Mr. Henry, we were invited to a dinner party at the Beauforts'. At the bottom left corner of the invitation was written, "Violin Recital."

"Adeline Beaufort is so original," said my mother over her toast and eggs, the morning we received the invitation. "Imagine. Who in Balfour County plays the violin?" Her voice indicated the amused tolerance extended to Adeline Beaufort, who had once been Adeline Ashton, of the Ashtons who had given their name to the town.

Hannah began to disassemble the chafing dish. "I hear she's paying some foreign man to play for her. He arrived from Raleigh last week. He's staying at Slater's."

"Real-ly?" said my mother, lengthening the word as she said it to express the notion that Adeline Beaufort, who lived in the one red brick mansion in Ashton, fronted by white columns and shaded by magnolias, should know better than to allow some paid performer staying at Slater's, with its sagging porch and mixed-color clientele, to play at her dinner party.

My father pushed back his chair. "Well, it'll be a nice change from that damned organist." He was already in his work shirt and jodhpurs.

"Language, Cullen," said my mother.

"Rose doesn't mind my damns, does she?" He stopped as he passed and leaned down to kiss the top of my head.

I decided then that I would grow up just like my father. I would wear a blue shirt and leather boots up to my knees, and damn anything I pleased. I looked like him already, although the sandy hair so thick that no brush could tame it, the strong jaw and freckled nose that made him a handsome man made me a very plain girl indeed. I did not need to look in a mirror to realize my plainness. It was there, in my mother's perpetual look of disappointment, as though I were, to her, a symbol of the town with its unpaved streets where passing carriages kicked up dust in the summer, and the dull green of the tobacco fields stretching away to the mountains.

After breakfast I ran to the Beauforts' to find Emma. The two of us had been friends since our first year at the Ashton Ladies' Academy. Together we had broken our dolls in intentional accidents, smuggled books like *Gulliver's Travels* out of the Ashton library, and devised secret codes that revealed exactly what we thought of the older girls at our school, who were already putting their hair up and chattering about beaux. I found her in the orchard below the house, stealing green apples. It was only the middle of June, and they were just beginning to be tinged with their eventual red.

"Aren't you bad," I said when I saw her. "You know those will only make you sick."

"I can't help it," she said, looking doleful. The expression did not suit her. Emma reminded me of the china doll Aunt Winslow had given me two summers ago, on my twelfth birthday. She had chestnut hair and blue eyes that always looked newly painted, above cheeks as smooth and white as porcelain, now round with the apple pieces she had stuffed into them. "Mama thinks I've grown too plump, so Callie won't let me have more than toast and an egg for breakfast, and no sugar for my coffee. I get so hungry afterward!"

"Well, I'll steal you some bread and jam later if you'll tell me about the violin player from Slater's."

We walked to the cottage below the orchard, so close to the river at the bottom of the Beauforts' back garden that it flooded each spring. Emma felt above the low doorway, found the key we always kept there, and let us both in. The cottage had been used, as long as we could remember, for storing old furniture. It was filled with dressers gaping where their drawers had once been and chairs whose caned seats had long ago rotted through. We sat on a sofa whose springs sagged under its faded green upholstery, Emma munching her apple and me munching another although I knew it would give me a stomachache that afternoon.

"His name is Johann Wilhelm," she finally said through a mouthful of apple. "He's German, I think. He played the violin in Raleigh, and Aunt Otway heard him there, and said he was coming down here, and that we might want him to play for us. That's all I know."

"So why is he staying at Slater's?"

"I dunno. I guess he must be poor."

"My mother said your mother was orig-inal for having someone from Slater's play at her house."

"Yeah? Well, your mother's a snobby Yankee."

I kicked Emma, and she kicked back, and then we had a regular kicking battle. Finally, I had to thump her on the back when she choked on an apple from laughing too hard. I was laughing too hard as well. We were only fourteen, but we were old enough to understand certain truths about the universe, and we both knew that mothers were ridiculous.

❦

IN THE WEEK that followed, I almost forgot about the scandalous violinist. I was too busy protesting against the dress Hannah was sewing for me to wear at the party, which was as uncomfortable as dresses were in those days of boning and horsehair.

"I'll tear it to bits before I wear it to the party," I said.

"Then you'll go in your nightgown, Miss Rose, because I'm not sewing you another party dress, that's for sure. And don't you sass your mother about it, either." Hannah put a pin in her mouth and muttered, "She's a good woman, who's done more for the colored folk in this town than some I could name. Now stand still or I'll stick you with this pin, see if I don't."

I shrugged to show my displeasure, and was stuck.

On the night of the party, after dinner off the Sèvres service that Judge Beaufort had ordered from Raleigh, we gathered in the back parlor, where chairs had been arranged in a circle around the piano. In front of the piano stood a man, not much taller than I was. Gray hair hung down to his collar, and his face seemed to be covered with wrinkles, which made him look like a dried-apple doll I had played with one autumn until its head was stolen by a squirrel. In his left hand he carried a violin.

"Come on, girl, sit by your Papa," said my father. We sat beside him although it placed Emma by Mr. Henry, who was complaining to Amelia Ashton, the town beauty, about the new custom of hiring paid performers.

The violinist waited while the dinner guests told each other to hush and be quiet. Then, when even the hushing had stopped, he said "Ladies and Gentlemen," bowed to the audience, and lifted his violin.

He began with a simple melody, like a bird singing on a tree branch in spring. Then came a series of notes, and then another, and I imagined the tree branch swaying in a rising wind, with the bird clinging to it. Then clouds rolled in, gray and filled with rain, and wind lashed the tree branch, so that the bird launched itself into the storm. It soared through turbulence, among the roiling clouds, sometimes enveloped in mist, sometimes with sunlight flashing on its wings, singing in fear of the storm, in defiance of it, in triumph. As this frenzy rose from the strings of the violin, which I thought must snap at any moment, the violinist began to sway, twisting with the force of the music as though he were the bird itself. Then, just as the music seemed almost unbearable, rain fell in a shower of notes, and the storm subsided. The bird returned to the branch and resumed its melody, then even it grew still. The violinist lifted his bow, and we sat in silence.

I sagged against my father, wondering if I had breathed since the music had started.

The violinist said "Thank you, ladies and gentlemen." The dinner guests clapped. He bowed again, drank from a glass of water Callie had placed for him on the piano, and walked out of the room.

"Papa," I whispered, "Can I learn to play the violin?"

"Sure, sweetheart," he whispered back. "As long as your mother says you can."

It took an absolute refusal to touch the piano, and a hunger strike lasting through breakfast and dinner, to secure my violin lessons.

"You really are the most obstinate girl, Rose," said my mother. "If I had been anything like you, my father would have made me stay in my room all day."

"I'll stay in my room all day, but I won't eat, not even if you bring me moldy bread that's been gnawed by rats," I said.

"As though we had rats! And there's no need for that. You'll have your lessons with Meister Wilhelm."

"With what?"

"Johann Wilhelm studied music at a European university. In Berlin, I think, or was it Paris? You'll call him Meister Wilhelm. That means Master, in German. And don't expect him to put up with your willfulness. I'm sure he's accustomed to European children, who are polite and always do as they're told."

"I'm not a child."

"Real–ly?" she said with an unpleasant smile, stretching the word out as long as she had when questioning Adeline Beaufort's social arrangements. "Then stop behaving like one."

"Well," I said, nervous under that smile, "should I go down to Slater's for my lessons?" The thought of entering the disreputable boarding house was as attractive as it was frightening.

"Certainly not. The Beauforts are going to rent him their cottage while he stays in Ashton. You'll have your lessons there."

MEISTER WILHELM LOOKED even smaller than I remembered, when he opened the cottage door in answer to my knock. He wore a white smock covered with smudges where he had rubbed up against something dusty. From its hem hung a cobweb.

"Ah, come in, Fraulein," he said. "You must forgive me. This is no place to receive a young lady, with the dust and the dirt every-where—and on myself also."

I looked around the cottage. It had changed little since the day Emma and I had eaten green apples on the sagging sofa, although a folded blanket now lay on the sofa, and I realized with surprise that the violinist must sleep there, on the broken springs. The furniture had been pushed farther toward the wall, leaving space in the center of the room for a large table cracked down the middle that had been banished from the Beauforts' dining room for at least a generation. On it were scattered pieces of bamboo, yards of unbleached canvas, tools I did not recognize, a roll of twine, a pot of glue with the handle of a brush sticking out of it, and a stack of papers written over in faded ink.

I did not know what to say, so I twisted the apron Hannah had made me wear between my fingers. My palms felt unpleasantly damp.

Meister Wilhelm peered at me from beneath gray eyebrows that seemed too thick for his face. "Your mother tells me you would like to play the violin?"

I nodded.

"And why the violin? It is not a graceful instrument. A young lady will not look attractive, playing Bach or Corelli. Would you not prefer the piano, or perhaps the harp?"

I shook my head, twisting the apron more tightly.

"No?" He frowned and leaned forward, as though to look at me more closely. "Then perhaps you are not one of those young ladies who cares only what the gentlemen think of her figure? Perhaps you truly wish to be a musician."

I scrunched damp fabric between my palms. I scarcely understood my motives for wanting to play the violin, but I wanted to be as honest with him as I could. "I don't think so. Mr. Henry says I have no musical talent at all. It's just that when I saw you playing the violin—at the Beauforts' dinner party, you know—it sounded, well, like you'd gone somewhere else while you were playing. Somewhere with a bird on a tree, and then a storm came. And I wanted to go there too." What a stupid thing to have said. He was going to think I was a complete idiot.

Meister Wilhelm leaned back against the table and rubbed the side of his nose with one finger. "It is perceptive of you to see a bird on a tree and a storm in my music. I call it *Der Sturmvogel*, the Stormbird. So you want to go somewhere else, Fraulein Rose. Where exactly is it you want to go?"

"I don't know." My words sounded angry. He did think I was an idiot, then. "Are you going to teach me to play the violin or not?"

He smiled, as though enjoying my discomfiture. "Of course I will teach you. Are not your kind parents paying me? Paying me well, so that I can buy food for myself, and pay for this bamboo, which has been brought from California, and glue, for the pot there, she is empty? But I am glad to hear, Fraulein, that you have a good reason for wanting to learn the violin. In this world, we all of us need somewhere else to go." From the top of one of the dressers, Meister Wilhelm lifted a violin. "Come," he said. "I will show you how to hold the instrument between your chin and shoulder."

"Is this your violin?" I asked.

"No, Fraulein. My violin, she was made by a man named Antonio Stradivari. Some day, if you are diligent, perhaps you shall play her."

I learned, that day, how to hold the violin and the bow, like holding a bird in your hands, with delicate firmness. The first time I put the bow to the strings I was startled by the sound, like a crow with a head cold, nothing like the tones Meister Wilhelm had drawn out of his instrument in the Beauforts' parlor.

"That will get better with time," he told me. "I think we have had enough for today, no?"

I nodded and put the violin down on the sofa. The fingers of my right hand were cramped, and the fingers of my left hand were crisscrossed with red lines where I had been holding the strings.

On a table by the sofa stood a photograph of a man with a beard and mustache, in a silver frame. "Who is this?" I asked.

"That is—was—a very good friend of mine, Herr Otto Lilienthal."

"Is he dead?" The question was rude, but my curiosity was stronger than any scruples I had with regard to politeness.

"Yes. He died last year." Meister Wilhelm lifted the violin from the sofa and put it back on top of the dresser.

"Was he ill?" This was ruder yet, and I dared to ask only because Meister Wilhelm now had his back to me, and I could not see his face.

"Nein. He fell from the sky, from a glider."

"A glider!" I sounded like a squawking violin myself. "That's what you're making with all that bamboo and twine and stuff. But this can't be all of it. Where do you keep the longer pieces? I know—in Slater's barn. From there you can take it to Slocumb's Bluff, where you can jump off the big rock." Then I frowned. "You know that's awfully dangerous."

Meister Wilhelm turned to face me. His smile was at once amused and sad.

"You are an excellent detective, kleine Rose. Someday you will learn that everything worth doing is dangerous."

༄

NEAR THE END of July, Emma left for Raleigh, escorted by her father, to spend a month with her Aunt Otway. Since I had no one to play with, I spent more time at the cottage with Meister Wilhelm, scraping away at the violin with ineffective ardor and bothering him while he built intricate structures of bamboo and twine.

One morning, as I was preparing to leave the house, still at least an hour before my scheduled lesson with the violinist, I heard two voices in the parlor. I crept down the hall to the doorway and listened.

"You're so fortunate to have a child like Emma," said my mother. "I really don't know what to do with Elizabeth Rose."

"Well, Eleanor, she's an obstinate girl, I won't deny that," said a voice I recognized as belonging to Adeline Beaufort. "It's a pity Cullen's so lax with her. You ought to send her to Boston for a year or two. Your sister Winslow would know how to improve a young girl's manners."

"I supposed you're right, Adeline. If she were pretty, that might be some excuse, but as it is . . . Well, you're lucky with your Emma, that's all."

I had heard enough. I ran out of the house, and ran stumbling down the street to the cottage by the river. I pounded on the door. No answer. Meister Wilhelm must still be at Slater's barn. I tried the doorknob, but the cottage was locked. I reached to the top of the door frame, pulled down the key, and let myself in. I banged the door shut behind me, threw myself onto the sagging sofa, and pressed my face into its faded upholstery.

Emma and I had discussed the possibility that our mothers did not love us. We had never expected it to be true.

The broken springs of the sofa creaked beneath me as I sobbed. I was the bird clinging to the tree branch, the tree bending and shaking in the storm Meister Wilhelm had played on his violin, and the storm itself, wanting to break things apart, to tear up roots and crack branches. At last my sobs subsided, and I lay with my cheek on the damp upholstery, staring at the maimed furniture standing against the cottage walls.

Slowly I realized that my left hip was lying on a hard edge. I pushed myself up and, looking under me, saw a book with a green leather cover. I opened it. The frontispiece was a photograph of a tired-looking man labeled "Lord Rutherford, Mountaineer." On the title page was written, "*The Island of Orillion: Its History and Inhabitants*, by

Lord Rutherford." I turned the page. Beneath the words "A Brief History of Orillion" I read, "The Island of Orillion achieved levitation on the twenty-third day of June, the year of our Lord one thousand seven hundred and thirty-six."

I do not know how long I read. I did not hear when Meister Wilhelm entered the cottage.

"I see you have come early today," he said.

I looked up from a corner of the sofa, into which I had curled myself. Since I felt ashamed of having entered the cottage while he was away, ashamed of having read his book without asking, what I said sounded accusatory. "So that's why you're building a glider. You want to go to Orillion."

He sat down on the other end of the sofa. "And how much have you learned of Orillion, liebling?"

He was not angry with me then. This time, my voice sounded penitent. "Well, I know about the painters and musicians and poets who were kicked out of Spain by that Inquisition person, Torquesomething, when Columbus left to discover America. How did they find the island in that storm, after everyone thought they had drowned? And when the pirate came—Blackbeard or Bluebeard or whatever—how did they make it fly? Was it magic?"

"Magic, or a science we do not yet understand, which to us resembles magic," said Meister Wilhelm.

"Is that why they built all those towers on the tops of the houses, and put bells in them—to warn everyone if another pirate was coming?"

Meister Wilhelm smiled. "I see you've read the first chapter."

"I was just starting the second when you came in. About how Lord Rutherford fell and broke his leg on a mountain in the Alps, and he thought he was going to die when he heard the bells, all ringing together. I thought they were warning bells?"

"Orillion has not been attacked in so long that the bells are only rung once a day, when the sun rises."

"All of them together? That must make an awful racket."

"Ah, no, liebling. Remember that the citizens of Orillion are artists, the children and grandchildren of artists. Those bells are tuned by the greatest musicians of Orillion, so that when they are rung, no matter in what order, the sound produced is a great harmony. From possible disorder, the bells of Orillion create musical order. But I think one chapter is enough for you today."

At that moment I realized something. "That's how Otto Lilienwhatever died, didn't he? He was trying to get to Orillion."

Meister Wilhelm looked down at the dusty floor of the cottage. "You are right, in a sense, Rose. Otto was trying to test a new theory of flight that he thought would someday allow him to reach Orillion. He knew there was risk—it was the highest flight he had yet attempted. Before he went into the sky for the last time, he sent me that book, and all of his papers. 'If I do not reach Orillion, Johann,' he wrote to me, 'I depend upon you to reach it.' It had been our dream since he discovered Lord Rutherford's book at university. That is why I have come to America. During the three years he lived on Orillion, Lord Rutherford charted the island's movements. In July, it would have been to the north, over your city of Raleigh. I tried to finish my glider there, but was not able to complete it in time. So I came here, following the island—or rather, Lord Rutherford's charts."

"Will you complete it in time now?"

"I do not know. The island moves slowly, but it will remain over this area only during the first two weeks of August." He stood and walked to the table, then touched the yards of canvas scattered over it. "I have completed the frame of the glider, but the cloth for the wings—there is much sewing still to be done."

"I'll help you."

"You, liebling?" He looked at me with amusement. "You are very generous. But for this cloth, the stitches must be very small, like so." He brought over a piece of canvas and showed me his handiwork.

I smiled a superior smile. "Oh, I can make them even smaller than that, don't worry." When Aunt Winslow had visited two summers ago, she had insisted on teaching me to sew. "A lady always looks elegant holding a needle," she had said. I had spent hours sitting in the parlor making a set of clothes for the china doll she had given me, which I had broken as soon as she left. In consequence, I could make stitches a spider would be proud of.

"Very well," said Meister Wilhelm, handing me two pieces of canvas that had been half-joined with an intricate, overlapping seam. "Show me how you would finish this, and I will tell you if it is good enough."

I crossed my legs and settled back into the sofa with the pieces of canvas, waxed thread and a needle, and a pair of scissors. He took *The Island of Orillion* from where I had left it on the sofa and placed it back on the shelf where he kept the few books he owned, between *The Empire of the Air* and *Maimonides: Seine Philosophie*. Then he sat on a chair with a broken back, one of his knees crossed over the other. Draping another piece of canvas over the raised knee, he leaned down so he could see the seam he was sewing in the dim light that came through the dirty windows. I stared at him sewing like that, as though he were now the hunchback of Notre Dame.

"You know," I said, "if you're nearsighted you ought to buy a pair of spectacles."

"Ah, I had a very good pair from Germany," he answered without looking up from his work. "They were broken just before I left Raleigh. Since then, I have not been able to afford another."

I sewed in silence for a moment. Then I said, "Why do you want to go to Orillion, anyway? Do you think—things will be better there?"

His fingers continued to swoop down to the canvas, up from the canvas, like birds. "The citizens of Orillion are artists. I would like to play my *Sturmvogel* for them. I think they would understand it, as you do." Then he looked up and stared at the windows of the cottage, as though seeing beyond them to the hills around Ashton, to the mountains rising blue behind the hills. "I do not know if human beings are better anywhere. But I like to think, liebling, that in this sad world of ours, those who create do not destroy so often."

❧

AFTER THE DAY on which I had discovered *The Island of Orillion*, when my lessons had been forgotten, Meister Wilhelm insisted that I continue practicing the violin, in spite of my protest that it took time away from constructing the glider. "If no learning, then no sewing—and no reading," he would say. After an hour of valiant effort on the instrument, I was allowed to sit with him, stitching triangles of canvas into bat-shaped wings. And then, if any time remained before dinner, I was allowed to read one, and never more than one, chapter of Lord Rutherford's book.

In spite of our sewing, the glider was not ready to be launched until the first week of August was nearly over. Once the pieces of canvas were sewn together, they had to be stretched over and attached to the bamboo frame, and then covered with three layers of wax, each of which required a day and a night to dry.

But finally, one morning before dawn, I crept down our creaking stairs and then out through the kitchen door, which was never locked. I ran through the silent streets of Ashton to Slater's barn and helped Meister Wilhelm carry the glider up the slope of the back pasture to Slocumb's Bluff, whose rock face rose above the waving grass. I had assumed we would carry the glider to the top of the bluff, where the winds from the rock face were strongest. But Meister Wilhelm called for me to halt halfway up, at a plateau formed by large, flat slabs of granite. There we set down the glider. In the gray light, it looked like a great black moth against the stones.

"Why aren't we going to the top?" I asked.

He looked over the edge of the plateau. Beyond the slope of the pasture lay the streets and houses of Ashton, as small as a dolls' town. Beyond them, a strip of yellow had appeared on the hilltops to the east. "That rock, he is high. I will die if the glider falls from such a height. Here we are not so high."

I stared at him in astonishment. "Do you think you could fall?" Such a possibility had never occurred to me.

"Others have," he answered, adjusting the strap that held a wooden case to his chest. He was taking his violin with him.

"Oh," I said, remembering the picture of Otto Lilienthal. Of course what had happened to Lilienthal could happen to him. I had simply never associated the idea of death with anyone I knew. I clenched and unclenched my hands.

"Help me to put on the glider," said Meister Wilhelm.

I held the glider at an angle as he crouched under it, fastened its strap over his chest, above the strap that held the violin case, and fitted his arms into the armrests.

"Rose," he said suddenly, "listen."

I listened, and heard nothing but the wind as it blew against the face of the bluff.

"You mean the wind?" I said.

"No, no," he answered, his voice high with excitement. "Not the wind. Don't you hear them? The bells, first one, then ten, and now a hundred, playing together."

I turned my head from side to side, trying to hear what he was hearing. I looked up at the sky, where the growing yellow was pushing away the gray. Nothing.

"Rose." He looked at me, his face both kind and solemn. In the horizontal light, his wrinkles seemed carved into his face, so that he looked like a part of the bluff. "I would like you to have my books, and my picture of Otto, and the violin on which you learned to play. I have nothing else to leave anyone in the world. And I leave you my gratitude, liebling. You have been to me a good friend."

He smiled at me, but turned away as he smiled. He walked back from the edge of the plateau and stood, poised with one foot behind the other, like a runner on a track. Then he sprang forward and began to sprint, more swiftly than I thought he could have, the great wings of the glider flapping awkwardly with each step.

He took one final leap, over the edge of the plateau, into the air. The great wings caught the sunlight, and the contraption of waxed canvas fastened on a bamboo frame became a moth covered with gold dust. It soared, wings outstretched, on the winds that blew up from the face of the bluff, and then out over the pasture, higher and farther into the golden regions of the sky.

My heart lifted within me, as when I had first heard Meister Wilhelm play the violin. What if I had heard no bells? Surely Orillion was there, and he would fly up above its houses of white stucco with their belltowers. The citizens of Orillion would watch this miracle, a man like a bird, soaring over them, and welcome him with glad shouts.

The right wing of the glider dipped. Suddenly it was spiraling down, at first slowly and then faster, like a maple seed falling, falling, to the pasture.

I heard a thin shriek, and realized it had come from my own throat. I ran as quickly as I could down the side of the bluff.

When I reached the glider, it was lying in an area of broken grass, the tip of its right wing twisted like an injured bird. Meister Wilhelm's legs stuck out from beneath it.

I lifted one side of the glider, afraid of what I might see underneath. How had Otto Lilienthal looked when he was found, crushed by his fall from the sky?

But I saw no blood, no intestines splattered over the grass—just Meister Wilhelm, with his right arm tangled in a broken armrest and twisted under him at an uncomfortable angle.

"Rose," he said in a weak voice. "Rose, is my violin safe?"

I lifted the glider off him, reaching under him to undo the strap across his chest. He rolled over on his back, the broken armrest still dangling from his arm. The violin case was intact.

"Are you going to die?" I asked, kneeling beside him, grass tickling my legs through my stockings. I could feel tears running down my nose, down to my neck, and wetting the collar of my dress.

"No, Rose," he said with a sigh, his fingers caressing the case as though making absolutely sure it was unbroken. "I think my arm is sprained, that is all. The glider acted like a helicopter and brought me down slowly. It saved my life." He pushed himself up with his left arm. "Is it much damaged?"

I rubbed the back of my hands over my face to wipe away tears.

"No. Just one corner of the wing."

"Good," he said. "Then it can be fixed quickly."

"You mean you're going to try this again?" I stared at him as though he had told me he was about to hang himself from the beam of Slater's barn.

With his left hand, he brushed back his hair, which had blown over his cheeks and forehead. "I have only one more week, Rose. And then the island will be gone."

Together we managed to carry the glider back to Slater's barn, and I snuck back into the house for breakfast.

Later that day, I sat on the broken chair in the cottage while Meister Wilhelm lay on the sofa with a bandage around his right wrist.

"So, what's wrong with your arm?" I asked.

"I think the wrist, it is broken. And there is much pain. But no more breaks."

His face looked pale and old against the green upholstery. I crossed my arms and looked at him accusingly. "I didn't hear any bells."

He tried to smile, but grimaced instead, as though the effort were painful. "I have been a musician for many years. It is natural for me to hear things that you are not yet capable of hearing."

"Well, I didn't see anything either."

"No, Rose. You would see nothing. Through the science—or the magic—of its inhabitants, the bottom of the island always appears the same color as the sky."

Was that true? Or was he just a crazy old man, trying to kill himself in an especially crazy way? I kicked the chair leg, wishing that he had never come to Ashton, wishing that I had never heard of Orillion, if it was going to be a lie. I stood up and walked over to the photograph of Otto Lilienthal.

"You know," I said, my voice sounding angry, "it would be safer to go up in a balloon instead of a glider. At a fair in Brickleford last year, I saw an acrobat go up under a balloon and perform all kinds of tricks hanging from a wooden bar."

"Yes, you are right, it would be safer. I spent many years in my own country studying with Count Von Zeppelin, the great balloonist. But your acrobat, he cannot tell the balloon where to go, can he?"

"No." I turned to face him again. "But at least he doesn't fall out of the sky and almost kill himself."

He turned away from me and stared up at the ceiling. "But your idea is a good one, Rose. I must consider what it is I did wrong. Will you bring me those papers upon the table?"

I walked over to the table, lifted the stack of papers, and brought it over to the sofa. "What is this, anyway?" I asked.

Meister Wilhelm took the stack from me with his left hand. "These are the papers my friend Otto left me." He looked at the paper on top of the stack. "And this is the letter he wrote to me before he died." Awkwardly, he placed the stack beside him on the sofa and lifted the letter to his nearsighted eyes.

"Let me read it to you," I said. "You'll make yourself blind doing that."

"You are generous, Rose," he said, "but I do not think you read German, eh?"

I shook my head.

"Then I will read it to you, or rather translate. Perhaps you will see in it another idea, like she of the balloon, that might help us. Or perhaps I will see in it something that I have not seen before."

He read the letter slowly, translating as he went, sometimes stumbling over words for which he did not know the English equivalent. It was nothing like the letters Emma and I were writing to each other while she stayed in Raleigh. There was no discussion of daily events, of the doings of family.

Instead, Otto Lilienthal had written about the papers he was leaving for his friend, which discussed his theories. He wrote admiringly of Besnier, the first to create a functional glider. He discussed the mistakes of Mouillard and Le Bris, and the difficulties of controlling a glider's flight. He praised Cayley, whose glider had achieved lift, and lamented Pénaud, who became so dispirited by his failures that he locked his papers into a coffin and committed suicide. Finally he wrote of his own ideas, their merits and drawbacks, and of how he had attempted to solve the two challenges of the glider, lift and lateral stability. He had solved the problem of lift early in his career. Now he would try to solve the other.

The letter ended, "My dear Johann, remember how we dreamed of gliding through the air, like the storks in our native Pomerania. I expect to succeed. But if I fail, do you continue my efforts. Surely one with your gifts will succeed, where I cannot. Always remember that you are a violinist." When he had finished the letter, Meister Wilhelm passed his hand, still holding a sheet of paper, over his eyes.

I looked away, out of the dirty window of the cottage. Then I asked, because curiosity had once again triumphed over politeness, "Why did he tell you to remember that you're a violinist?"

Meister Wilhelm answered in a tired voice, "He wanted to encourage me. To tell me, remember that you are worthy to mingle with the citizens of Orillion, to make music for them before the Monument of the Muse at the center of the city. He wanted—"

Suddenly he sat up, inadvertently putting his weight on his right hand. His face creased in pain, and he crumpled back against the seat of the sofa. But he said, in a voice filled with wonder, "No. I have been stupid. Always remember, Rose, that we cannot find the right answers until we ask the right questions. Tell me, what did the glider do just before it fell?"

I stared at him, puzzled. "It dipped to the right."

He waved his left forefinger in the air, as though to punctuate his point. "Because it lacked lateral stability!"

I continued to look puzzled.

He waved his finger again, at me this time. "That is the problem Otto was trying to solve."

I sat back down. "Yes, well he didn't solve it, did he?"

The finger waved once again, more frantically this time. "He solved it in principle. He knew that lateral stability is created with the legs, just as lift is controlled with the position of the body in the armrests. His final flight must have been intended to test which position would provide the greatest amount of control." Meister Wilhelm sat, pulling himself up this time with his left hand. "After his death, I lamented that Otto could never tell me his theory. But he has told me, and I was too stupid to see it!" He rose and began pacing, back and forth as he spoke, over the floor of the cottage. "I have been keeping my legs still, trying not to upset the glider's balance. Otto was telling me that I must use my body like a violinist, that I must not stay still, but respond to the rhythm of the wind, as I respond to the rhythm of music. He thought I would understand."

He turned to me. "Rose, we must begin to repair the glider tomorrow. And then, I will fly it again. But this time I will fly from the top of Slocumb's Bluff, where the winds are strongest. And I will become one with the winds, with the great music that they will play through me."

"Like the Stormbird," I said.

His face, so recently filled with pain, was now filled with hope. "Yes, Rose. Like Der Sturmvogel."

☙

SEVERAL DAYS LATER, when I returned for dinner after a morning spent with Meister Wilhelm, Hannah handed me a letter from Emma.

"Did the post come early?" I asked.

"No, child. Judge Beaufort came back from Raleigh and brought it himself. He was smoking in the parlor with your Papa, and I'm gonna have to shake out them parlor curtains. So you get along, and don't bother me, hear?"

I walked up the stairs to my room and lay on top of the counterpane to read Emma's letter. "Dear Rose," it began. "Aunt Otway, who's been showing me an embroidery stitch, asks what I'm going to write." That meant her letter would be read. "Father is returning suddenly to Ashton, but I will remain here until school begins in September." She had told me she was returning at the end of August. And Emma never called Judge Beaufort "Father." Was she trying to show off for Aunt Otway? Under the F in "Father" was a spot of ink, and I noticed that Emma's handwriting was unusually spotty. Under the b and second e in "embroidery," for instance. "Be" what? The letters over the remaining spots spelled "careful." What did Emma mean? The rest of her letter described a visit to the Museum of Art.

Just then, my mother entered the room. "Rose," she said. Her voice was gentler than I had ever heard it. She sat down on the edge of my bed. "I'm afraid you can't continue your lessons with Meister Wilhelm."

I started at her in disbelief. "You don't want me to have anything I care about, do you? Because you hate me. You've hated me since I was born. I'll tell Papa, and he'll let me have my violin lessons, you'll see!"

She rose, and her voice was no longer gentle. "Very well, Elizabeth. Tell your father, exactly as you wish. Until he comes home from the Beauforts', however, you are to remain in this room." She walked out, closing the door with an implacable click behind her.

Was this what Emma had been trying to warn me about? Had she known that my mother would forbid me from continuing my lessons? But how could she have known, in Raleigh?

As the hours crept by, I stared at the ceiling and thought about what I had read in Lord Rutherford's book. I imagined the slave ship that had been wrecked in a storm, and the cries of the drowning slaves. How they must have wondered, to see Orillion descending from the sky, to walk through its city of stucco houses surrounded by rose gardens. How the captain must have cursed when he was imprisoned by the citizens of Orillion, and later imprisoned by the English as a madman. He had raved until the end of his life about an island in the clouds.

Hannah brought my dinner, saying to me as she set it down, "Ham sandwiches, Miss Rose. You always liked them, didn't you?" I didn't answer. I imagined myself walking between the belltowers of the city, to the Academy of Art. I would sit on the steps, beneath a frieze of the great poets from Sappho to Shakespeare, and listen to Meister Wilhelm playing his violin by the Monument of the Muse, the strains of his *Sturmvogel* drifting over the surface of the lake.

After it had grown dark, I heard the bang of the front door and the sound of voices. They came up the stairs, and as they passed my door I heard one word—"violin." Then the voices receded down the hall.

I opened my door, cautiously looking down the hall and then toward the staircase. I saw a light under the door of my father's study and no signs of my mother or Hannah.

Closing my bedroom door carefully behind me, I crept down the hall, stepping close to the wall where the floorboards were less likely to creak. I stopped by the door of the study and listened. The voices inside were raised, and I could hear them easily.

"To think that I let a damned Jew put his dirty fingers on my daughter." That was my father's voice. My knees suddenly felt strange, and I had to steady them with my hands. The hallway seemed to sway around me.

"We took care of him pretty good in Raleigh." That was a voice I did not recognize. "After Reverend Yancey made sure he was sacked from the orchestra, Mr. Empie and I visited him to get the money for all that bamboo he'd ordered on credit. He told us he hadn't got the money. So we reminded him of what was due to decent Christian folk, didn't we, Mr. Empie?"

"All right, Mr. Biggs," said another voice I had not heard before. "There was no need to break the man's spectacles."

"So I shook him a little," said Mr. Biggs. "Serves him right, I say."

"What's done is done," said a voice I knew to be Judge Beaufort's. "The issue before us is, what are we to do now? He has been living on my property, in close proximity to my family, for more than a month. He has been educating Mr. Caldwell's daughter, filling her head with who knows what dangerous ideas. Clearly he must be taken care of. Gentlemen, I'm open for suggestions."

"Burn his house down," said Mr. Biggs. "That's what we do when niggers get uppity in Raleigh."

"You forget, Mr. Biggs," said Judge Beaufort, "that his house is my house. And as the elected judge of this town, I will allow no violence that is not condoned by law."

"Than act like a damned judge, Edward," said my father, with anger in his voice. "He's defaulted on a debt. Let him practice his mumbo jumbo in the courthouse jail for a few days. Then you can send him on to Raleigh with Mr. Biggs and Mr. Empie. Just get him away from my daughter!"

There was silence, then the sound of footsteps, as though someone were pacing back and forth over the floor, and then a clink and gurgle, as though a decanter had been opened and liquid were tumbling into a glass.

"All right, gentlemen," said Judge Beaufort. I leaned closer to the door even though I could hear his voice perfectly well. "First thing tomorrow morning, we get this Wilhelm and take him to the courthouse. Mr. Empie, Mr. Biggs, I depend on you to assist us."

"Oh, I'll be there all right," said Mr. Biggs. "Me and Bessie." I head a metallic click.

My father spoke again. "Put that away, sir. I'll have no loaded firearms in my home."

"He'll put it away," said Mr. Empie. "Come on, Biggs, be sensible, man. Judge Beaufort, if I could have a touch more of that whiskey?"

I crept back down the hall with a sick feeling in my stomach, as though I had eaten a dozen green apples. So this was what Emma had warned me about. I wanted to lie down on my bed and sob, with the counterpane pulled over my head to muffle the sounds. I wanted to punch the pillows until feathers floated around the room. But as I reached my door, I realized there was something else I must do. I must warn Meister Wilhelm.

I crept down the stairs. As I entered the kitchen, lit only by the embers in the stove, I saw a figure sitting at the kitchen table. It was my mother, writing a note, with a leather wallet on the table beside her.

She looked up as I entered, and I could see, even in the dim light from the stove, that her face was puffed with crying. We stared at each other for a moment. Then she rose. "What are you doing down here?" she asked.

I was so startled that all I could say was, "I heard them in the study."

My mother stuffed the note she had been writing into the wallet, and held it toward me.

"I was waiting until they were drunk, and would not miss me," she said. "But they think you're already asleep, Rose. Run and give this to Meister Wilhelm."

I took the wallet from her. She reached out, hesitantly, to smooth down my mop of hair, but I turned and opened the kitchen door. I walked through the back garden, picking my way through the tomato plants, and ran down the streets of Ashton, trying not to twist my ankles on invisible stones.

When I reached the cottage, I knocked quietly but persistently on the door. After a few minutes I heard a muffled grumbling, and then a bang and a word that sounded like an oath. The door opened, and there stood Meister Wilhelm, in a white nightshirt and nightcap, like a ghost floating in the darkness. I slipped past him into the cabin, tossed the wallet on the table, where it landed with a clink of coins, and said, "You have to get out of here, as soon as you can. And there's a note from my mother."

He lit a candle, and by its light I saw his face, half-asleep and half-incredulous, as though he believed I were part of some strange dream. But he read the note. Then he turned to me and said, "Rose, I hesitate to ask of you, but will you help me one final time?"

I nodded eagerly. "You go south to Brickleford, and I'll tell them you've gone north to Raleigh."

He smiled at me. "Very heroic of you, but I cannot leave my glider, can I? Mr. Empie would find it and take it apart for its fine bamboo, and then I would be left with what? An oddly shaped parachute. No, Rose, I am asking you to help me carry the glider to Slocumb's Bluff."

"What do you mean?" I asked. "Are you going to fly it again?"

"My final flight, in which I either succeed, or— But have no fear, liebling. This time I will succeed."

"But what about the wing?" I asked.

"I finished the repairs this afternoon, and would have told you about it tomorrow, or rather today, since my pocket watch on the table here, she tells me it is after midnight. Well, Rose, will you help me?"

I nodded. "We'd better go now though, in case that Mr. Biggs decides to burn down the cottage after all."

"Burn down—? There are human beings in this world, Rose, who do not deserve the name. Come, then. Let us go."

The wind tugged at the glider as we carried it up past the plateau where it had begun its last flight, toward the top of Slocumb's Bluff. In the darkness it seemed an animated thing, as though it wanted to fly over the edge of the bluff, away into the night. A little below the top of the bluff, we set it down beneath a grove of pine trees, where no wind came. We sat down on a carpet of needles to wait for dawn.

Through the long, dark hours, Meister Wilhelm told me about his childhood in Pomerania and his days at the university. Although it was August, the top of the bluff was chilly, and I often wished for a coat to pull over my dress. At last, however, the edges of the sky looked brighter, and we stood, shaking out our cold, cramped legs.

"This morning I am an old man, liebling," said Meister Wilhelm, buckling the strap of the violin case around his chest. "I do not remember feeling this stiff, even after a night in the Black Forest. Perhaps I am too old, now, to fly as Otto would have me."

I looked at the town. In the brightening stillness, four small shapes were moving toward Judge Beaufort's house. "Well then, you'd better go down to the courthouse and give yourself up, because they're about to find out that you're not at the cottage."

Meister Wilhelm put his hand on my shoulder. "It is good that you have clear eyes, Rose. Help me to put on the glider."

I helped him lift the glider to his back and strap it around his chest, as I had done the week before. The four shapes below us were now moving from Judge Beaufort's house toward Slater's barn.

Meister Wilhelm looked at me sadly. "We have already said our goodbye, have we not? Perhaps we do not need to say it again." He smiled. "Or perhaps we will meet, someday, in Orillion."

I said, suddenly feeling lonelier than I had ever felt before, "I don't have a glider."

But he had already turned away, as though he were no longer thinking of me. He walked out from under the shelter of the trees and to the top of the bluff, where the wind lifted his gray hair into a nimbus around his head.

"Well, what are you waiting for?" I asked, raising my voice so he could hear it over the wind. Four shapes were making their way toward us, up the slope above Slater's barn.

"The sun, Rose," he answered. "She is not yet risen." He paused, as though listening, then added, "Do you know what day this is? It is the ninth of August, the day that my friend Otto died, exactly one year ago."

And then the edge of the sun rose over the horizon. As I had seen him do once before, Meister Wilhelm crouched into the stance of a runner. Then he sprang forward and sprinted toward the edge of the bluff. With a leap over the edge, he was riding on the wind, up, up, the wings of the glider outspread like the wings of a moth. But this time those wings did not rise stiffly. They turned and soared, as thought the wind were their natural element. Beneath them, Meister Wilhelm was twisting in intricate contortions, as though playing an invisible violin. Then the first rays of the sun were upon him, and he seemed a man of gold, flying on golden wings.

And then, I heard them. First one, then ten, then a hundred—the bells of Orillion, sounding in wild cacophony, in celestial harmony. I stood at the top of Slocumb's Bluff, the wind blowing cold through my dress, my chin lifted to the sky, where the bells of Orillion were ringing and ringing, and a golden man flying on golden wings was a speck rapidly disappearing into the blue.

"Rose! What in heaven's name are you doing here?" I turned to see my father climbing over the top of the bluff, with Judge Beaufort and two men, no doubt Mr. Biggs and Mr. Empie, puffing behind. I looked into his handsome face, which in its contours so closely resembled mine, so that looking at him was like looking into a mirror. And I answered, "Watching the dawn."

∾

I MANAGED TO remove *The Island of Orillion* and the wallet containing my mother's note from the cottage before Mr. Empie returned to claim Meister Wilhelm's possessions in payment for his bamboo. They lie beside me now on my desk, as I write.

After my father died from what the Episcopal minister called "the demon Drink," I was sent to school in Boston because, as Aunt

Winslow told my mother, "Rose may never marry, so she might as well do something useful." When I returned for Emma's wedding to James Balfour, who had joined his uncle's law practice in Raleigh, I read in the Herald that the Wrights had flown an airplane among the dunes near Kitty Hawk, on the winds rising from the Atlantic. As I arranged her veil, which had been handed down through generations of Ashton women and made her look even more like a china doll, except for the caramel in her right cheek, I wondered if they had been searching for Orillion.

And then, I did not leave Ashton again for a long time. One day, as I set the beef tea and toast that were all my mother could eat, with the cancer eating her from the inside like a serpent, on her bedside table, she opened her eyes and said, "I've left you all the money." I took her hand, which had grown so thin that blue veins seemed to cover it like a net, and said, "I'm going to buy an airplane. There's a man in Brickleford who can teach me how to fly." She looked at me as though I had just come home from the river by the Beauforts', my mouth stained with blackberries and my stockings covered with mud. She said, "You always were a troublesome child." Then she closed her eyes for the last time.

I have stored the airplane in Slocumb's barn, which still stands behind the remains of the boarding house. Sometimes I think, perhaps Orillion has changed its course since Lord Rutherford heard its bells echoing from the mountains. Perhaps now that airplanes are becoming common, it has found a way of disguising itself completely and can no longer be found. I do not know. I read Emma's letters from Washington, in which she complains about the tedium of being a congressman's wife and warns about a war in Europe. Even without a code, they transmit the words "be careful" to the world. Then I pick up the wallet, still filled a crumbling note and a handful of coins. And I consult Lord Rutherford's charts.

CONRAD

WHEN HAD HE realized that Aunt Susan was trying to kill him? He shook his head to clear away the clouds that always seemed to gather around him, like the clouds outside his window, gray and filled with rain, obscuring the garden. From his bed, he could see the tops of the yew trees. His father had hated them, had said they made the garden look like a graveyard. But they had been planted by the first Randolph Slovak, who had lost his name at Ellis Island. Someone had written Slovak where his last name should have been on the form, and he had been Slovak for the rest of his life. They had mistaken his first name as well. It should have been something else, something that sounded to Conrad, when his father said it, like coughing. Randolph Senior had come to Ellis Island with nothing but the clothes on his back and a pocket filled with soil from the forest around his village, and died one of the richest men in Manhattan. Slovak Inc. had bought the house on the upper East Side, with the garden in which the yew trees stretched their branches over the graves of Randolphs Senior and Junior. As Conrad's mother had pointed out, the garden was indeed a graveyard.

And now there was another grave, although he had not seen it. When he had caught that cold and Aunt Susan had come, bringing Dr. Stanton, and the clouds— He drifted again, over the streets of Manhattan, and then the playing fields and dormitories of St. Andrew's, where Simon McGreevy and Barnabas Ringe were arguing about the Peloponnesian War. And then out to sea, where his father, who had refused to name him Randolph, was also drifting in the waves beside his mother, who had seaweed in her hair. And the waves were saying—

"Conrad! I don't think he's paying attention to us at all. Dr. Stanton said it sometimes happens. You must have read about the accident, on the front page of the *Times*. Mary, that was my sister, and Randolph Slovak. Obituary pages aren't good enough for the Slovaks! I'd never fly in one of those small planes myself. Far too dangerous, whatever they tell you. And Randolph, I wouldn't call him a drunkard. I won't speak ill of the dead. But I warned Mary. Drunk at the wedding, with that friend of his from college, both of them singing something that would make a decent woman blush. But would she listen to me? An old maid, she called me, though I was only ten years older than she was. That's ten years worth of advice I could have given her. Conrad!" Aunt Susan's beads clinked as she leaned over him. He tried to count the strands. First there were five, and then seven. "Conrad, are you awake?"

He turned his head on the pillow.

"This is your nurse. You're going to have a nurse, Conrad. This is Nurse Gray."

That must mean he was dying. He had never had a nurse, although Dr. Stanton came once a week, on Thursdays. When had he realized? It had something to do with Dr. Stanton, who came once a week, on—

"Conrad, Nurse Gray is going to give you your pill."

He looked at Nurse Gray. She was as gray as her name, with gray hair drawn back from her face, and thin gray lips. Even her uniform was gray. She looked formidable—he remembered the word from a spelling test at school. She was walking toward him as silently as a cat, on a nurse's rubber-soled shoes.

He noticed these things automatically, without interest. What else did he have to think about, except the yews, planted by Randolph Senior to remind him of the forest around his village? They had each been planted, his mother had told him, with the soil from that forest at their roots. Why, Conrad had asked. But she didn't know. She had never met Randolph Senior, who had died before Conrad's father had graduated from Princeton, although she remembered Randolph Junior as a grim presence at her wedding. Long after midnight, with the diamonds she had worn to a party still in her hair, she had told him the stories that his father had heard as a child, about bears who became men, and women who lived in trees and married the woodcutters who spared them. Conrad's father had hated those stories, as much as he hated being the Third and the offices of Slovak Inc., where he never showed up before noon if he could help it. They had given him nightmares. But Conrad had liked them. No more questions, Conrad, his mother had said, and she had brushed his hair back from his forehead, and he had fallen asleep—

"Nurse, if you have everything—"

"Yes, Madam. I see that the patient has water in his carafe."

She was holding it in the palm of her hand, a small red pill the size of a button. That was it, of course. He had walked down the hall to the bathroom, the night his bedside carafe was empty—he could still walk, then—and heard them in what had been his mother's sitting room and was now hers.

"It happens often enough. I had a patient, a women, who collapsed after her fiancé's death. She spent three years in bed before they called me in. I fixed her up, of course."

"Was she pretty?" Conrad had never heard her so—simpering. That was the word. He had found that one in the dictionary.

"Is my little girl worried?" There were noises he could not identify, noises like a cat lapping at a bowl of milk, until he realized, with disgust, that they were kisses. "There's nothing to worry about. You're the only patient I've ever fallen in love with. And you know what's coming, don't you? In six months, seven, who knows—no more than a year. You don't mind waiting a year? It's so much safer that way. Then we can have everything we wanted, together. Everything we ever wanted, baby. You'll have diamonds to put in your hair, just like your sister." Then there were more kisses.

"Your pill, Conrad," said Nurse Gray. She held it in the palm of her hand. When had it occurred to him that the pill might be poisoned? Perhaps because it was red, like a stop sign. Red meant stop, it meant danger. And once—yes, this was part of it, once Aunt Susan had left a bottle of pills on his bedside table, and he had seen that they were prescribed by Dr. Stanton. But how could he keep himself from swallowing the pill? Aunt Susan always gave it to him herself, and watched until he swallowed. He tried to think of a way, but the clouds drifted in and he could not think clearly.

Nurse Gray had closed her hand. Why, when she wanted Conrad to take the pill? His hand was already halfway to hers, reaching for it. She opened her hand again. The pill was still there, in her palm, but it was—how could it be?—white. He took it automatically and put it into his mouth. Aunt Susan, standing at the foot of the bed, had seen nothing. Before he swallowed it, he tasted—sugar.

Aunt Susan let out a small sigh, and her beads clinked as her hand fumbled nervously among them. "Nurse Gray will be staying with us, Conrad. You must do everything she says. She's here to make you well."

Nurse Gray, looking as formidable as ever, nodded once, then turned and followed Aunt Susan out of the room.

CONRAD LISTENED FOR footsteps. Aunt Susan must not find him sitting on the window seat. Or even Nurse Gray, because could he be sure, absolutely sure, that she was on his side? For a week now, she had turned the red pills into white, the bitter into sweet. But without a word for him, without a smile even. Slowly, over the past week, the clouds had dissipated, and he had begun to think. To think! How wonderful that was. He had never realized before how wonderful it was, simply to think. And to plan.

But what could he plan? He knew that there was money. What else was Aunt Susan in this for? And where there was money, there were lawyers. But if he found them and said, "My Aunt Susan is poisoning me because she wants the money for herself," they would not believe him. No one believed you when you were twelve years old, no matter how precocious you were—another spelling word, and besides the headmaster had used it, after looking at his IQ test. In fact, the more precocious you were, the less they believed you, because they assumed you were imaginative—another word the headmaster had used—and made things up. Not that lawyers would particularly be convinced by Aunt Susan. But they would absolutely be convinced by Dr. Stanton, because he was a psychiatrist, and people were convinced by psychiatrists. Conrad wasn't sure why, but he knew they were.

Aunt Susan had sent away Mrs. Martin, the housekeeper, who might have helped him, and Janet, the maid, who probably would not have. She had looked like a rabbit, and was always rubbing her nose.

She would have been too scared of Aunt Susan. But anyway, he didn't know where they had gone. Which brought the issue back to Nurse Gray, because it was Dr. Stanton who had suggested a nurse.

"And how is our patient?" he had asked yesterday morning. It had been the day of his weekly visit.

"Much the same, Doctor," said Nurse Gray in a disapproving voice. Conrad suspected that she would have sounded equally disapproving if she had said that he would make a full recovery, or be dead by that afternoon.

"Then we must work hard to make him better," said Dr. Stanton, smiling in a way that showed his teeth. He had very straight and even teeth. "Let's take a look at you, Conrad."

He had anticipated this, had thought of ways to convince Dr. Stanton that he was still as sick as he had been a week ago, but his heart was beating and he could feel sweat on his palms. If he could imagine the clouds, drifting in front of his eyes—

"I'll sit him up for you, Doctor," said Nurse Gray. She was pulling him up, pulling up the pillows behind him. Had someone opened the window? No, she had breathed on his face. He was cold, cold, and the clouds had come again, he was not imagining them, they surrounded him like a gray wall, and suddenly he was not afraid that Dr. Stanton would find out.

It had been then, while Nurse Gray had left the room to fetch her book. Dr. Stanton was packing his bag, and Aunt Susan was standing beside him, and he said to her, "That's strange, it's working faster than I thought. He's got another month or two, maybe."

Aunt Susan said, "I can't thank you enough for recommending Nurse Gray. She's so respectful. And reliable! When Mary was in high school, she had influenza, and we had to hire a nurse. You can't imagine. The woman drank. She positively reeked of whiskey. And when she left—my mother dismissed her as soon as Mary looked at all well—we discovered that Mama's cameo was missing, and a hundred dollars. Where did you find her?"

"Where does anyone find nurses?" said Dr. Stanton. "Someone or other recommended her. Probably a patient of mine. You know how nurses move around. This one seems less talkative than most, thank goodness."

And that was when, as they were walking out of the room, leaving Conrad lying alone on the pillow, they had mentioned Cousin Ralph.

"Another letter came yesterday. He keeps writing," said Aunt Susan, "asking to see the boy."

"What sort of person is he?" asked Dr. Stanton.

"Oh, terrible, just like Randolph," said Aunt Susan. "I met him once, at Mary's wedding. He and Randolph were hanging on to each other, equally drunk. Later, he sang one of those fraternity songs with a lampshade on his head."

"What did you tell him?" They were outside the door now, and Conrad could barely hear them.

"The same thing. That the doctor had said no visitors."

"Quite right. And so I do."

So someone remembered him, someone was trying to see him. Conrad remembered Cousin Ralph playing the piano and singing a song he wasn't supposed to hear—at least, his mother had sent him to bed. His mother, telling him stories—but he wasn't going to think about that. He rubbed his eyes, hard. He didn't know how much faith to have in Cousin Ralph. But once again the clouds were beginning to dissipate, and for the first time he did not feel completely alone.

Now he was sitting on the window seat, looking out at the snow. In the garden, the graves of the three Randolphs stood together, as the Randolphs had never stood while alive. Snow swirled around the yew trees. He breathed on the window.

How things had changed, since the last time he had breathed on this window—when he had realized that his cold was not getting better, was in fact getting worse, and that Dr. Stanton was somehow responsible—and he had written the word "HELP" on the pane with his finger. He breathed on the window again, turning it a translucent white. The word reappeared. It had been there, invisible, all along. Was Nurse Gray there to help him, or not?

Startled, he pressed his nose to the window. Surely he had seen her, walking between the yews, with snow on her shoulders? No, it was the wind, making the snow whirl up, like a whirlpool but in reverse. No, it was Nurse Gray after all, looking straight up at him. Like one of the yews herself, against the snow.

By the time she entered the room, he was under the covers.

NURSE GRAY OFTEN read to herself, from a green book. Once, she had left it on the bedside table, and Conrad had looked at the spine: *The Complete Poetical Works of William Wordsworth*. She read to herself in an undertone, not loud enough for Aunt Susan to hear in her sitting room, but loud enough so that Conrad could hear her. Most of the poems were boring, but listening helped him lie silently through the long hours, thinking and planning—or trying to, because he had not come up with a plan yet, other than running away, and where was he going to go, in the snow, in his pajamas?

But there was a poem she had read several times already that he liked. It was about a Chief—Conrad imagined him with eagle feathers in a braid of black hair—who had been put in prison. But his friends were coming to free him. "Live and take comfort," went the poem.

Thou hast left behind
Powers that will work for thee: air, earth, and skies:
There's not a breathing of the common wind
That will forget thee. Thou hast great allies . . .

Conrad liked that even the wind was going to help free the Chief, probably by blowing down the prison walls. But it reminded him that he, Conrad, was also imprisoned, and made him wish that he had great allies. He couldn't call Cousin Ralph a great ally. If he had sent Aunt Susan another letter, Conrad had not heard of it. And Nurse Gray did nothing, day after day, but give him white pills, and look at him disapprovingly, and read from her book.

Where was she now? She had said something about a cup of tea, and he was lying alone in the gray light, with the snow falling outside. It had been falling for days. And suddenly, for the first time since he had caught that cold and been confined to bed, he felt like screaming, so that Aunt Susan would hear it, so that the sound of it would echo through the house and out into the garden—evidence, although he did not realize it, like the ache in his legs, that he was healthier than he had been for a long time.

"You! Did you let him into this house?" Aunt Susan shouting, somewhere downstairs. And then a door slamming.

"Calm down, Susan. I know he's sick. I just want to see him. I won't even wake him up."

"Get out, get out! And don't expect me to give you a reference."

"Cousin Ralph," said Conrad. How hoarse he sounded. It was the first thing he had said for weeks. "He's not my cousin really," he said to Nurse Gray, "just a friend of Dad's. But we used to go fishing together, when my Dad—" Was alive. And where had she come from? She had not been there a moment ago.

159

Nurse Gray held out her hand. In it was a plastic bottle, filled with pills: red as a fire truck, as a rose.

"Show him," she said. "They're not what they're supposed to be." As disapproving as ever.

"Cousin Ralph, Cousin Ralph," shouted Conrad as he ran down the stairs in his pajamas. "Help me, I'm being poisoned by Aunt Susan and Dr. Stanton!" And then his face was pressed against a wool coat, wet with melted snow, and Cousin Ralph was saying "Hey, now, what are you doing out of bed? You're not even wearing slippers. What would Mrs. Martin say? You know she wrote to me, asking how you were, and I didn't know what to write back. Is this any way to treat an invalid, Susan?"

❧

THE CROCUSES WERE just beginning to open. They grew, blue and purple and yellow, around the gravestones, although the ground was still covered with snow.

"What do you think will happen to Aunt Susan?" asked Conrad.

"Depends on what the jury decides," said Cousin Ralph. "She'll probably be sent to one of those women's prisons. Those pills of yours—you know, that doctor Trevor and Callahan hired, the expert witness? Told me they're used to knock out dogs. Hey, Conrad, is Trevor treating you well? Because if he's not— I mean, he's giving you an allowance and all that, right?"

"He's great. I mean, he's giving me whatever I want. I don't need that much, mostly books. And a chess set. I'm in the chess club this year."

"Good. I mean, for you. Not a game I ever understood. Your Dad and I—we weren't much for intellectual games. Give us a soccer ball. But anyway, if you need anything, just let me know, OK?"

Conrad nodded and kicked his toe into the earth beside Randolph Senior, After His Labors He Rests. "So, I'm been meaning to ask," although he hadn't quite known how. "Who did let you into the house? Someone must have, right? I mean, the door must have been locked."

Cousin Ralph stopped by Randolph Junior, He Rests in the Lap of the Lord, and put his hands in his pockets. "There was someone, and if I could find her again—" And, unbelievably, he blushed. "She had this, you know, uniform, that fit her like—well, a glove. And brown hair. She was the prettiest damn— Sorry. And you know, I even asked Stanton who she might have been, though I wanted to spit in his eye the whole time I was doing it. But he said the only other person in the house was a nurse, who must have been sixty." He kicked the earth, in unconscious imitation.

"The one who disappeared."

"Right you are, boy genius. Did Trevor tell you? He wanted to call her as a witness, but her room was empty, and none of Stanton's patients had heard of her though he swore she was recommended. But hey, you probably don't remember her, after being drugged like a German Shepherd."

"No, I remember—"

Conrad investigated for himself, wandering around the upstairs rooms while Cousin Ralph walked through the garden, smoking a cigarette. He looked in what must have been her room, but there was no mark of her in it. Not a hairpin on the floor, no reflection of her in the mirror over the dresser. But in his room, the room where he had lain for what had once seemed like forever, he did find something. Already, it seemed to have happened so long ago, and the important things were the dormitories of St. Andrews, covered with ivy in which sparrows nested, and his algebra test, and whether Simon McGreevy would beat him at chess. But he sat on the window seat and read the letters written in the white circle of his breath. Yes, she had left him something.

Powers that will work for thee: air, earth, and skies.

He did not know what it meant, but she had probably thought it was an explanation, and that was enough.

Cousin Ralph was wearing a yellow crocus in his buttonhole. "Ready, Conrad?"

"Yes, I'm ready," he said. He ran his fingers over Randolph III and His Wife Mary, At Peace, then turned away from the Randolphs, resting beneath their yews. "Let's go. I'll race you to the car!"

A STATEMENT IN THE CASE

SURE, I KNOW István Horvath. We met about a year before Eva died. That's my wife, Eva. You knew that? Yeah, I figured you were pretty thorough.

It was the year of the blizzard, when snow covered the cars parked on the streets and even the Post Office shut down. I didn't have to go to work for a week. So one night, I think it was Thursday, Eva says, "Mike, I only have one of the blue pills left." This was when we still thought the chemo was doing something. When we discovered it wasn't, she turned her head toward me on the pillow—she was so beautiful, like the day we got married—and said, "Mike, I think the Lord wants me home." After that, she refused to take the pills. But I couldn't throw them out. Every morning I opened the medicine cabinet, and there they were, the blue ones, the orange ones that made her throw up, the green ones that made her hair fall out, the purple ones that caused constipation. When she died, I flushed them down the toilet. But you don't want to hear about Eva. I was talking about the day I met István Horvath.

Well, there she was saying there were no more blue pills, and how was I going to get to Walgreens? The snow was up to my armpits, and the subway wasn't running. Then Eva said, "What about that store around the corner?" Now, we always went to Walgreens. You know the guy in Alabama who sold aspirin as that stuff you take for cholesterol? So we were always careful. We never went to the store around the corner. For one thing, the sign said Apothecary, which looked kind of foreign, and we wanted our pills one hundred percent American. For another, the front of the store was kind of dirty. You know, like nobody washed the windows.

But we had to have the blue pills. So I put on my boots and walked through the snow to the Apothecary. And I tell you, it was just around the corner, but by the time I got there I felt like I was going to have a heart attack. It was some work, walking through all that snow.

I figured the store would be closed, and I'd have to knock on the other door, the one for the apartment above the store, which had a sign on it that said Pharmacist. But the sign in the window—which was written in magic marker, can you believe it—said Open. So I walked in.

When the bell on the door rang, István stood up from behind the counter. Not that I knew his name, then. He was wearing a white coat, so I figured he was the pharmacist. "Hello," he said, in a foreign kind of voice, like I'd expected. I figured he was probably Russian. We had a lot of Russians in the neighborhood, in those days. Nothing wrong with that. My grandfather came through Staten Island. We're all immigrants, right? Even the Indians came from someplace else. Now Gorski, what's that, Polish? Ernie at the Post Office, he's Polish. Do you mind if I get some water, Sergeant Gorski? I'm not used to talking so much, since Eva died. Nowadays, you get these lawyers and doctors moving in. They like the "neighborhood atmosphere." Then the old people can't afford it anymore, so they go to Florida, to the retirement communities. And suddenly there's nobody to talk to. But Eva and I had some savings, and with my pension—well, I'm not ready to leave the neighborhood yet.

So István stands up from behind the counter and says, "Hello. Today, I did not expect customers. I was setting traps for the mice. Not to hurt them, you understand. I take them outside, to the cemetery."

Later, I told him they would come back. Mice are smart, they know their way home. But he said, "Then I will trap them again. It is pleasant in the cemetery, with the grass and trees. I will leave them bread, and perhaps they will learn to like it there." Can you imagine? A regular mouse vacation. But that was István all over. He wouldn't swat the flies on the walls. He'd catch them and put them outside, and half an hour later they'd get in again through the holes in the screen. So you're not going to convince me that he murdered his wife.

Now, I have to admit I didn't like the look of the place, when I first came in. There was dust on the shelves, and the boxes of Ace bandages looked like they'd been there a while. Toward the back there were bottles of what looked like dried leaves and flowers, with labels—in magic marker, what did you expect—saying things like Tansy, Agrimony, Rue. But the bottle of blue pills he gave me looked just like it came from Walgreens. When he handed it to me he said, "Tell her to take it always with a piece of bread, so the nausea is not so bad." And you know, he was right.

I won't say I stopped going to Walgreens after that, but I got to buying little things at the Apothecary. Tweezers, antacids, Vicks VapoRub. One day I noticed a chess board on the counter. "Colonel Borodin, she left it," he told me. He could never get his genders right. To him, everyone was a she. "She has a problem with the liver, all that vodka. But she cannot pay the bill, so she gives me this. It is beautiful, no?"

It was beautiful, with ebony and ivory pieces. My grandfather taught me to play chess. He said, in Italy all the men would play in the park, while the women were cooking Sunday dinner. That was the way to live, he said. I sure wouldn't mind living that way.

So István and I started to play together. Usually we played in the Apothecary, on the counter, but a couple of times I invited him over to meet Eva. That was when I found out he was Hungarian. Eva's grandmother was Hungarian, and she knew a few words: yes, no, hello, goodbye, thank you. I think he liked to hear them. Once, he brought a plastic bag full of yellow and white flowers. "Chamomile," he said. "It helps the stomach." Later, he showed me where he dried things, in the basement. He had racks down there, with plants hanging from them. I know that's not what you found. Don't they teach you patience, at the police academy? Chamomile tea was the only thing Eva drank, the month before she died. Toward the end, when she couldn't talk, he told her stories. About girls who lived in rivers, and hens that laid eggs covered with diamonds and rubies. They were so fancy, they were sent to the Russian Tzar. He said he had learned them from his mother. Eva loved those stories. She would smile, and then for a while she'd be able to sleep. She didn't sleep much, in those days.

Before she died, we didn't have a lot of friends. She hadn't gone out for a long time, except to the hospital, and I didn't want to invite the guys from the Post Office to the funeral. Ernie, for example, he can't stand hallways, especially if they're narrow. Stan doesn't like bushes. And none of us likes going to funerals. Your father was in Vietnam? Yeah, you know what I'm talking about.

Our parents, they died a while back, and her brother was out in Tucson. So it was just me and István at the cemetery. He brought a bunch of Easter lilies, exactly the kind of flowers Eva would have liked.

I didn't see him for a while after that. I felt like keeping to myself. I went to work, came home, opened a bottle of beer, and watched TV. I didn't even answer the telephone. It was always someone trying to sell me something, like a time share in Florida, or asking what I thought about the mayor. And István left me alone. That's the kind of guy he was, sensitive. Like Eva.

But one day, he knocked on the door. "Mike," he said, after I'd let him in and asked if he wanted a beer, "I have to go to Budapest. My mother, she is dying. The doctors are not so good there. And now I think they will not put me in prison."

See, the Berlin Wall had come down. I watched them take it down on TV. I figured, this was what we had fought for. To defeat the Commies, right? That's what Ernie said: the day that wall came down, we won the Vietnam war. I don't know. It didn't feel won to me.

"The first time I tried to escape," he told me—I was drinking beer, he was drinking chamomile tea—"they found me. I was stupid, I tried to escape on the train. I was only fifteen. The guards, they laughed and beat the soles of my feet. They sent me back to my mother and told her I would not run away any more. The second time, I was a pharmacist, finished with university. A German friend came to Budapest on vacation. His car, the back seat, it was hollow. I stayed there until we crossed the border into West Germany."

He sat with his hands wrapped around the mug. "I wonder if I was wrong to leave my country. A pharmacist, she is useful everywhere." He looked down into his tea. "I do not know what my mother looks like, now. When I left, her hair was brown. Perhaps it is white."

"You can't change the past," I said. And you can't. It's the one thing you can't do.

He asked if I would take care of the store, just check on it once in a while to make sure no one broke in and the mice didn't eat everything. Then he gave me the key.

I didn't see him again for a couple of months. Then one day I heard a knock on the door. It was him, even thinner than usual, like he hadn't been eating. And standing next to him was this girl.

Of course it was her. Don't worry, I'm getting to that. She had on this coat that looked like it came from the Salvation Army, and a cap on her head that was the color of—well, anyway, it was brown. She was ugly, then. Pale, like she hadn't been out in the sun in years. And she had dark circles under her eyes. I mean, she looked like she'd been raised in a box.

István said, "My friend Mike!" and kissed me on both cheeks. Now, I don't hold with men kissing, you understand. But he'd been away for a while, and they do things different in those foreign countries.

"This is Ildiko," he said, "my wife." She'd been taking care of his mother, he explained. After his mother died, she had nowhere to go. She had no family, and there were no jobs in Budapest. If the country became Communist again, the borders would close, and she'd have no way out. Now isn't that István all over. He marries this girl because he feels sorry for her. He might as well have invited the flies into his apartment.

The first thing I noticed, when I went to the Apothecary for some Pepto Bismol and maybe a game of chess, was the sign. It wasn't in magic marker any more. It was one of those regular signs that other stores had, the Pizza Express and Lou's Shoe Repair and the Vacuum Emporium. The window had been cleaned. In it were a row of combs and brushes, and some of those plastic things women put in their hair. Clips and things. Not the sorts of things Eva would ever have worn. Though toward the end, she almost always wore a turban.

Ildiko was standing behind the counter, with her hair back in one of those plastic clips. "István not here," she said, and rang me up. She was looking a little better, like she'd gotten some sleep. But I don't like skinny women, or ones that don't say hello or thank you. She stared at me like I had no right to be in that store. I tell you, I knew even then that something was wrong. You don't believe me? Well, you're the one trying to figure out who burned down the Apothecary.

About a week later, István invited me over to play chess. He told me he'd been at a pharmacist's convention. It had been Ildiko's idea, like the combs and brushes. Everything was Ildiko's idea, then.

This time there was a rack of magazines by the register: *Woman's Day*, *Soap Opera Digest*, *The National Enquirer*. Those bottles of leaves and flowers that he'd dried himself—they'd been replaced on the shelves with soap and shampoo. There were jars of face cream. It was cleaner, sure, and more like Walgreens. But I didn't like it.

Ildiko was behind the counter again, but I almost didn't recognize her. For one thing, she'd dyed her hair. It was blond, like Marilyn Monroe, though you could still see the roots. And she was wearing bright red lipstick. Her fingernails were bright red too. She was something to look at, all right. But I sure wouldn't have wanted to be her husband.

István, he thought she was wonderful. "She loves America," he told me, setting up the chess pieces. We were upstairs, in the apartment. She didn't want him playing chess on the counter. It would make the customers think there wasn't enough business. "She wants this to be a real American store. She thinks we should name it Drug Mart. You see, she is so clever about the window. We need a display, she says. Something to bring in the women. And her Russian is better than mine. The old men, the majors and colonels, they like her." I bet they did. "I wish she and Eva could have met. I'm certain they would have liked each other." I wasn't so certain. Eva was—well, she was a lady, if you know what I mean. And Ildiko Horvath—well, I don't want to say what she was.

At that moment we heard her laughing, and a "Da, da" coming from downstairs.

You think I'm being unfair? One night, this was about two weeks later, I was walking down the street, smoking a cigarette. Eva would never let me smoke in the apartment, and I still go outside. I don't know why. I guess I imagine her saying, "Mike, you're going to get that smoke all over my curtains."

Anyway, when I passed the Apothecary, I heard her voice from the upstairs window. "Do you think I enjoy taking care of that stupid woman? Do you think I enjoy cleaning up when she cannot go to the toilet? And then I find out she doesn't leave me a forint, not a forint!" She was shouting so loud I thought she would wake up Lou. He still lives above the Shoe Repair, though he retired last year. István answered her in Hungarian, or that's what I figured it was. "Why you think I marry you?" I had to give her one thing, her English was getting better. "I deserve—yes, *deserve*, every forint of that money!"

So don't get on your high horse to me about Ildiko Horvath. The *Herald* can go on about the tragic story: young wife found in a basement, burned to death. But I know what kind of woman she really was.

We started playing chess every week, me and István, and every week there was something new at the store. Boxes of Whitman's Samplers. Marlboro Lights. Those pantyhose in eggs. Ildiko sat at the counter with her blond hair and red nails, in dresses I'd be ashamed to see on Eva.

All right, all right, I'll stick to the facts. That day, I went over to play chess. She wasn't at the counter. István was there instead, with a liquor bottle open beside him. I'd never seen him drink anything stronger than chamomile tea. "Come join me, friend Mike," he said, and poured some into a glass. It was called—now, what was it? Pálinka. Peach brandy, though it didn't taste much like peaches. It burned my throat going down.

Yeah, I guess it could account for the smell. So the firemen noticed that, did they?

"We've been friends for a long time, no?" he said, and I nodded. I guess he was as close to a friend as I had. "I can tell you, things are not well." His speech was slurred, and it was hard figuring out what he was saying, with that accent. He was drunk of course, and I figured I was in for the whole story. That's what guys do when they're drunk, they tell you the whole story. And then they cry in their beer. Waste of good beer, if you ask me. But he got up from the counter and said, "Come, I will show you. She said she will shop for dresses at Filene's, and then she will watch a movie. She said I should not expect her until evening."

He was swaying from side to side, like one of those toys that kids punch, and they don't fall down. But he managed to unlock the door to the basement. I followed him down the stairs.

When he switched on the light, I saw that the racks of drying plants were gone. Instead—how can I describe it? Eva liked movies where people wore costumes. You know, *Dr. Zhivago*. In those movies, rich people always have tables with things on them, like statues. That basement was full of tables and chairs, and on them were statues, of women dancing, and all kinds of dogs. There were pieces of lace, just lying on the tables. Silver teapots and trays, piles of teaspoons. Glass bowls and vases, dark red and that yellow color, what do they call it? Amber. The legs of the tables were carved so they had feet, and the backs of the chairs were inlaid. You know, where they use a different wood to make designs, like birds or flowers. Stan does it as a hobby, but I've never seen him do anything like that. On one table there was a box filled with jewelry, rings and necklaces and what looked like a crown. The kind Miss America wears. On another there was a collection of eggs, and I knew what those were. Eva took me to the museum once, to see those eggs. Fabergé, they call them. The most expensive eggs in the world. The whole room looked like it belonged in Las Vegas.

"What the hell?" I said. I couldn't think of anything else to say.

"My country is poor now," said István. "Many people sell what belonged to their parents or grandparents. And Ildiko knows people who will carry these things across the border. I don't know how, she does not tell me. Mike, how can she know such people?"

"What the hell is she going to do with all this?" I couldn't stop staring. I picked up the crown. It was heavier than I'd expected.

"She sells to Americans. First she sold only a few pieces, then with the money she bought more, and now she sells the treasures of my country." He held out his hands, as though he didn't know what to say. "She tells me, this is America, land of opportunity. I have been here so long, I should be rich by now. But this is not the worst. No—"

Above us, I heard the store bell ring.

"I must go see the customer," he said, "or Ildiko will be angry." He swayed up the stairs, leaving me in the basement.

I looked around me. All that stuff in the light of one bare bulb, shining off the carved wood, the polished silver. It was like being in Aladdin's cave.

Then I heard something. Don't ask me to describe it to you. It came from the back of the basement, behind the tables. Where the light didn't exactly reach. I heard it again.

You think it was Ildiko Horvath? You mean, you think he knocked her on the head, hid her in the basement, then took me down to see what she'd been doing? What kind of fool would do a thing like that? No offense, Gorski, but I don't know how you made sergeant. Sure, he might have been too drunk to care. But that's not what happened. I told you she'd gone to the movies. I saw her come home myself, around six o'clock.

No, what I saw were cages. Cages stacked on top of each other, in the darkness. Now, I'm going to tell you what was in those cages. But I want you to remember, I'd been drinking that pálinka. I was probably drunk. Would a sober man have seen a goat with the head of a boy, maybe fifteen, sixteen? Or a girl, but only about three feet tall, and covered with scales? She had gills on the sides of her neck, just like a fish. There wasn't enough room in the cage for her to stand, so she sat there, rocking back and forth like a monkey at the zoo. There was a cage full of snakes, except they had wings, a bunch of them on some of the bigger ones. There wasn't room to fly, but they beat the air with their wings, and hissed at me. There was a hen with only one leg, not on one side as though the other had been chopped off, but right in the middle. When I looked in that cage, I realized where all those Fabergé eggs had come from. Then the goat boy bleated—that was the sound I'd heard—and something in a cage I'd thought was empty, except for what looked like a rubber poncho on the floor, opened its eyes. Its hell of a lot of eyes, all different colors, blue and gray and green. I turned and ran out of that basement, up the stairs and past the counter where István was ringing up a customer. He looked up, startled, as I ran past him and out the door. I didn't stop until I was across the street and smoking a cigarette. I stood there, across the street from the store, until it got dark, smoking most of a pack, not wanting to go home to the empty apartment, not wanting to return to the Apothecary. I think István realized why I had run out of there, because after that customer left he went upstairs to the apartment and sat at the kitchen table with his head in his hands. Yeah, he went down again once, but then he went back to the kitchen. A couple more customers came by, but he didn't answer the bell.

That's how I saw when Ildiko came home, right around six o'clock as I said. She went upstairs and said something to him. When he didn't answer she threw her coat down on the chair, and her purse on top of it. Then she turned on the stove and started cooking dinner.

Now what you want to know is, how did the store burn down, with her body in the basement? I'll tell you what I'm going to swear to in court. I'm going to swear that I saw Ildiko Horvath go down to the store and open the basement door, then go down to the basement. You can see the door through the store window. And I'll swear that I saw

István fall asleep on the kitchen table, spilling the bottle of pálinka. Remember, the stove was on. It was a small kitchen—easy enough for some of the pálinka to spill on the flames. That would explain why the firemen smelled peaches. You don't think I could see that far? Check my army record. I was a sniper in Vietnam. My vision's still better than twenty twenty.

Oh, but I wasn't drunk by then. I'd been standing out there about an hour. I'd had plenty of fresh air. All right, so Ildiko had a bruise on her head. Maybe she got that trying to escape the fire. It spread so fast, I barely got István out. Someone should talk to the mayor about these old buildings.

I thought you would find the cages. Of course they were empty. You don't think I actually saw those things? István probably kept the cages for catching raccoons.

But I'm going to tell you something, Sergeant. Off the record. You don't have one of those wires, do you? I've watched cop shows on TV. That's why I wanted to meet here, instead of at the station. István Horvath, he wouldn't hurt a fly. Those things—I don't know what they were, but I think he cared about them. Remember the stories he told Eva. I think that's what he really meant, when he talked about the treasures of his country. I mentioned how he let the mice out in the cemetery? Once, when I was sitting there by Eva's grave, I saw her. The scaled girl. She was sitting on the grass by the pond, and sort of humming. And once I saw the biggest bat I've ever seen. Two feet across, it must have been, like a black kite. I don't even want to talk about its eyes. But it was getting dark, so I could have been mistaken.

What if, off the record now, István did start that fire? First, he would have set those things free. Some things shouldn't be in cages. You can understand that, right? You're Polish, your people are from the old country. And Ildiko Horvath? Like I said, István wouldn't hurt a fly. But she wasn't a fly, more like a spider in her web, or a cat waiting for the mouse to come out of its hole. What if, when she went down to the basement, István followed her, with the bottle of pálinka in his hand? What if he showed her the empty cages, then poured what was left in the pálinka bottle over those pieces of lace, and told her he would burn the things in the basement before he'd let her sell them? And then he lit a match. I figure she would fly at him with those red nails of hers. If he hit her with the bottle, well, that's self-defense. It wouldn't be his fault that the fire spread so quickly. But hey, I'm just telling a story. There are no windows in the basement. If something happened down there, I wouldn't have seen it, even if I wanted to. Anyway, I tell you, whatever she got she deserved. And I think Eva would agree.

But that's between you and me. István's not talking. I told him, this is America. We have rights in this country. So I'm your only witness. As far as I'm concerned, the fire was an accident. And I'm not going to say different, not if I have to swear on the Bible, so help me God.

DEATH COMES FOR ERVINA

"YOU HAVE A visitor."

THERE IS SOMETHING vaguely bovine about the nurse, whose name Ervina has once again forgotten. She reminds Ervina of the cows that she milked during the war. She would wake in the darkness, before the rooster crowed from his perch on the hay wagon, and fetch the water so her mother could make breakfast: boiled potatoes on which she dripped lard for flavoring. Then she would milk the cows, whose names were, she remembers, Rózsa and Piroska. In winter, when a rim of ice formed on the milk pail, she would warm her hands in their breaths. When Rózsa stopped giving milk, she was taken to the butcher, and Ervina cried for three days.

"Jésus Mária," said her mother, who always appears in her memories wearing an apron, "all those tears for a cow."

Then she would collect the eggs. Surely, at first, there were eggs with the potatoes, fried in lard? And later there were no eggs, no lard, and finally no potatoes, just boiled cabbage flavored with salt. The faces of the children at school became pale above their uniforms, which were ragged from being worn every day of the week, for doing chores or playing football. They had no other clothes.

After her father came back from the war, without Dénes or Ödön, it was her mother's turn to cry. She could not, Ervina supposes, have cried for three years, but that is what she remembers. When she began school again, with a new uniform and a red kerchief around her neck, her cheeks were damp with her mother's tears.

∾

"MISS KÓVACS, DID you hear me? You have a visitor. Someone from the ballet school. You want I should open the window? I don't know how you stand it in here, under all those blankets."

∾

HER FATHER DID not want her to go to the ballet school.

"She's just a child," he said. "Who will raise her in Budapest? You say she will be raised by the school, but I spent a week in the city during the war. It's filled with gypsies and prostitutes. Why should I send my daughter to such a place?"

Because, explained the teacher, his daughter had a talent for the ballet, and it was his duty to the Party—and why, by the way, hadn't he joined the Party, didn't he know it was created to benefit farmers such as himself?—to use her talent in the service of the People's Republic.

Ervina listened from behind the kitchen door. Budapest was as unreal to her as the frog prince in the fairy tale. Once, she had tried to kiss a frog she had found in the reeds by the river Tisza, with no result. Not that she wanted the frog to become a prince. But she wanted, herself, to become a princess, with a gold ball. After she had milked the cows, she would stand by the barn door to make her révérence, and the cows would stare at her with appreciative brown eyes. But when her father returned from the war, alone and leaning heavily on a cane, her mother went back to milking the cows and collecting the eggs, while Ervina sat at the kitchen table practicing her sums.

It seemed strange that she should be taken to Budapest because she could point her toes or arch her back better than the other children in her class, away from the mother who no longer told her fairy tales but cried into the cabbage soup, the father who told her to practice her sums so she could train to be an accountant, because on the farm she would never be as useful as a boy.

The smell of exhaust and roasting eggplant fills the room. When she first moved to this apartment in Brooklyn, there was a Hungarian bakery across the street. Each morning she would buy a slice of poppy seed beigli and eat it slowly, in miniature bites, with her morning coffee, as though to reward herself for a lifetime of hunger.

At the ballet school in Budapest, breakfast was two pieces of toast, a boiled egg, and a sliced tomato. How hungry they were, the girls whose shoulder blades appeared through their leotards, like vestigial wings. How proud they were of their hunger, the girls from farms as far away as Debrecen, as they watched their muscular waists become slender, watched the suppleness of their legs, which had once struggled in farm boots through fields to be mown for hay. Even the fourteen-year-olds drank their coffee black and smoked Bulgarian cigarettes.

Now the Hungarian bakery has been replaced by an Armenian restaurant. But she can no longer eat sweets, she thinks approvingly, looking at her wrists, which have never been so thin: blue veins covered by layers of tulle, like the skirts of the Swans Maidens surrounding Odette, who wears a crown that to the audience looks like gold, although Ervina knows that it is gilded papier maché. She has worn it often enough.

~

"ISN'T THAT BETTER? It's about time you got some fresh air. He says his name is Victor. He says he knows you from the ballet school. Miss Kóvacs? Should I tell him you're too tired? Or should I tell him to come in?"

~

BUT IT WAS not in *Swan Lake* that she first met Victor Boyd.

She danced in *Swan Lake* the first time she came to New York. It was an era when cultural exchange was encouraged, and the Budapest Ballet had been invited to Carnegie Hall. From their rooms in a hotel on West 83rd Street, the ballerinas could hear the continual honking of taxis, and smell hot dogs being sold in the park.

Perhaps it was that, although she was Ervina Kóvacs, whose photograph hung in the ballet school dormitory, who had a sponge cake named after her at Gundel's, who had received a standing ovation from Chairman Brezhnev himself, she had to share a room with Ilona Nagy, who danced Odile. Perhaps that, from the car window as the ballerinas were driven to Carnegie Hall, she could see buildings taller than any she had seen in Budapest, or Prague, or even Moscow, whose windows reflected clouds. Perhaps she was tired of dancing Petipa, of Jardins Animés or bayadères endlessly pirouetting across the stage behind her. Perhaps it was only the smell of hot dogs.

That day, while Siegfried began his pas de deux with Odile, she pulled out the hairpins that held on her crown, threw a coat that the janitor had left on a hook over her shoulders, and left through a back door. She waved her arms on the street until a taxi swerved to the curb, splashing her pointe shoes with mud.

"New York Ballet," she had said, repeating it three times until the driver understood. Her pronunciation was not so good in those days. He cursed her when, in front of the ballet school, she jumped out of the taxi and handed him a purse full of forints.

The door opens again and Victor walks into the room, looking as when she first saw him, in jeans and a t-shirt with Rolling Stones written on it, the blond hair ragged around his shoulders, as awkward and graceful as a young swan.

But no, this Victor has gray hair above his ears. This Victor is wearing a gray suit and a watch with Bulova written on it, and his name is Mr. Boyd. There are traces, still, in his movements of the boy to whom she once said, "If you would only apply yourself, Vic, you would be the greatest ballet dancer in the company, perhaps in the world. I mean, of course, after me."

∾

"ERVINA," HE SAYS, taking her hands, which are as pale as milk, with blue veins running through them. She approves of their delicacy. "Madame Petrovna told me you were sick."

∾

SHE WAS ALREADY a teacher then, training to succeed Larissa Petrovna, who had trained with the Kirov Ballet and was the most famous teacher at the ballet school. She had already danced in Paris, in

London, in Tokyo, and in a public television special. But she could feel that her calloused feet, which had long ago conformed to the shape of a pointe shoe, were no longer as subtle as they had been, and that her back could no longer bend like a reed in the river current. She had already stopped dancing the roles that Mr. D had created for her, the Blue Note in *Symphony in Blue*, Elena in *Three Sisters*, the Hyacinth Girl. She was preparing, with a pragmatism she supposed she had inherited from her father, who was lying in his grave in Szent Miklós, presumably no longer shocked that she had become a ballerina, which was no better than a prostitute, for the day when she could no longer dance. It had not been easy, realizing that she would soon have to stop dancing even Odette. But one could still, she had thought, be useful, one could still have a sort of fame, after one no longer wore the papier maché crown.

She had thought of her mother, one of those interchangeable widows dressed in black at the Museum of Cultural History in Debrecen, who issued visitors felt slippers so the floors would not be scuffed. In her last letter she had sounded almost happy, had written about a geranium she was growing in the apartment window. She had sent Ervina her gingerbread recipe. So, Ervina supposed, old age contracted one's interests until such things were enough. Perhaps, she thought, one day I will no longer care if the audience applauds.

And then into the studio had walked Mr. D, leading a young man with ragged hair around his shoulders. He had said, "Ervina, this is Victor Boyd. You must teach him to dance."

"But he is too old!" Ervina had said.

And then Victor had danced for her. Had she fallen in love with him that day? Or had it been later, on a day that they danced together in the studio, as the Black Pawn and White Queen in *Chess* perhaps, or the Herons in *Birds*?

He had been badly taught. It would take months before she could unteach him all he had learned, before she could teach him what he needed to know. Months in which, after mornings at the barre, he would meet with her individually. In the afternoons, with sunlight slanting through the studio windows, they would watch him move in the mirror, while the pianist played Prokofiev or Tchaikovsky with the endless precision of a machine.

WHAT IS HE telling her? "Did she mention that Juliette left me? The day Jim left for college. She said, 'Now that the children are out of the house, there's no reason for us to stay together, is there?' Her suitcase was already packed. She's living with an investment banker on Long Island. But you're not interested in this. How are you doing, Ervina? Rosemarie said you're getting excellent care."

That's why the nurse reminds her of a cow. Rosemarie is the name that she's forgotten.

"So we're finally through." He begins to laugh, then stops abruptly. When did his face become wrinkled? She prefers it to the blank twenty-year-old face he had when he told her, "I'm going to marry Juliette."

"You warned me, didn't you?" he says, looking down at her hands, absentmindedly running his fingers over the veins. "You said, 'Juliette Biró will never be more than a soloist, and if you marry her you will never be the dancer you were meant to be.' That was the night we danced Oberon and Titania together."

IT HAD BEEN a benefit for the New York Diabetes Foundation, his debut and her farewell performance. They had danced Mr. D's *A Midsummer Night's Dream*, the last ballet he would create for her and, she realized with chagrin, one suitable for her diminished talents. Despite her elaborate costume, which was covered with leaves that had to be sewn on by hand, Titania's role was largely ornamental, while Oberon had been choreographed for a dancer who could leap like a stag, from one end of the stage to the other. With Oberon's antlers on his head, dressed only in a bronze loincloth and bronze paint, Victor looked like a god of the forest. She pirouetted to meet him, the green tulle fastened to her shoulders fluttering like wings. With fairies piquéing around them, Peaseblossom, Cobweb, Moth, and Mustardseed, students from the ballet school, she met him not in the embrace Mr. D had choreographed, but with a kiss worthy of a forest god and the queen of fairies. And afterward he had told her, behind the curtain, "I'm going to marry Juliette."

"SO HERE I am. This morning I met with the planning committee. This afternoon I'm going to a fundraiser for the school." He laughs again, uncomfortably, then abruptly leans forward until his forehead is resting on the backs of her hands. "You were right, you know." His voice is muffled, but she hears it as clearly as the call before the raising of a curtain. "You were right about everything. But you scared the shit out of me. You were the great Ervina Kóvacs, and what was I? A kid from Oklahoma who grew up on basketball and got stuck in a dance class because the coach thought it would help him jump." He raises his head and looks at her, so that she sees herself in his eyes: the gray hair lying on the pillow, the face like a wrinkled sheet. "I just wanted you to know that."

THERE IS SOMETHING she must tell him, about mornings during the war when she milked the cows, and nothing for breakfast but potatoes. She must tell him that he has misunderstood her. But it is she who has misunderstood: the revelation comes slowly, like sunlight filtering through the mud in the river Tisza, illuminating the carp that slide beneath the surface. It wasn't you I loved, she wants to tell him. It wasn't you after all. It was—but she's not certain how to finish.

She feels her eyebrows extend into antennae.

He takes off his jacket, unbuttons his white shirt. It is not the body she remembers, the shoulders almost too muscular for the waist, which was as slender as a girl's. This waist has filled out, but it is still firm, the skin glittering like bronze. And his kiss, as he bends over the bed, is still the kiss of a forest god. His antlers rise like the branches of an oak tree. Then he moves away from her in a series of soubresauts and stands in front of the window, through which she can hear the noise of traffic, holding out his hands as though waiting for her to join him.

"DID YOU HAVE a nice visit with Mr. Boyd?" asks Rosemarie. "He looks so distinguished, like a doctor on *General Hospital*. I bet he was a dreamboat when he was a boy." Oberon stands in front of the window, antlered and naked except for a bronze loincloth. "You want I should bring you some lunch? I made chicken broth with dumplings, just like you taught me."

THE CHAIR ON which he had been sitting has sprouted, and the forest is rising around her, cardboard branches casting shadows under the spotlight of a moon. Music is playing from a unseen orchestra, and fairies flit through the forest on wings of tulle, with antennae painted over their eyes. In the forest, Oberon is waiting. Yes, she thinks, this is it, this is what I wanted all along. Titania rises from her bank of flowers.

❧

"MISS KÓVACS?"

❧

SHE PIROUETTES, REVELING in the strength of her feet, the suppleness of her back as she leans over Oberon's arm, looking toward the darkness where an audience is watching. She sees her mother, holding a potted geranium; her father, dour and disapproving; Ödön and Dénes. A teacher from her school in Szent Miklós, waving a red flag. Students she remembers from ballet class, taking notes. Larissa Petrovna, swinging her famous string of pearls in time to the music. Even Rózsa is standing in the aisle. She can see them all, in the darkness beyond the footlights. Perhaps, she thinks, for what I have done or not done, I have been forgiven. In the wings, hidden behind a curtain, Mr. D is nodding his approval. She smiles at him, then looks again at Oberon as the music begins for their pas de deux.

THE BELT

MY STORY HAS the contours of a fairy tale. Once, there was a shoemaker's daughter named Sophia. She lived in the city you see from your morning-room windows, in a part of it that you don't see. A poor part, a shabby part, where the shoemakers lived, and the laundresses, and the sellers of coal. Her father was, as I have mentioned, a shoemaker, who served neither the merchants, nor the professors at the university, but their clerks and students, men who wished, at relatively small expense, to dress like their masters. He served also members of the theatrical profession. His most celebrated shoe was worn by Herr Grünwald, in the character of Macbeth.

Her mother, a grocer's daughter, died when Sophia was just old enough to understand that the priest who performed the burial rites could offer no consolation. I tell you this because if her mother had lived until Sophia's seventeenth birthday, my story would not have happened.

One day, after delivering a pair of short boots to a clerk who worked—exalted position!—in the Hauptbank, within sight of the Winterpalast, Sophia decided that she would walk home by way of the park. For the first time in three days, the snow had stopped. She was tired of being cooped up in the back room of the shoemaker's shop, with its smell of beeswax and alcohol, and wanted to see the branches of the trees encased in ice. They sparkled in the sunlight— your diamonds, Madam, are as nothing to them—and filled her heart with delight so that, as she walked home along the frozen streets, she looked up at the sky and sang a little song under her breath, one of the country songs her mother had sung to her in the cradle.

That is why she slipped on a patch of ice and fell to the ground.

The hands that lifted her up were encased in leather gloves trimmed with ermine—their tails hung over the wrist. When she looked up, dazzled and in pain, for she had twisted her ankle, she discovered that the person assisting her was a young man, with a very white face and very blue eyes, and an ermine hat.

I am not like your men of letters, who can write *he said* and *she said* for seven hundred pages. Before my mother died, she told me stories, by firelight after I had finished my schoolwork, while my father sat in a corner preparing leather for a riding boot or stitching satin for a lady's slipper. I can only tell you this story as she would have done.

For three months, Nicholas sat in the shoemaker's shop, courting Sophia. Once, he asked her to marry him. Twice, he asked her. And the third time she said yes. Why did she wait so long, why did she risk losing what was obviously a match beyond her most extravagant expectations? For Nicholas had explained his position to her father, the timber harvested from northern forests, the mines that gave forth coal, the mills that produced cloth. And it was obvious to both father and daughter that Nicholas was in love. The shoemaker had not gone to school past the age of fourteen, but he was an able judge of men, for the city had made him so, and Sophia had taken in with her mother's milk not only the romantic ideas that made her tell stories of princes and beggar maids by firelight but also the shrewdness of a grocer's daughter, who understood two things as thoroughly as though she had studied them at the university: customers and money.

And they were not deceived. For when Sophia stood in the cathedral, in the satin wedding dress that had been her mother's one extravagance and shoes that her father had made for her, and said that she would love and obey her husband, she became a Baroness, the owner of a village in the south and a townhouse in the city. Her father would never make shoes again, except for pleasure. It was her seventeenth birthday.

You think this is the end of my story. Wait, Madam. This is its true beginning.

After the wedding, Nicholas told Sophia that he would take her to a hunting lodge he owned in the Eisenwald. They rode in the carriage for hours, with the mountains rising on either side of them, the fir trees covered with snow. He held her hands. Once, he let them go to wrap her cloak more tightly around her. It was a cloak of ermine, which he had given her as a wedding gift. Occasionally they talked, in the way people do who have a great deal of time together, and no immediate need for conversation.

Once, he pressed his lips to her hands, and she realized, with a start, *Why, he loves me more than I love him.* It was a revelation for her, that love in marriage could be unequal, and for the first time she wondered what her mother would have said to Nicholas' proposal. *I believe,* she thought, *that Mama would have told me to send him away.* For she guessed, and in this I think she was right, that her mother would have shared the scruple which had kept her from accepting his proposal for three months. *I cannot give him as much as he gives me, and that is a bad bargain.* There, you see, spoke the grocer's daughter.

At last, they arrived. It was late, and the stars were shining, more stars than she had ever seen, in the city with its gas lamps. Nicholas himself lit a fire in the great stone fireplace, beneath the head of a stag, and himself unpacked the basket of food they had brought. He filled the wine glasses.

"I have told the driver to sleep in the village," he said. "I wanted our first night to be altogether alone."

She realized that she had seen no servants. She would not have expected them in her former life, but here their absence seemed to make the rooms more silent, and lent a strangeness to their meal. She wondered who would unlace her dress and blushed, then felt foolish for blushing. She smiled, to show him that she appreciated this romantic gesture. Already, you see, a note of pity had crept into her relation to him. She promised herself that she would turn it into tenderness, for she had taken her marriage vows seriously, and intended to love and obey him.

So she appeared neither shocked nor disgusted when he showed her the belt. "Without it," he said, looking down at the bearskin laid across the carpet, as though ashamed of his confession, "I can do nothing. If you would wear it?" It was an ordinary leather belt, but with a buckle at the back, to which were attached two smaller belts, whose use was evident enough. His white hands held it toward her, and his blue eyes pleaded.

He buckled it over her waist, and buckled her wrists behind her.

I know, Madam, what you are expecting. But if my story contains perversions, they are not the ones you imagine. Nicholas' and Sophia's marital relations were as proper as your own, and merited the blessings of the Church. The only difference was, that Sophia wore the belt.

In the morning, when she woke in his arms, Nicholas begged her, "Wear it, just for today." What could she do? Stronger than the constraint of the belt was the constraint of her pity: she did not love him as he loved her, and so she must treat him with tenderness. In addition, her enjoyment of their wedding night had been adequate, but had not equaled his ecstasy. And when he had asked her, in the morning, she had resorted to a fib. For this she felt shame, but an even greater sense of injustice, as though she had cheated a customer by placing her thumb on the scale.

He dressed her with gentleness and considerable skill. She was surprised to see that he was not hindered by the belt. He found ways to modify her costume to accommodate its limitations.

That day, they walked through the forest, and when he shouted her name, icicles crashed from the trees, like a symphony of breaking glass. He breathed on her cheeks to warm them, and showed her a white owl as it flew through the trees. They ate cold chicken, and potatoes he had roasted in the fireplace. The wine came from a hillside in Italy. He told her they would go there someday, and roam through the galleries of Florence, and swim in the Mediterranean. She imagined it as a sheet of water as blue as his eyes.

That night, when he asked her to wear the belt for another day, she knew she had a problem. It was this: she knew that if she asked him to remove it, he would do so. But she could not ask him. She was her mother's daughter, and her sense of pity, and of justice, forbade it. And then, too, she had promised in the presence of the Holy Mother to love and obey him. Since she did not love him as she ought, she must try to do the other. But he would never remove the belt of his own volition. She had begun to understand that, had seen it in his blue eyes, in the joy with which he looked at her, and the helplessness. So what was she to do?

She sat on the bearskin before the fireplace and said, "Tell me about the belt."

He looked down at his hands, and then a blush rose from his neck to his cheeks, making him look as though he had a fever. When he looked at her again, his eyes were filled with tears.

"Do you know what I saw in your face, that first day, when you slipped on the ice?" he asked. "I saw that we were alike, you and I. And when I brought you home, and spoke to your father, I discovered it was true. You lost your mother when you were young. I lost my father. Your father raised you, while my mother—" He looked into the fire.

Startled, Sophia thought, *It is as though he has looked into a mirror and seen my face, and assumed it is identical to his own. But a face seen in a mirror is not identical, but opposite, to its original.*

His mother had been a possessive woman, of a hysterical temperament. After his father's funeral, she had brought Nicholas to the hunting lodge. She had dismissed the servants, and arranged for deliveries of whatever they might need from the village. Then, she had presented him with the belt. He was just fourteen. It had been made according to her request by one of the shoemakers in the city, perhaps one of the shoemakers in the quarter where Sophia had lived with her father.

For three years Nicholas had worn the belt. For three years she had fed him and bathed him and clothed him, attending to all his needs.

"You see," he said, blushing again, like sunset on a mountain covered with snow, "she loved me. She wanted me to be her child. But I did not understand her. On my seventeenth birthday, I accused her of imprisoning me, like the witch in a fairy tale. I told her that she was cruel, and that I hated her, that I would always hate her. That day, she unbuckled the belt. I ran through the forest to the village, and ordered a room at the inn. I spent the night drinking and listening to the men tell hunting stories. I paid for all their drinks, with money I had stolen from her bureau. They slapped me on the back and teased me about girls, as though I were one of them. The next morning, they told me she was dead. The village woman who brought our milk had found her. Since her payment was not on the doorstep, she had knocked on the door until it swung open. My mother had hung herself from one of the beams, with the belt."

He looked into the fire again, then said, "Would you like to see a picture of her?"

In the miniature, Sophia recognized his blue eyes, the indeterminate chin that was hidden in his case by a small beard. The painted lips looked as though about to tremble. His long, mobile mouth had come from his father. But suddenly, she saw that it was trembling as well.

"So you see, I am a murderer. And a liar as well, because I loved her, almost as much as I love you."

Sophia thought, *And I love him. I do. So I will endure this thing which after all he endured before me.* And again she felt for him a great pity.

But on the second day that she wore the belt, something happened. While she was standing by the kitchen door, watching Nicholas throw the crumbs of their breakfast to the sparrows, she realized that she was bored.

You think, Madam, that the opposite of love is hatred, but it is not. The opposite of love is boredom. When the mind is bored, the heart cannot love, nor can it have pity, because the mind asks, *What do I care for such things?*

In that moment, Sophia thought, *This man is a stranger to me, and this is not my home.*

And yet she could not ask him to unbuckle the belt. She was constrained by all that she had previously thought and promised to herself. Perhaps you think, she should have been more practical. But she was her mother's daughter, and both her sense of justice and her romanticism prevented her from breaking a promise. Besides, what girl was ever practical at seventeen? Yourself excepted, Madam.

But she was a shoemaker's daughter, and if there was one thing she understood, it was leather. That evening, when Nicholas asked if she would like some wine, she said, "I have drunk already," and he was so joyful in his love for her, in the feel of his fingers tangled in her hair, that he did not wonder how she could have drunk without his help. On the next day, she insisted that she was not thirsty, and once she coughed when he put a glass of water to her lips, so that it spilled.

By the evening of that third day, her wedding ring could slip from her finger, and her hands could slip from the leather straps at the back of the belt. Remember that it had been made for him, and she was a shoemaker's daughter, who had not been fed all her life on beef and cream. Even when buckled on the smallest holes, it did not fit her as tightly as it had fit him at fourteen.

That night, she slept in the belt.

The next morning, she woke before him and slipped her hands out of the straps. She unbuckled the belt from her waist, and placed it on the bed beside him. She waited for three minutes by his pocket watch, which he had left on the table, one minute for each day that she had worn the belt, and each year that he had worn it. *Or*, she thought, *one minute for the Son, the Father, and the Holy Ghost.* That was the time she had decided to wait, in memory of her former love and pity. *If he wakes now*, she told herself, *I will put it on again, and God, and not myself, will have decided.*

But she knew that while a shoemaker's daughter wakes at dawn, a Baron's son does not wake until the maid brings him his coffee and rolls. On previous mornings, she had woken before him. This morning, he did not wake.

She followed the road until she came to the village, and the carriage driver recognized her as the Baroness, so she ordered her breakfast on credit.

And that is the end of my story.

Forgive me, Madam. I forgot that in your father's court you were taught philosophy and geography and French, but that you were never told even one small fairy tale. If you had been, you would not need me to explain further. Someday, you must let me tell you the stories my mother told me. They are the stories of your people, and even an Empress should know them.

Well then. The ending of a fairy tale is as inevitable as death. I, Madam, am a murderess. After Nicholas' body was taken down from the beam, Sophia had the belt cut and sewn into a pair of shoes, which she wore to Mass every Sunday. I have them still, although I no longer wear them. One becomes bored, eventually, even of penance. Do not blame Sophia, Madam. Boredom is a healthy impulse. It is a sign of the will to live. Fear the man who is not bored by suffering.

I will tell you, too, that every fairy tale has a moral. The moral of my story may be that love is a constraint, as strong as any belt. And this is certainly true, which makes it a good moral. Or it may be that we are all constrained in some way, either in our bodies, or in our hearts or minds, an Empress as well as the woman who does her laundry. Indeed, perhaps you are more constrained, Madam. For your laundress, whose name you do not know, can do something that you, whose fingers are covered with diamonds, cannot—she can walk through the streets of the city at night and look up at the stars. Perhaps it is that a shoemaker's daughter can bear restraint less easily than an aristocrat, that what he can bear for three years she can endure only for three days. That is a moral your husband and his counselors, Madam, would do well to learn, for a shoemaker's daughter is very like a laundress, or the seller of violets on the street corner. And what if someday there should be no shoes or violets, and the laundry should not be washed? Even now, in a part of the city that you don't see, men are marching with placards: shoemakers and sellers of coal, but also clerks from the Hauptbank and university students. Your husband has not told you this, I think. Or perhaps my moral is that our desire for freedom is stronger than love or pity. That is a wicked moral, or so the

Church has taught us. But I do not know which moral is the correct one. And that is also the way of a fairy tale.

PHALAENOPSIS

IT WAS A phalaenopsis orchid. He had chosen it himself, had walked down the central aisle of the greenhouse (sweat rolling down his neck, making the back of his neck prickle: it was hot) between two rows of orchids. Some looked like magenta purses, like those purses his mother had carried in the sixties. Some looked like yellow butterflies. Some were brown, like spiders. Some were pure white, hanging like—well, like white flowers, like themselves. And he knew those wouldn't do. They were beyond him. He needed something simpler, more obvious: something with color. So he chose a phalaenopsis orchid, with three flowers above the oval leaves, white and pink.

"Why orchids?" he had asked Brother Simon.

"Theoretically, of course, any flower would do," Bother Simon answered. They were walking along the cloister, and it was raining. He liked the rain, liked hearing it fall on the slate roof of the monastery. He had grown up not far from here, although when he stood at the library window, looking out on the river that wound between its manicured banks and the boathouses of ancient colleges, it seemed as distant as Mars—in the tenements near the railroad tracks. But rain fell on the rich and poor alike. It reminded him of home.

"Theoretically, even a vegetable would do—the whorls of a cabbage, for instance. The point is to have a focal—well, point. The point is to have a point. For the Buddhist, that point is a sound: the sound of his breath, of the exhalation OM. But perhaps we—and I don't mean Catholics specifically, but we westerners—aren't as spiritual as the Buddhists, spirit of course coming from *spiritus*, meaning breath. For us, seeing is believing. A rose now, a rose would probably do. Although a rose, like a cabbage, is convoluted, it does not come to a point. So come to think of it, the mind might—well, wander more than it ought to. And there is the symbolism, of a rose I mean—although it's vanity, not wanting to be accused of sentiment. But there it is, we are not as spiritual as we should be." Brother Simon stood in the corridor, considering the possibilities, his head, with looked like a turtle's, sticking out of the cowl that lay around his thin neck. "Yes, it might allow the mind to wander, and then what would be the—well, point?" He poked John gently in the ribs with his finger, and chuckled. "But in practice, you know," he said, serious again, "we find that an orchid is best, and the prices have come down remarkably with the new hybrids."

So here it was, his orchid, on the table in front of him. It was not raining, but it might rain later; the sky was gray with clouds. But he should not look out the window, at the sky or the maple branch that bisected it, with a single brown leaf still hanging on, or the clouds beyond them. Or the wall with the metal cane leaning against it. He had asked Brother Simon if he should learn how to use it, but Brother Simon answered, "That will come soon enough." He had sat here, in this chair, every night for the last two years, reading from Genesis to Revelations, then starting at Genesis again, underlining every text that seemed important to him.

When Moses asked to see God's face, for example, and God said to him, thou canst not see my face, for there shall no man see me and live. And he told Moses to stand on a rock, and covered Moses with his hand, and when he took his hand away, there was God's backside. Or, as his father had once said, "All that work, and he gets to see God's ass." But the point—here he was, talking about points like Brother Simon—the point was, that it was blasphemy, wanting to see God. And yet the Psalmist asked for exactly that: O Lord God, to whom vengeance belongeth, O God, to whom vengeance belongeth, shew thyself. This was Brother Martin's God—he could not imagine Brother Simon's God being vengeful. But perhaps Brother Simon was mistaken, perhaps he was too influenced by Buddhist philosophy, which he had studied—Brother Martin had told him this—at Harvard. Like music in the supermarket, that you find yourself humming after you leave the store, the psalm kept rolling through his head: Lord, how long shall the wicked, how long shall the wicked triumph? And, they break in pieces thy people, O Lord, and afflict thy heritage. They slay the widow and the stranger, and murder the fatherless. He had been a stranger, and fatherless. Yet no one had done anything to him. He had done it all himself. He had slain the widow, metaphorically. Which meant that he was one of the wicked—that much, at least, he had understood in prison. Yet surely it was, also, the promise of the Gospels, which were not vengeful, not generally, except for the sheep and the goats, which was another issue, and maybe Jesus was in a bad mood that day. That's what the Gospels promised: blessed are the pure in heart, for they shall see God. One night, when he had been at the monastery for only a couple of months, he realized that his candle was the only one lit, along all the stone corridors, in all the stone rooms, the only one. And he had been afraid.

He was afraid now. Afraid to look at the orchid, so he looked down at Bernie's head lying across his feet, in wool socks and Birkenstock sandals. Should he reach down and run the Saint Bernard's soft ears through his hands, bury his fingers in the abundant hair at his neck? Let Bernie sleep. He would have enough to do afterward.

He wondered what his father would have said. He was looking at the orchid now, afraid but looking anyway. His mother had been the Catholic, had brought him to Saint Mary Magdalen when his father was riding the train, from Boston to all points south, New York through Philadelphia, all the way down to Washington. "Don't tell your father," she said, and she made him put on his white shirt and go to Mass with her, every Sunday that his father was gone. He should have hated it, should have wanted to be outside, playing baseball with the boys from John F. Kennedy Junior High. But he liked the way the church smelled, like his mother's handkerchief, and he liked the clink of her rosary, and the way her face became peaceful in the silence before the organ uttered its first note. It made her look the way she should have, but seldom did, like an older version of the girl in her wedding picture, rather than the pale, gray woman he had always known. Afterward, she would introduce him to the other women: terribly old, they seemed to him, most of them from Poland or Latvia or Romania, some country that no longer existed, or existed again, on the map of Europe. His mother would say, "This is my Johnny, he's a good boy," and pat his arm, which she had threaded through hers, and he would be happy.

One day, his father came home before he was expected. There had been an accident on the line. When John arrived home from Mass with his mother, his father was waiting, still in his conductor's uniform. His father didn't shout, he was a big man but a quiet one, but he said, "My son isn't going to be a pansy." After that, he went with his father to the Union meetings, and if his mother went to church, she must have done it alone, while he was in school or playing baseball with his friends.

That was one of the days that had broken her heart, he now realized. Like the day his father died. The Union had voted to strike: something about pensions, it was always about pensions. The strike was going well, Union members marching with placards, the engineers, the signalmen, his father with the Brotherhood of Railway Conductors, all wearing their uniforms, when someone, probably a security guard, shot into the air. But they didn't know that, they thought they were being shot at, and some of them panicked. By the time an ambulance got through, his father was dead of a heart attack. Like the day he dropped out of school, the day he was sent to prison. Now she lay in a nursing home upstate, with a broken heart despite the bypass and two angioplasties.

"That guilt is your burden," Brother Martin had said. "Carry it like Christ carried the cross. We live in a culture, John, where we're told not to feel guilty. But guilt is good for us. It's the one thing that can make us truly humble."

Well, he had felt humble enough, after getting out of prison. Humble enough for a herd of donkeys.

But he had forgotten the orchid. The flower at the top of the stalk was fully open—the lower ones were still mostly closed, like mouths. The flower at the top had three petals, unless you counted those other two, what were they, like leaves, although not leaves because they were white. But thinner than the other petals, and almost hidden behind them. So five—were they called petals? He should have read something, like a book about orchids. And suddenly he thought, this will never work, never, because I didn't read a book about orchids, and he felt a tremendous sense of relief. Because if it didn't work, he could walk out of here, and rent an apartment, and maybe work in a convenience store.

"Get thee behind me," he whispered—the first thing he had said since coming into the room and putting the orchid on the table, and sitting in his chair, and starting to look.

"Your goal isn't to understand, but to *see*," Brother Simon had said. Brother Martin knew the words but Brother Simon knew the reasons behind the words, or so it seemed to him. Brother Martin was smart, in his own way: he had been a high school math teacher, and he believed in the Bible like he believed in algebra. But Brother Simon had been at the monastery for twenty-two years. He had also been in Vietnam. When John asked him why he had come to the monastery, Brother Simon said, "I'd seen enough. I wanted to stop seeing."

"Did you?" he asked.

"No," said Brother Simon. "I learned to see again."

No, his father would not have approved. "That's what religion is, Johnny," he had said, sitting at the kitchen table, late one night, after coming home from another run. "The opiate of the masses. Mumbo-jumbo to scare women like your mother."

The upper petal was white. The lower petals were tinged with pink, radiating outward from the center. As though the lower petals were blushing. And that upper petal, it was like a hillside covered with snow. He could slide down it, as he had slid down the slope of a neighbor's yard, one winter when it snowed so much that even in Boston, they closed the schools.

And what would his mother think, if she knew? Because he had told her that he was joining a monastery, but not which one, not one that the church—the orchid looked like the Pope's face, white with a flush on his cheeks, which could have been makeup for the TV cameras but was probably his heart condition—disavowed. Like his mother, the Pope had a broken heart. Anyone who prayed for that many people would have to. The Holy Father, he corrected himself. After two years, he should have learned some things.

"The strangest thing about you, John," Brother Martin had said, "is that you don't think like a Catholic. And yet you're here."

"I didn't have anywhere else to go," he answered, but that wasn't strictly true. He could have gone back to his mother—she was still living in Boston, then. Someone would have given him a job, despite the prison record. If you explained that it was for selling marijuana, people understood that you weren't a rapist or a murderer, although they might check the cash register after your shift. Once an addict, always an addict, that's what people believed. And perhaps they were right. Perhaps this was a way to replace the pot, which he still craved sometimes. Perhaps this was another way to get high.

At the center of the orchid was a frill, like the frill on a girl's collar, or the gill on a fish. Was that the point he was supposed to focus on? He found it difficult to focus. His mind kept going—back, mostly.

After all, he could have gone elsewhere, to the Franciscans for instance. But it was here that he had found something other than the gray wall that had always been his life. Was it accurate to say always? There must have been a time before, when he was still playing baseball, and eating hamburgers at the Burger King next to the hardware store where he worked after school, and dating girls. But even at Emerson High it was being built, the gray wall that surrounded him, that cut off any view of the landscape, of the river for instance, although it was only a trolley-ride away. It separated him from his mother, from any girl he had ever dated. If he imagined it now, he could see it, behind the orchid. On it was engraved one word: WHY? At first, WHY? had meant, why did my father have to die? Later it meant, why am I doing this? Whatever this was, writing a paper for his English class, working at the hardware store to make money for college, having sex with Jennifer Lewinsky in the back seat of her father's car. Celibacy had not been difficult for him. After prison, he was used to it. Even in prison, there had been opportunities, or at least one. There had been someone who suggested—but he had said no, and after that he was left alone. The guy who'd made the suggestion—in for armed robbery—had made sure of that. You didn't know how decent people could be, until you met them in prison. But he remembered sex, with Jennifer Lewinsky after prom, and another woman—was her name Christine or Kimberly?—in college, through the haze of pot, as quickly over and not particularly fulfilling. It had been a bigger sacrifice giving up cigarettes. And finally, it had become a universal WHY?

Brother Simon had said, "Don't you see, John. By going to prison, you surrounded yourself with the wall that you've been experiencing all your life. You literalized your metaphor."

"You mean," he responded, "that I'm even dumber than I look." So that's what one learned at Harvard.

It had been here, where he had come after meeting Brother Simon in rehab, that he had begun to find answers. Here it was quiet, and you could hear yourself think. Here there was a maple branch outside your window, whose leaves turned red in autumn, and some mornings a chickadee perched on it, singing its two notes. Here, you could lie in your bed at night, listening as the rain beat on the tiles. Here there was Bernie, who had moved in his sleep and was now breathing, hot and moist, like the air in the greenhouse where he had picked out his orchid, on his ankles.

Which brought him to what frightened him most. How did they do it? Was it surgery? Was it—but anything else was inconceivable to him. He had seen Brother Martin's eyes, once. Brother Martin removed his glasses to rub the bridge of his nose. They had been arguing for an hour, and he said, "John, you're giving me a headache. The problem with you is, you're trying to find answers to specific questions. Why did my father die? Why do children all over the world go to sleep hungry at night? Well, the Bible's not going to answer you.

Only God is going to answer you, and you have to understand that answer in your heart."

"I thought it was all in the eyes," he said, bitterly. Because there in front of him were Brother Martin's eyes, clouded and blank. How did they do it? Maybe they all caught an infectious disease. Although why hadn't he caught it already, then? Maybe it was something in the soup that Brother Andrew dispensed every day with a wooden ladle. Lentil soup, carrot soup. What he wouldn't give for a hamburger. Maybe they stared at the sun, stood all day staring at the sun together—but when did the sun shine here for more than a couple of hours at a time? At least in autumn (and it was autumn). Maybe they used a special kind of lamp.

"You see, a Protestant would misunderstand that." Roy, Brother Martin's dog, sat up and put his muzzle on his master's knee. Without pausing, Brother Martin pulled a biscuit from a pocket within his habit and fed it to Roy. "A Protestant would take that literally: Jesus made the blind man see. And Jesus said, what wilt thou that I shall do unto thee? And he said, Lord, that I may receive my sight. And Jesus said unto him, receive thy sight, thy faith hath saved thee. And immediately he received his sight and followed him, glorifying God. What kind of miracle was that, if all he saw was a muddy street in Jerusalem? God makes you see with the heart. Here we see as through a glass, darkly. There we shall see face to face. We will see God face to face. That's your answer."

"So the eyes aren't important at all."

"No, the eyes aren't important. Unless you're concerned about bumping into tables." Brother Martin pushed his glasses up the bridge of his nose, ran his hand along Roy's back, took hold of the German Shepherd's harness, and said, "Come on, Roy. I hear the bell for vespers."

The bell was ringing now, although he did not know the time—was it sext or none?—and the orchid had turned into the face of his mother, with rouge on her cheeks. She looked younger than he remembered, younger than the first day she had taken him to church and said, "Pray for your father, Johnny, so he won't go to hell."

Then her face dissolved and became the face of Jennifer Lewinsky, made up for prom. Afterward, sitting in her father's car, she had talked about getting married and having four children, about the names she would give them: Tiffany and Stephanie were two of them, he remembered. He could see them curled into the lower petals of the orchid, Tiffany and Stephanie, and one said, "Don't you want to know, to know, to know?" like the tolling of a bell. "Don't you want to know what they all know, and you don't?" The other said, "Do you want to be blind, like them?" But he didn't know which was which, they looked so exactly alike.

"You are of the Devil," he whispered, wondering if they were simply of Common Sense, and they opened their mouths and laughed, their teeth as white as the upper petal of the orchid. And then it was a moon, and he was surprised that one of them, he did not know which, would be so rude, so irreverent.

He thought of the word "phalaenopsis," but it changed and became "falling-oops." Which was what he was doing, falling into the orchid, into its frilled center, between the petals which he suddenly realized were hips or thighs. But at their center, where he had expected darkness, there was light.

And the woman on the hillside covered with snow said to him, "I never sinned, therefore between my thighs there is light." At the foot of the hill was his mother, saying her rosary with the steady clink he remembered, and a whispered "Blessed art thou among women, and blessed is the fruit of thy womb." He was surrounded by a subtle fragrance, which he supposed was the fragrance of the orchid, but reminded him of incense.

The woman on the hillside wore a dress covered with frills, like a flapper, and she said, "Only I can lead you into the heart of things."

He said, "Holy Mother, I have some questions."

She leaned down and patted Bernie's head. Bernie, who was sitting on his haunches beside her, looked up, whined, and licked her hand. She said, "They don't matter, John. They didn't matter before, but you couldn't see. You were a blind man, like a man in a whirlstorm. But look, the heart of things is still."

And it was, on that hillside, with his mother praying below and the woman in white, in her frilled dress, with Bernie by her side and the sky blushing above them, as though somewhere, unseen, the sun was beginning to set.

"Except me," he said. "I've never been still, all my life. Maybe because my father was a conductor. I couldn't sit still in class. I couldn't stay with any girl. When I smoked—what I smoked, it was to get away, as far away as I could. The hardest thing about prison was learning to stay in one room. But I never got anywhere. I always felt like I was surrounded by a wall, that wherever I went, I was just walking in a circle. Around and around."

"Here there are no walls," she said, "and no need to escape from them."

He could see that. Behind her the hills stretched away to the mountains, whose slopes were covered with snow, and when he turned around he could see in the distance a gray line that was probably the sea. His mother said "Amen," and looked up at him.

"I love you, Johnny," she said. "I don't think I ever told you that. I should have, I realize that now. But you knew anyway, didn't you?"

"Yes, Ma," he said. "I knew."

She nodded, then picked up her purse, which was magenta and shaped like an orchid. She began to walk toward the mountains.

"It's time for you to go back," said the woman on the hill.

"What do you mean, go back?" he said. "I thought I was supposed to come here."

"You were," she said, "but man cannot live at the heart of things. You were made to live on the outside, looking in."

"Why?" he asked.

"That was the way God made you," she answered. "Your purpose in the creation is to see it, as his purpose," she stroked Bernie's head, "is to guide you."

Bernie barked once in the cold air.

"But why—" he began.

She said, "There is only one answer to all of your questions, John. Only one, and that is the will of God. Once, there was a man who lost everything he had. And he said to his friends, yet in my flesh shall I see God, whom I shall see for myself, and mine eyes shall behold, and not another. That was all he got, after all his suffering, and it was enough. Do you understand?"

"Yes," he said. "But I'm not sure I like it."

She smiled. "That's what it means to be outside, out in the cold. Now look inside, John. Look inside God's creation, and I will give you peace."

"How do I do that?"

She pointed up at the sky. There was an orchid, with three petals, the upper one white as snow, the lower two flushed with pink, the center surrounded by a frill, and two—were they petals or leaves, also white? "Look," she said. "It's there, in every atom of God's creation. Look at a snowflake, at a spider's leg, the wing of a butterfly, or the petal of a flower. Look, and see inside."

He looked and saw a phalaenopsis orchid in a terracotta pot, sitting on the table. It had three flowers and oval leaves, one of them beginning to wilt. He looked at the flowers on the stalk, at the uppermost flower, which was fully open: it had three or perhaps five petals. He looked and he saw it, saw its atoms dancing like stars, the will of God in the veins of each leaf, in a drop of water that hung, he now saw, on the edge of a petal. Why had he not see that? How many things had he not seen, before? It was clear, so clear, the specificity of creation. So clear and so bright. He could never have imagined how bright, and he had been walking through it his entire life, like a blind man. He cried out.

"Do you see?" asked Brother Simon.

"Yes," he answered, as breathless as though he had run up the side of a mountain.

"Brother Andrew saved some soup for you, from lunch. Lentil again, I'm afraid, with that macrobiotic bread he insists on baking. Do you need any help?"

"No," he said. "I've got Bernie right here." Bernie stood and gave a low bark. "Good dog."

"Then follow me, Brother John. You must be famished."

They walked together, canes tapping on the stone floor, to the refectory, in the light.

PIP AND THE FAIRIES

"WHY, YOU'RE PIP!"

She has gotten used to this, since the documentary. She could have refused to be interviewed, she supposes. But it would have seemed— ungrateful, ungracious, particularly after the funeral.

"Susan Lawson," read the obituary, "beloved author of *Pip and the Fairies*, *Pip Meets the Thorn King*, *Pip Makes Three Wishes*, and other Pip books, of ovarian cancer. Ms. Lawson, who was sixty-four, is survived by a daughter, Philippa. In lieu of flowers, donations should be sent to the Susan Lawson Cancer Research Fund." Anne had written that.

"Would you like me to sign something?" she asks.

White hair, reading glasses on a chain around her neck—too old to be a mother. Perhaps a librarian? Let her be a librarian, thinks Philippa. Once, a collector asked her to sign the entire series, from *Pip and the Fairies* to *Pip Says Goodbye*.

"That would be so kind of you. For my granddaughter Emily." A grandmother, holding out *Pip Learns to Fish* and *Under the Hawthorns*.

She signs them both "To Emily, may she find her own fairyland. From Philippa Lawson (Pip)."

This is the sort of thing people like: the implication that, despite their minivans and microwaves, if they found the door in the wall, they too could enter fairyland.

"So," the interviewer asked her, smiling indulgently, the way parents smile at their children's beliefs in Santa Claus, "Did you really meet the Thorn King? Do you think you could get me an interview?"

And she answered as he, and the parents who had purchased the boxed set, were expecting. "I'm afraid the Thorn King is a very private person. But I'll mention that you were interested." Being Pip, after all these years. Maintaining the persona.

Her mother never actually called her Pip. It was Pipsqueak, as in, "Go play outside, Pipsqueak. Can't you see Mommy's trying to finish this chapter? Mommy's publisher wants to see something by Friday, and we're a month behind on the rent." When they finally moved away from Payton, they were almost a year behind. Her mother sent Mrs. Payne a check from California, from royalties she had received for the after-school special.

Philippa buys a scone and a cup of coffee. There was no café when she used to come to this bookstore, while her mother shopped at the food co-op down the street, which is now a yoga studio. Mrs. Archer used to let her sit in a corner and read the books. Then she realizes there is no cupholder in the rental car. She drinks the coffee quickly. She's tired, after the long flight from Los Angeles, the long drive from Boston. But not much farther now. Payton has stayed essentially the same, she thinks, despite the yoga studio. She imagines a planning board, a historical society, the long and difficult process of obtaining permits, like in all these New England towns.

As she passes the fire station, the rain begins, not heavy, and intermittent. She turns on the windshield wipers.

There is Sutton's dairy, where her mother bought milk with cream floating on top, before anyone else cared about pesticides in the food chain. She is driving through the country, through farms that have managed to hold on despite the rocky soil. In the distance she sees cows, and once a herd of alpacas. There are patches too rocky for farms, where the road runs between cliffs covered with ivy, and birches, their leaves glistening with rain, spring up from the shallow soil.

Then forest. The rain is heavier, pattering on the leaves overhead. She drives with one hand, holding the scone in the other (her pants are getting covered with crumbs), beneath the oaks and evergreens, thinking about the funeral.

It was not large: her mother's coworkers from the Children's Network, and Anne. It was only after the documentary that people began driving to the cemetery in the hills, leaving hyacinths by the grave. Her fault, she supposes.

The interviewer leaned forward, as though expecting an intimate detail. "How did she come up with Hyacinth? Was the character based on anyone she knew?"

"Oh, hyacinths were my mother's favorite flower."

And letters, even contributions to the Susan Lawson Cancer Research Fund. Everyone, it seems, had read *Pip and the Fairies*. Then the books had gone out of print and been forgotten. But after the funeral and the documentary, everyone suddenly remembered, the way they remembered their childhoods. Suddenly, Susan Lawson was indeed "beloved."

Philippa asked Anne to drive up once a week, to clear away the letters and flowers, to take care of the checks. And she signed over the house. Anne was too old to be a secretary for anyone neater than Susan Lawson had been. In one corner of the living room, Philippa found a pile of hospital bills, covered with dust. She remembers Anne at the funeral, so pale and pinched. It is good, she supposes, that her mother found someone at last. With the house and her social security, Anne will be all right.

Three miles to Payne House. Almost there, then. It had been raining too, on that first day.

"Look," her mother said, pointing as the Beetle swerved erratically. If she looked down, she could see the road though the holes in the floor, where the metal had rusted away. Is that why she has rented one of the new Beetles? Either nostalgia, or an effort to, somehow, rewrite the past. "There's Payne House. It burned down in the 1930s. The Paynes used to own the mills at the edge of town," now converted into condominiums, Mrs. Archer's successor, a woman with graying hair and a pierced nostril, told her, "and one night the millworkers set the stables on fire. They said the Paynes took better care of their horses than of their workers."

"What happened to the horses?" She can see the house from the road, its outer walls burned above the first story, trees growing in some of the rooms. She can see it through both sets of eyes, the young Philippa and the old one. Not really old of course, but—how should she describe it?—tired. She blames the documentary. Remembering all this, the road running through the soaked remains of what was once a garden, its hedges overgrown and a rosebush growing through the front door. She can see it through young eyes, only a few weeks after her father's funeral, the coffin draped with an American flag and the minister saying "fallen in the service of his country" although really it was an accident that could have happened if he had been driving to the grocery store. And old eyes, noticing that the rosebush has spread over the front steps.

As if, driving down this road, she were traveling into the past. She felt this also, sitting beside the hospital bed, holding one pale hand, the skin dry as paper, on which the veins were raised like the roots of an oak tree. Listening to the mother she had not spoken to in years.

"I have to support us now, Pipsqueak. So we're going to live here. Mrs. Payne's going to rent us the housekeeper's cottage, and I'm going to write books."

"What kind of books?"

"Oh, I don't know. I guess I'll have to start writing and see what comes out."

How did it begin? Did she begin it, by telling her mother, over her milk and the oatmeal cookies from the food co-op that tasted like baked sawdust, what she had been doing that day? Or did her mother begin it, by writing the stories? Did she imagine them, Hyacinth, the Thorn King, the Carp in the pond who dreamed, so he said, the future, and the May Queen herself? And, she thinks, pulling into the drive that leads to the housekeeper's cottage, what about Jack Feather? Or did her mother imagine them? And did their imaginations bring them into being, or were they always there to be found?

She slams the car door and brushes crumbs from her pants. Here it is, all here, for what it is worth, the housekeeper's cottage, with its three small rooms, and the ruins of Payne House. The rain has almost stopped, although she can feel a drop run down the back of her neck. And, not for the first time, she has doubts.

"One room was my mother's, one was mine, and one was the kitchen, where we took our baths in a plastic tub. We had a toaster oven and a crock pot to make soup, and a small refrigerator, the kind you see in hotels. One day, I remember having soup for breakfast, lunch, and dinner. Of course, when the electricity was turned off, none of them worked. Once, we lived for a week on oatmeal cookies." The interviewer laughed, and she laughed with him. When they moved to California, she went to school. Why doesn't she remember going to school in Payton? She bought lunch every day, meatloaf and mashed potatoes and soggy green beans. Sometimes the principal gave her lunch money. She was happier than when the Thorn King had crowned her with honeysuckle. "Young Pip," he had said, "I pronounce you a Maid of the May. Serve the May Queen well."

That was in *Pip Meets the May Queen*. And then she stops—standing at the edge of the pond—because the time has come to think about what she has done.

What she has done is give up *The Pendletons*, every weekday at two o'clock, Eastern Standard Time, before the afternoon talk shows. She has given up being Jessica Pendleton, the scheming daughter of Bruce Pendleton, whose attractive but troublesome family dominates the social and criminal worlds of Pinehurst.

"How did your mother influence your acting career?"

She did not answer, "By teaching me the importance of money." Last week, even a fan of *The Pendletons* recognized her as Pip.

She has given up the house in the hills, with a pool in the back yard. Given up Edward, but then he gave her up first, for a producer. He wanted, so badly, to do prime time. A cop show or even a sitcom, respectable television. "I hope you understand, Phil," he said. And she did understand, somehow. Has she ever been in love with anyone—except Jack Feather?

What has she gained? She remembers her mother's cold hand pulling her down, so she can hear her whisper, in a voice like sandpaper, "I always knew they were real."

But does she, Philippa, know it? That is why she has come back, why she has bought Payne House from the Payne who inherited it, a Manhattan lawyer with no use for the family estate. Why she is standing here now, by the pond, where the irises are about to bloom. So she can remember.

The moment when, in *Pip and the Fairies*, she trips over something lying on the ground.

"OH," SAID A voice. When Pip looked up she saw a girl, about her own age, in a white dress, with hair as green as grass. "You've found it, and now it's yours, and I'll never be able to return it before he finds out!"

"What is it?" asked Pip, holding up what she had tripped over: a piece of brown leather, rather like a purse.

"It's Jack Feather's Wallet of Dreams, which he doesn't know I've taken. I was just going to look at the dreams—their wings are so lovely in the sunlight—and then return it. But 'What You Find You May Keep.' That's the law." And the girl wept bitterly into her hands.

"But I don't want it," said Pip. "I'd like to look at the dreams, if they're as nice as you say they are, but I certainly don't want to keep them. Who is Jack Feather, and how can we return his wallet?"

"How considerate you are," said the girl. "Let me kiss you on both cheeks—that's the fairy way. Then you'll be able to walk through the door in the wall, and we'll return the wallet together. You can call me Hyacinth."

Why couldn't she walk through the door by herself? Pip wondered. It seemed an ordinary enough door, opening from one of the overgrown rooms to another. And what was the fairy way? She was just starting to wonder why the girl in the white dress had green hair when Hyacinth opened the door and pulled her through.

On the other side was a country she had never seen before. A forest stretched away into the distance, until it reached a river that shone like a snake in the sunlight, and then again until it reached the mountains.

Standing under the trees at the edge of the forest was a boy, not much taller than she was, in trousers made of gray fur, with a birch-bark hat on his head. As soon as he saw them, he said, "Hyacinth, if you don't give me my Wallet of Dreams in the clap of a hummingbird's wing, I'll turn you into a snail and present you to Mother Hedgehog, who'll stick you into her supper pot!"

—From *Pip and the Fairies*, by Susan Lawson

HOW CLEARLY THE memories are coming back to her now, of fishing at night with Jack Feather, searching for the Wishing Stone with Hyacinth and Thimble, listening to stories at Mother Hedgehog's house while eating her toadstool omelet. There was always an emphasis on food, perhaps a reflection of the toaster and crock pot that so invariably turned out toast and soup. The May Queen's cake, for example, or Jeremy Toad's cricket cutlets, which neither she nor Hyacinth could bear to eat.

"I hope you like crickets," said Jeremy Toad. Pip and Hyacinth looked at one another in distress. "Eat What You Are Offered," was the Thorn King's law. Would they dare to break it? That was in *Jeremy Toad's Birthday Party*.

She can see, really, where it all came from.

"I think the feud between the Thorn King and the May Queen represented her anger at my father's death. It was an accident, of course. But she blamed him for leaving her, for going to Vietnam. She wanted him to be a conscientious objector. Especially with no money and a daughter to care for. I don't think she ever got over that anger."

"But the Thorn King and the May Queen were reconciled."

"Only by one of Pip's wishes. The other—let me see if I remember. It was a fine wool shawl for Thimble so she would never be cold again."

"Weren't there three? What was the third wish?"

"Oh, that was the one Pip kept for herself. I don't think my mother ever revealed it. Probably something to do with Jack Feather. She—I—was rather in love with him, you know."

The third wish had been about the electric bill, and it had come true several days later when the advance from the publisher arrived.

Here it is, the room where she found Jack Feather's wallet. Once, in *Pip Meets the Thorn King*, he allowed her to look into it. She saw herself, but considerably older, in a dress that sparkled like stars. Years later, she recognized it as the dress she would wear to the Daytime Emmys.

And now what? Because there is the door, and after all the Carp did tell her, in *Pip Says Goodbye*, "You will come back some day."

But if she opens the door now, will she see the fields behind Payne House, which are mown for hay in September? That is the question around which everything revolves. Has she been a fool, to give up California, and the house with the pool, and a steady paycheck?

"What happened, Pip?" her mother asked her, lying in the hospital bed, her head wrapped in the scarf without which it looked as fragile as an eggshell. "You were such an imaginative child. What made you care so much about money?"

"You did," she wanted to and could not say. And now she has taken that money out of the bank to buy Payne House.

If she opens the door and sees only the unmown fields, it will have been for nothing. No, not nothing. There is Payne House, after all. And her memories. What will she do, now she is no longer Jessica

Pendleton? Perhaps she will write, like her mother. There is a certain irony in that.

The rain on the grass begins to soak through her shoes. She should remember not to wear city shoes in the country.

But it's no use standing here. That is, she has always told herself, the difference between her and her mother: she can face facts.

Philippa grasps the doorknob, breathes in once, quickly, and opens the door.

❧

"I'VE BEEN WAITING forever and a day," said Hyacinth, yawning. She had fallen sleep beneath an oak tree, and while she slept the squirrels who lived in the tree had made her a blanket of leaves.

"I promised I would come back if I could," said Pip, "and now I have."

"I'm as glad as can be," said Hyacinth. "The Thorn King's been so sad since you went away. When I tell him you're back, he'll prepare a feast just for you."

"Will Jack Feather be there?" asked Pip.

"I don't know," said Hyacinth, looking uncomfortable. "He went away to the mountains, and hasn't come back. I didn't want to tell you yet, but—the May Queen's disappeared! Jack Feather went to look for her with Jeremy Toad, and now they've disappeared too."

"Then we'll have to go find them," said Pip.

—From *Pip Returns to Fairyland*, by Philippa Lawson

LESSONS
WITH MISS GRAY

THAT SUMMER, WE were reporters: intrepid, like Molly McBride of the Charlotte *Observer*, who had ridden an elephant in the Barnum and Bailey circus, and gone up in a balloon at the Chicago World's Fair, and whose stagecoach had been robbed by Black Bart himself. Although she had told him it would make for a better story, Black Bart had refused to take her purse: he would not rob a lady.

We were sitting in the cottage at the bottom of the Beauforts' garden, on the broken furniture that was kept there. Rose, on the green sofa with the torn upholstery, was chewing on her pencil and trying to decide whether her yak, on the journey she was undertaking through the Himalayas, was a noble animal of almost human intelligence, or a surly and unkempt beast that she could barely control. Emma, in an armchair with a sagging seat, was eating gingerbread and writing the society column, in which Ashton had acquired a number of Dukes and Duchesses. Justina, in another armchair, which did not match—but what was Justina doing there at all? She was two years older than we were, and a *Balfour*, of the Balfours who reminded you, as though you had forgotten, that Lord Balfour had been granted all of Balfour County by James I. And Justina was beautiful. We had been startled when she had approached us, in the gymnasium of the Ashton Ladies' Academy, where all of us except Melody went to school, and said, "Are you writing a newspaper? I'd like to help." There she was, sitting in the armchair, which was missing a leg and had to be propped on an apple crate. It leaned sideways like a sinking ship. She was writing in a script that was more elegant than any of ours—Rose's page was covered with crossings out, and Emma's with gingerbread crumbs—about Serenity Sage, who was, at that moment, trapped in the Caliph's garden, surrounded by the scent of roses and aware that at any moment, the Caliph's eunuchs might find her. She would always, afterward, associate the scent of roses with danger. How, Justina wondered, would Serenity escape? How would she get back to Rome, where the Cardinal, who had hired her, was waiting? Beside him, as he sat in a secret chamber beneath the cathedral, were a trunk filled with gold coins and his hostage: her lover, the revolutionary they called The Mask. We did not, of course, insist that everything in our newspaper be true. How boring that would have been. And Melody was sitting on the other end of the sofa, reading the Charlotte *Observer*, trying to imitate the advertising.

"Soap as white as, as—" she said. "As soap."

"As the snows of the Himalayas," said Rose, who had decided that her yak was surly, and the sunlight on the slopes blinding. But surely her guide, who was intrepid, would lead her to the fabled Forbidden Cities.

"As milk," said Emma. "I wish I had milk. Callie's gingerbread is always dry."

"For goodness sake," said Rose. "Can't you think of anything other than food?"

"As the moon, shining over the sullied streets of London," said Melody, in the voice she used to recite poetry in school.

"What do you know about London?" said Emma. "Make it the streets of Ashton."

"I don't think they're particularly sullied," said Rose.

"Not in front of your house, Miss Rose," said Melody, in another voice altogether. Rose kicked her.

"As the paper on which a lover has written his letter," said Justina. Serenity Sage was sailing down the Tiber.

"If he's written the letter, it's not going to be white," said Emma. "Obviously."

And then we were silent, because no one said "obviously" to a Balfour, although Justina had not noticed. The Mask was about to take off his mask.

"I don't understand," said Melody, in yet another voice, which made even Justina look up. "Lessons in witchcraft," she read, "with Miss Emily Gray. Reasonable rates. And it's right here in Ashton."

"Do you think it's serious?" asked Emma. "Do you think she's teaching real witchcraft? Not just the fake stuff, like Magical Seymour at the market in Brickleford, who pulls Indian-head pennies out of your ears?"

"You're getting crumbs everywhere," said Rose, who was suddenly and inexplicably feeling critical. "Why shouldn't it be real? You can't put false advertising in a newspaper. My father told me that."

And suddenly we all knew, except Justina, who was realizing the Cardinal's treachery, that we were no longer reporters. We were witches.

∽

"WHERE DID YOU say she lived?" asked Melody. We were walk-ing down Elm Street, in a part of town that Melody did not know as well as the rest of us.

"There," said Emma. We didn't understand how Emma managed to know everything, at least about Ashton. Although her mother was a whirlpool of gossip: everything there was to know in Ashton made its way inevitably to her. She had more servants than the rest of us: Mrs. Spraight, the housekeeper, as well as the negro servants, Callie, who cooked, and Henry, who was both gardener and groom. Rose's mother made do with a negro housekeeper, Hannah, and Justina, who lived with her grandmother, old Mrs. Balfour, had only Zelia, a French mulatto who didn't sleep in but came during the day to help out. And Melody—well, Melody was Hannah's niece, and she had no servants at all. She lived with her aunt and her cousin Coralie, who taught at the negro school, across the train tracks. We didn't know how she felt about this—we often didn't know what Melody felt, and when we asked, she didn't always answer.

"Don't you think it's unfair that you have to go to that negro school, with only a dusty yard to play in? Don't you think you should be able to go to the Ashton Ladies' Academy, with us? Don't you think—" And her face would shut, like a curtain. So we didn't often ask.

"The white house, with the roses growing on it," said Emma. "It used to be the Randolph house. She was a witch too, Mrs. Randolph, at least that's what I heard. She died, or her daughter died, or some-body, and afterward all the roses turned as red as blood."

"They're pink," said Melody.

"Well, maybe they've faded. I mean, this was a long time ago, right?" Rose looked at the house. The white trim had been freshly painted, and at each window there were lace curtains. "Are we going in, or not?"

"It looks perfectly respectable," said Emma. "Not at all like a witch's house."

"How do you know what a witch's house looks like?" asked Melody.

"Everyone knows what a witch's house looks like," said Rose. "I think you're all scared. That's why you're not going in."

At that, we all walked up the path and to the front door, although Justina had forgotten where we were and had to be pulled. Justina often forgot where we were, or that the rest of us were there at all. Rose raised her hand to the knocker, which was shaped like a frog—the first sign we had seen that a witch might, indeed, be within—waited for a moment, then knocked.

"Good afternoon," said a woman in a gray dress, with white hair. She looked like your grandmother, the one who baked you gingerbread and knitted socks. Or like a schoolteacher, as proper as a handkerchief. Behind her stood a ghost.

∾

THAT SUMMER, WE each had a secret that we were keeping from the others.

Rose's secret was that she wanted to fly. She had books hidden under her bed, books on birds and balloons and gliders, on everything that flew. She read every story that she could find about flight—Icarus, and the Island of Laputa, and the stories of Mr. Verne. There was no reason to keep this a secret—the rest of us would not have particularly cared, although Melody might have said that if God intended us to fly, he would have given us wings. Her aunt had said that to a passing preacher, who had told the negro people to rise up, rise up, as equal children of God. And Justina might have looked even more absent than usual, with the words "away, away" singing through her head. But Rose would have been miserable if she had told: it was the only secret she had, and it gave her days, and especially nights, when she was exploring the surface of the moon, meaning. And what if her mother found out? Elizabeth Caldwell's lips would thin into an elegant line, and Rose would see in her eyes the distance between their house with its peeling paint, beneath a locust tree that scattered its seedpods over the lawn each spring, and the house where her mother had grown up, in Boston. She would see the distance between herself and the girl who had grown up in that house, in lace dresses, playing the piano or embroidering on silk, a girl who had never been rude or disobedient. Who had never, so far as Rose knew, wanted to climb the Himalayas, or to fly.

Justina's secret was that her grandmother, the respectable Mrs. Balfour who, when she appeared in the Balfour pew at the Episcopal Church, resembled an ageing Queen Victoria, was going mad. Two nights ago, she had emptied the contents of her chamberpot over the mahogany suite in the parlor, spreading them over the antimacassars, over the Aubusson carpet. Justina had washed everything herself, so Zelia would not find out. And Zelia had apparently not found out, although the smell— She still had a bruise where her grandmother had gripped her arm and whispered, "Do you see the Devil, with his hooves like a goat's and his tongue like a lizard's? *I can*." "Away, away" the words sang through her head, and she imagined herself as Serenity Sage, at the mercy of the Cardinal, but with a curved dagger she had stolen from the Caliph hidden in her garter. Then she would be away, away indeed, sailing across the Mediterranean, with the wind blowing her hair like a golden flag.

Emma's secret was that her mother had locked the pantry. Adeline Beaufort had been a Balfour—Emma was Justina's second or third cousin—and no daughter of hers was going to be *fat*. For two weeks now she had been bribing Callie, with rings, hair ribbons, even the garnet necklace that her father had given her as a birthday present. That morning, she had traded a pair of earrings for gingerbread. Callie was terrified of Mrs. Beaufort. "Lordy, Emma, don't tempt me again! She'll have me whipped, like in the old slave days," she had whispered. But she could not resist fine things, even if she had to keep them under a floorboard, as Emma could not resist her hunger. They were trapped, like a couple of magpies, fearful and desiring.

Melody's secret was that she wanted to go to college. There was a negro college in Atlanta that admitted women, the preacher had told her. So they could be teachers, for the betterment of the negro race. Because white teachers went to college, and why should only negro children be taught by high school graduates—if that? And Melody wanted to better the negro race. Sometimes she wondered if she should be with us at all, instead of with the other girls in her school—perhaps, as her aunt often said, she should stick with her own. But her own filled her with a sense of both loyalty and despair. Why couldn't those girls look beyond Ashton, beyond the boys they would one day marry, and the families they would work for? And there was a streak of pragmatism in this, as in many of her actions, because the rest of us checked books out of the library for her, more books than even we read. She had never been told that colored folk could not enter the library, but colored folk never did, and what if she was told to leave? Then she would know she was not welcome, which was worse than suspecting she would not be. So every morning, after her chores were done and before school, when other girls were still ironing their dresses and curling their hair, she went to the houses of the wealthy negro families, of the Jeffersons, who traded tobacco and were, if the truth were told, the wealthiest family in Ashton, and the Beauforts, whose daughters were, as everyone knew, Emma's fourth or fifth cousins, and cleaned. She put the money she earned, wrapped in an old set of her aunt's drawers, in a hole at the back of her closet. For college.

THE GHOST WAS, of course, a girl, and we all knew her, except Justina. She lived near the railroad tracks, by the abandoned tobacco factory that not even the Jeffersons used anymore, with her father. He was a drunkard. We did not know her name, but we could identify her without it. She was the ghost, the white girl, the albino: white hair, white face, and thin white hands sticking out from the sleeves of a dress that was too short, that she must have outgrown several years ago. Only her eyes, beneath her white eyebrows, had color, and those were a startling blue. Her feet were bare, and dirty.

We knew that we weren't supposed to play with her, because she was poor, and probably an idiot. What else could that lack of coloring mean, but idiocy? There was an asylum in Charlotte—her father should be persuaded to put her there, for her own good. But he was a drunkard, and could even Reverend Hewes persuade a drunkard? He rarely let her out. Look at the girl—did he remember to feed her? She looked like she lived on air. Adeline Beaufort and Elizabeth Caldwell agreed: it would be for her own good. Really a mercy, for such a creature.

"Come inside, girls," said Miss Gray. "But mind you wipe your feet. I won't have dirt in the front hall."

It was certainly respectable. The parlor looked like the Beauforts', but even more filled with what Emma later told us were bibelots or objets d'art: china shepherdesses guarding their china sheep; cranberry-colored vases filled with pink roses and sprays of honeysuckle; and painted boxes, on one of which Justina, who had studied French history that year, recognized Marie Antoinette. And there were cats. We did not notice them, initially—they had a way of being inconspicuous, which Miss Gray later told us was their own magic, a cat magic. But we would blink, and there would be a cat, on the sofa where we were about to sit, or on the mantel where we had just looked. "How they keep from knocking down all those—music boxes and whatnots,

I don't know," Emma said afterward. But we didn't say anything then. We didn't know what to say.

"Please sit down, girls." We did so cautiously, trying to keep our knees away from the rickety tables, with their lace doilies and china dogs. Trying to remember that we were in a witch's house. "I've made some lemonade, and Emma will be pleased to hear that I've baked walnut bars, and those cream horns she likes." There was also an angel cake, like a white sponge, and a Devil's Food cake covered with chocolate frosting, and a jelly roll with strawberry jelly, and meringues. We ate although Melody whispered that one should never, ever eat in a witch's house. The ghost ate too, cutting her slice of angel cake into small pieces with the side of her fork and eating them slowly, one by one.

"Another slice, Melody, Justina, Rose?" We did not wonder how she knew our names. She was a witch. It would have been stranger, wouldn't it, if she hadn't known? We shook our heads, except for Emma, who ate the last of the jelly roll.

"Then it's time to discuss your lessons. Please follow me into the laboratory."

It must have been a kitchen, once, but now the kitchen table was covered with a collection of objects in neat rows and piles: scissors; a mouse in a cage; balls of string, the sort used in gardens to tie up tomatoes; a kitchen scale; feathers, blue and green and yellow; spectacles, most of then cracked; a crystal ball; seashells; the bones of a small alligator, held together with wire; candles of various lengths; butterfly wings; a plait of hair that Rose thought must have come from a horse—she liked horses, because on their backs she felt as though she were flying; some fountain pens; a nest with three speckled eggs; and silver spoons. At least, that's what we remembered afterward, when we tried to make a list. We sat around the table on what must have once been kitchen chairs, with uncomfortable wooden backs, while Miss Gray stood and lectured to us, exactly like Miss Harris in Rhetoric and Elocution.

"Once," said Miss Gray, "witchcraft was seen as a—well, a craft, to be taught by apprenticeship and practiced by intuition. Nowadays, we know that witchcraft is a science. Specific actions will yield specific results. Rose, please don't slouch in your chair. Being a witch should not prevent you from behaving like a lady. Justina, your elbow has disarranged Mortimer, a South American alligator, or the remains thereof. A witch is always respectful, even to inanimate objects. Please pay attention. As I was saying, nowadays witchcraft is regarded as a science, as reliable, for an experienced practitioner, as predicting the weather. It is this science—not the hocus-pocus of those terrible women in *Macbeth*, who are more to be pitied than feared in their delusion—that I propose to teach you. We shall begin tomorrow. Please be prompt—I dislike tardiness."

As we walked down the garden path, away from the Randolph house, Emma said to the ghost, "How did you know about the lessons?"

"My Papa was sleeping under the *Observer*," she said. Her voice was a rusty whisper, as though she had almost forgotten how to use it.

"Here, I don't want this," said Emma, handing her the last cream horn, somewhat crumbled, which she had been keeping in her pocket.

None of us realized until afterward that Miss Gray had never told us what time to come.

"THE FIRST LESSON," said Miss Gray, "is to see yourselves."

We were looking into mirrors, old mirrors speckled at the edges, in tarnished gold frames—Justina's had a crack across her forehead, and

Emma stared into a shaving-glass. Justina thought, "I look like her. My mother looked like her. They say my mother died of influenza, but perhaps she died at the asylum in Charlotte, chained to her bed, clawing at her hair and crying because of the lizards. Perhaps all the Balfours go mad, from marrying each other. Is that why Father left?" Because to the best of her knowledge, her father was in Italy, perhaps in Rome, where Serenity glared out through the bars of her prison, so far beneath the cathedral that no daylight crept between the stones, at the Inquisitor and his men, monks all, but with pistols at their sides. Justina looked into her eyes, large and dark, for signs of madness.

Rose scowled, which did not improve her appearance. What would she have looked like, if she had taken after the Winslows rather than her father? She imagined her mother and her aunt Catherine, who had never married. How daunting it must have been, taking for a moment her father's perspective, to marry that austere delicacy, which could only have come from the City of Winter. In Boston, her mother had told her, it snowed all winter long. Rose imagined it as a city of perpetual silence, where the snow muffled all sounds except for the tinkling of bells, sleigh bells and the bells of churches built from blocks of ice. Within the houses, also built of ice, sat ladies and gentlemen, calm, serene, with noses like icicles, conversing politely—probably about the weather. And none of them were as polite or precise as her mother or her aunt Catherine, the daughters of the Snow Queen. When they drove in their sleigh, drawn by a yak, they wore capes of egret feathers. If she were more like them, more like a Snow Princess, instead of—sunburnt and ungainly—would she, Rose wondered, love me then?

Emma imagined herself getting fatter and fatter, her face stretching until she could no longer see herself in the shaving glass. If she suddenly burst, what would happen? She would ooze over Ashton like molasses, covering the streets. Her father would call the men who were harvesting tobacco, call them from the fields to gather her in buckets and then tubs. They would give her to the women, who would spread her over buttered bread, and the children would eat her for breakfast. She shook her head, trying to clear away the horrifying image.

Melody thought, "Lord, let me never wish for whiter skin, or a skinnier nose, or eyes like Emma's, as blue as the summer sky, no matter what."

We did not know what the ghost thought, but as she stared into her mirror, she shook her head, and we understood. Who can look into a mirror without shaking her head? Except Miss Gray.

"No, no, girls," said Miss Gray. "All of the sciences require exact observation, particularly witchcraft. You must learn to see, not what you expect to see, but what is actually *there*. Now look again."

It was Melody who saw first. Of course she had been practicing: Melody always practiced. It was hot even for July—the flowers in all the gardens of Ashton were drooping, except for the flowers in Miss Gray's garden. But in the laboratory it was cool. We were drinking lemonade. We were heartily sick of looking into mirrors.

"Come, girls," said Miss Gray. "I would like you to see what Melody has accomplished." We looked into Melody's mirror: butterflies. Butterflies everywhere, all the colors of sunrise, Swallowtails and Sulfurs, Harvesters and Leafwings, Fritillaries, Emperors, and Blues, like pieces of silk that were suddenly wings—silk from evening gowns that Emma's mother might have worn, or Rose's. "O latest born and loveliest visions far of all Olympus' faded hierarchy! Butterflies are symbols of the soul," said Miss Gray. "And also of poetry. You, Melody, are a poet."

"That's stupid," said Melody.

"But nevertheless true," said Miss Gray.

"It's like—a garden, or a park," said Emma, when she too saw. And we could also see it, a lawn beneath maple trees whose leaves were beginning to turn red and gold. They were spaced at regular intervals along a gravel path, and both lawn and path were covered with leaves that had already fallen. The lawn sloped down to a pond whose surface reflected the branches above. Beside the path stood a bench, whose seat was also covered with leaves. On either side of the bench were stone urns, with lichen growing over them, and further along the path we could see a statue of a woman, partially nude. She was dressed in a stone scarf and bits of moss.

"How boring," said Emma, although the rest of us would have liked to go there, at least for the afternoon, it was so peaceful.

And then, for days, we saw nothing. But finally, in the ghost's mirror, appeared the ghost of a mouse, small and gray, staring at us with black eyes.

"He's hungry," said the ghost. Emma handed her a piece of gingerbread, and she nibbled it gratefully, although we knew that wasn't what she meant. And from then on, we called her Mouse.

"If you'd only apply yourself, Rose, I'm sure you could do it," said Miss Gray, as Miss Osborn, the mathematics teacher, had said at the end of the school year while giving out marks. Rose scowled again, certain that she could not. And it was Justina whom we saw next.

"It's only a book," she said. It was a large book, bound in crimson leather with gilding on its spine, and a gilt title on the cover: *Justina*.

"Open it," said Miss Gray.

"How?" But she was already reaching into the mirror, opening the book at random—to a page that began, "And so, Justina opened the book." The rest of the page was blank. "Who writes in it?" asked Justina, as the words "'Who writes in it,' asked Justina" wrote themselves across the page.

"That's enough for now," said Miss Gray as she reached into the mirror and closed the book. "Let's not get ahead of ourselves."

On the day that Rose finally saw herself, the rest of us were grinding bones into powder and putting the powder into jars labeled lizard, bat, frog. Mouse was sewing wings on a taxidermed mouse.

"That's it?" asked Rose, outraged. "I've been practicing all this time for a stupid rosebush? It doesn't even have roses. It's all thorns."

"Wait," said Miss Gray. "It's early yet for roses," although the pink roses—La Reine, she had told us—were blooming over the sides of the Randolph house, and their perfume filled the laboratory.

Sitting in the cottage afterward, we agreed: the first lesson had been disappointing. But we rather liked grinding bones.

ROSE'S HEART SWUNG in her chest like a pendulum when Miss Gray said, "It's time you learned how to fly." She told us to meet in the woods, at the edge of Slater's Pond. Mouse was late, she was almost always late. As we stood waiting for her, Emma whispered, "Do you think we're going to use broomsticks? Witches use broomsticks, right?"

Miss Gray, who had been looking away from us and into the woods, presumably for Mouse, turned and said, "Although Emma seems to have forgotten, I trust the rest of you remember that a lady never whispers. The use of a broomstick, although traditional, arose from historical rather than magical necessity. All that a witch needs to fly is a tree branch—the correct tree branch, carefully trained. It must have fallen, preferably in a storm—we are fortunate, this summer, to have had so many storms—and the tree from which it fell must be compatible with the witch. The principle is a scientific one: a branch, which has evolved to exist high above the earth, waving in the wind, desires to return to that height. Therefore, with the proper encouragement, it has the ability to carry the witch up into the air, which we experience as flying. Historically, witches have disguised their branches as brooms, to hide them from—those authorities who did not understand that witchcraft is a science. It is part of the lamentable history of prejudice against rational thinking. I myself, when I worked with Galileo—Sophia, I'm afraid you're late again."

"I'm sorry," mumbled Mouse, and we walked off into the woods, each separately searching for our branches, with Miss Gray's voice calling instructions and encouragement through the trees.

Justina's branch was a loblolly pine, that only she could ride: it kicked and bucked like an untrained colt. Melody rode a tulip poplar that looked too large for her. It moved like a cart horse, but she said that it was so steady, she always felt safe. Rose found an osage-orange that looked particularly attractive, with its glossy leaves and three dried oranges, now brown, still attached, but they did not agree—she liked to soar over the treetops, and it preferred to navigate through the trees, within a reasonable distance of the ground. When she flew too high, it would prick her with its thorns. So she gave it to Emma, who rode it until the end of summer and afterward asked Henry to carve a walking stick out of it, so she would not forget her flying lessons. Rose finally settled on a winged elm, which she said helped her loop-de-loop, a maneuver only she would try. Mouse took longer than all of us to find her branch: she was scared of flying, we could see that. Finally, Miss Gray gave her a shadbush, which never flew too high and seemed as skittish as she was. Miss Gray herself flew on a sassafras, which never misbehaved. She rode side-saddle, with her back straight and her skirt sweeping out behind her, in a steady canter.

"Straighten your back," she would say, as we flew, carefully at first and then with increasing confidence, over the pasture beneath Slocumb's Bluff, the highest point in Ashton. "Rose, you look like a hunchback. Melody, you must ride your branch with spirit. Think of yourself as Hippolyta riding her favorite horse to war."

"Who's Hippolyta?" asked Emma, gripping her branch as tightly as she could. She had just avoided an encounter with the rocky side of the bluff. Mouse was the most frightened, but Emma was the most cautious of us.

"Queen of the Amazons," said Melody, attempting to dodge two Monarchs. Since the day she had seen herself in the mirror, butter-flies had come to her, wherever she was. They sat on her shoulders, and early one morning, when she was cleaning the mirror in Elspeth Jefferson's bedroom, she saw that they had settled on her hair, like a crown.

That day, none of us were being Amazon Queens. Rose was fly-ing close to the side of the bluff and over the Himalayas, in a cloak of egret feathers. She could see the yak she had once ridden, sulking beneath her. She was, for the first time she could remember, perfectly happy. Somewhere among those peaks were the Forbidden Cities. She could see the first of them, the City of Winter, where the Snow Queen ruled in isolated splendor and the Princesses Elizabeth and Caroline rode thought the city streets in a sleigh drawn by leopards as white as snow. She flew upward, over the towers of the city, which were shining in the sunlight. And there were the people, serene and splendid, looking up at her, startled to see her flying above them with her cloak of egret feathers streaming out behind her, although they were too polite to shout. But then one and another raised their hands to wave to her, and the bells on their wrists jingled, like sleigh bells.

She raised her hand to wave back, and plunged down the side of the bluff.

"What were you thinking!" said Emma, when Rose was sitting on a boulder at the bottom of the bluff, with her ankle bound up in Miss Gray's scarf.

"I pulled out of it, didn't I?" said Rose.

"But you almost didn't," said Melody. "You really should be more careful."

Rose snorted, and we knew what Miss Gray would say to that. A lady never snorts. But Miss Gray had other problems to take care of.

"Justina!" she called, but Justina wasn't listening. Serenity Sage was floating over the Alps in a balloon. In a castle in Switzerland, The Mask was waiting for her. He had not been captured by the Inquisition after all, and knowing that he was free had given her the resolve to starve herself until she was slender enough to slip through the prison bars, and then up through the darkness of the stone passages under the cathedral. There, through a rosewood fretwork, she had seen the secret rites of the Inquisition, and they had marked her soul forever. But today she was free and flying in the sunlight over the mountains. For three days now, her grandmother had been sick. Zelia had been sitting with her, Zelia had taken care of everything, and the cut on Justina's shoulder was healing, although the paperweight with a view of the Brighton Pavilion would never be the same. Three days, three days of freedom, thought Serenity, watching the mountains below, which looked like a bouquet of white roses.

"Justina!" called Miss Emily. "Are you simply going to float up into the sky? Stop at once."

The loblolly stopped, although Justina almost didn't. She lurched forward and looked around, startled, at Miss Gray.

"I don't want to be an Amazon Queen," said Emma, watching from below, "and I don't want to learn to fly."

"How can you not want to fly?" asked Rose.

"Because I'm not you. How can you never remember to comb your hair?"

Rose ran her fingers through her hair, which did look like it had been in a whirlwind.

"Stop arguing," said Melody. "I'm worried about Mouse."

"She's doing all right," said Rose. What Mouse lacked in courage, she made up for in determination: she was sputtering over the meadow, her thin legs stuck out on either sides of the branch, her body bent forward to make it go faster, her hair falling into her face.

"That's not what I'm worried about," said Melody. "Have you noticed how thin she's getting?"

"You'd be so much better if you practiced," said Rose. "Melody practices. That's why she's the best flyer, after me and Justina."

"I don't think you're so much better than Justina," said Emma.

"You're not listening," said Melody. "I said—" but just then a flock of Painted Ladies rose about her, so thick that she had to brush them away with her hands.

We all learned to fly, although it took longer than we expected, and by the time we could all soar over the bluff—except Emma, who preferred to stay close to the ground—the summer storms had passed. We could feel, in the colder updrafts, the coming of autumn.

Despite what Emma had said, Rose was the best of us, the most accomplished flyer. She had explored the Himalayas, had found each of the Forbidden Cities hidden among their peaks, including the city that was simply a stone maze, the City of Birds, where she had practiced speaking bird language, and the temporary and evanescent City of Clouds.

AUTUMN WAS COMING, and these were the things we knew: how to, in a mirror or still pond, see Historical Scenes (although we were heartily sick of the Battle of Waterloo and the Death of Cleopatra, which Miss Gray seemed to particularly enjoy); summon various animals, including possums, squirrels, sparrows, and stray dogs; turn small pebbles into gold and turn gold into small pebbles (to which we had lost another pair of Emma's earrings); and speak with birds. We could now speak to the crows that lived in the trees beside the Beauforts' cottage, although they never said anything interesting. It was always about whose daughter was marrying whom, and how that changed the rules of precedence, which were particularly arcane among crows.

We thought of them first, when we decided to do something about Mouse.

"Can't we ask the birds? Maybe they know where she is." Melody sat curled in a corner of the green sofa, like one of Miss Gray's cats. "We haven't seen her for days." But the crows, who told us everything they knew about mice, knew nothing about Mouse.

"Try the mirror," said Justina. "If we can watch the Battle of Waterloo over and over, surely we can see where Mouse has gone." We were startled: since we had learned how to fly, Justina had seemed more distant than ever, and although she still spent mornings with us at the cottage, she always seemed to be somewhere else.

The only mirror in the cottage had once been in the Beauforts' front hall; it was tall and in a gilt frame, the sort of hall mirror that had been fashionable when old Mrs. Balfour and Mrs. Beaufort, Emma's grandmother, had ruled the social world of Ashton, whose front halls had to be widened to accommodate their crinolines. When Adeline Beaufort entered the house after Grandma Beaufort's funeral, she said, "That mirror has to go."

Justina wiped the dust from it with her handkerchief, which turned as gray and furry as a mouse.

"Please," she said, as politely as Miss Gray had taught us, because one should always be polite, even to dead alligators, "show us Mouse."

"Not Cleopatra again!" said Emma. We were sitting around Justina, who sat on the floor in front of the mirror. "You know, I don't think she's beautiful at all. I don't know what Mark Anthony saw in her."

"Please show us America," said Justina. "And nowadays, not in historical times." We were no longer looking at the obelisks of Egypt, but at a group of teepees, with Indians sitting around doing what Indians did, we supposed, when they weren't scalping settlers. We had all learned in school that Indians collected scalps like Rose's mother collected Minton figurines.

"Thank you," said Justina. "But here in Ashton." We saw a city, with buildings three or four stories high and crowds in the streets, milling around the trolleys and their teams of horses. "That's New York," said Melody, and we remembered that she had lived there, once—when her mother was still alive. Then ships in a harbor, their sails raised against the sky, and then Emma's mother, staring into a mirror, so that we started back, almost expecting to see ourselves reflected behind her. She spread Dr. Bronner's Youth Cream over her cheeks and what they call the décolletage, and then slapped herself to raise the circulation. She leaned toward the mirror and touched the skin under her eyes, anxiously.

Emma turned red. "Parents are so stupid."

"Yes, thank you," said Justina patiently, "but we really want to see Mouse. No, that's—what's Miss Gray doing with Zelia?" They were walking in the Balfours' garden, their heads bent together, talking as though they were planning—what?

And there, finally, was Mouse.

We saw at once why Mouse had been missing our lessons with Miss Gray: she was tied up. There was a rope tied around one of her ankles, with a knot as large as the ankle itself.

"It looks like—the dungeons of the Inquisition," said Justina.

"It looks like the old slave house at the Caldwell plantation," said Melody. It had burned during the war, and other than the slave house, only the front steps of the plantation, which were made of stone, remained to mark where it had been.

"It's a good thing we can't smell through the mirror," said Emma. "I bet it stinks."

In the mirror, Mouse was waving her hands as though conducting a church choir. And as she waved, visions rose in the air around her. Trees grew, taller and paler than we had ever seen. Melody later told us they were paper birches—she had found a picture in a library book. Mouse was sitting on what seemed to be moss, but there was a low mist covering her knees like a blanket, and we could only see the ground as the mist shifted and swirled. The birches around her glowed in the light of—was it the sun, as pale as the moon, that shone through the gray clouds? The forest seemed to go on in every direction, and it was wet—leaves dripped, and Mouse's eyelashes were beaded with waterdrops. Then a pale woman stepped out from one of the birches—from behind it or within it, we could not tell, and all the pale women stepped out, and they moved in something that was not a dance, but a pattern, and the hems of their dresses, which were made of the thinnest, most translucent bark, made the mist swirl up in strange patterns. Up it went, like smoke, and suddenly the vision was gone. Mouse sat, curled in a corner, with the rope around her ankle.

"I don't think she learned that from Miss Gray," said Emma.

"What are we going to do?" asked Rose. "We have to do something." And we knew that we had to do something, because we felt in the pits of our stomachs what Rose was feeling: a sick despair.

"Rescue her," said Melody. She looked around at the rest of us, and suddenly we realized that we were going to do exactly that, because Melody was the practical one, and if she had suggested it, then it could be done.

"How?" asked Rose. "We don't even know where she is."

"On our branches," said Justina. "Mirror, show us—slowly, show us the roof. Now the street. Look, it's one of the drying sheds by the old tobacco factory. All we need to do is follow the railroad tracks."

"How can we fly on our branches?" asked Emma. "We'll be seen."

"No, we won't," said Justina. She looked at us, waiting for us to understand, and one by one, as though candles were being lit in a dark room, we knew. "Rose, how long has it been since your mother asked where you spend your afternoons? How long has it been since anyone asked any of us, even Melody? Why has Coralie started doing her afternoon chores? And when Emma burned one of her braids, when we were making butterscotch on the Bunsen burner and Miss Gray came in suddenly and startled us, did anyone notice?" No one had. "I don't think anyone has seen what we've been doing, all summer. We've become like Miss Gray's cats, invisible until you're about to sit on them. I think we could fly through Brickleford on market day and no one would notice."

So we flew through the streets of Ashton, as high as the roofs of the houses, seeing them from the air for the first time. Ashton seemed smaller, from up there, and each of us thought the same thing—I will leave here one day. Only Emma was sorry to think so.

We landed by the shed that the mirror had shown us. One by one, we dismounted from our branches. Justina—we had not known she could be such a good leader—opened the door. It did look like a dungeon of the Inquisition, and smelled just as Emma had expected—the smell of death and rotting meat. Mouse was sitting in her corner, with her arms around her knees and her head down, crying. She did not look up when we opened the door.

"Mouse," said Rose. "We've come to rescue you." It sounded, we realized, both brave and silly.

Mouse looked up. We had never seen her face so dirty. Each tear seemed to have left behind a streak of dirt. "Why?" she asked.

"Because—" said Emma. "Because you're one of us, now."

We could not untie the knot. It was too large, too tight: the rope must once have been wet and shrunk.

"There's a knife, next to the bowl," said Mouse. "I can't reach it from here, the rope won't let me—I tried and tried."

The smell of rotting meat came from that bowl, and it was covered with flies. When Justina had finished cutting the rope from Mouse's ankle—the rest of us were standing as close as we could to the boarded-up window, where the crookedness of the boards let in chinks of light—she said, "I think I'm going to be sick."

The door banged open. "What do you brats think you're doing here?" It was a man, who brought with him a stench worse than rotting meat—the stench of whiskey.

"The drunkard father," whispered Emma. We all stood still, too frightened to move, and from Mouse came a mouse-like whimper.

"You little bitch," he said. "I know you. You're Judge Beaufort's daughter. You know how many times your father's put me in that prison of his? You goddamned Beauforts, sneering down your noses at anyone who isn't as high and all goddamn mighty as you are. Wait until he sees what I'm going to do with you—I'll whip you like a nigger, until your backside is as raw as—as raw meat."

Emma shrieked, a strangled sort of shriek, and dropped her branch.

"You're not a man but a toad," said Justina.

He stared at her, as though she had suddenly appeared in front of his eyes. "What—"

"No, not a man at all," said Rose. "You're a toad, a nasty toad with skin like leather, and you eat flies."

"You don't live here," said Melody. "You live in the swamp by the Picketts' house, where the water is dark and still."

Somewhere, in some other country, where we were still Justina, Rose, Melody, and Emma, instead of witches, we thought, but we haven't learned transformations yet.

"That's right," said Emma. "Go home, toad. Go back to the swamp where you belong. You don't belong here."

"Sophie," he said, looking at Mouse. "I'm your father, Sophie." He looked at her as though, for once, asking for something, asking with fear in his eyes.

"You know you are, Papa," she said. "You know you're a toad. I've tried to love you, but you haven't changed. You'll always be a toad in your heart."

"Go home, toad," said Justina. "We don't want you here any-more."

"Yes, go back to your swamp," said Melody. "And I hope Jim Pickett catches you one day, and Mrs. Pickett puts you into her supper pot. The Picketts like toad. They say it tastes like chicken."

Mouse's father, the drunkard, hopped out through the door and away, we assumed in the direction of the swamp. We let out a sigh, together, as though we had been holding our breaths all that time.

We made Mouse a bed in the cottage, on the green sofa. Emma said, "Callie won't let me have any more food. Since the revival came, she says she's found religion, and she's got jewels waiting for her in heaven that are more beautiful than earthly trinkets. She's given me back my rings and necklaces." So Rose stole some bread and jam from the cup-board when Hannah wasn't looking, and Mouse ate bread with jam until she was full. Melody gave her a dress, because the rest of us were too big, although Melody didn't have many dresses of her own. Emma brought soap and water so Mouse could wash her face, and combed her hair. Properly combed, it was as fine and flyaway as milkweed.

Before we went home to our suppers, Melody read to her from *The Poetical Works of Keats*, which Emma had taken out of the library for her, while the rest of us curled up on the sofa in tired silence.

"Good night," said Mouse, when we were leaving. "Good night, good night." And because she was one of us now, we knew that she was happy.

The next day, Rose and Melody were punished for taking bread and jam without permission and for losing a perfectly good dress, which Hannah had just darned.

∾

"THE NEXT LESSON," said Miss Gray, "is gaining your heart's desire. For which you will need a potion that includes hearts. Today, I want you to go out and find hearts."

"You don't want us to kill squirrels, or something?" said Emma, incredulously.

"Don't be ridiculous," said Miss Gray. "Have you learned nothing at all this summer? The heart is the center, the essence, of a thing. It is what gives a stone gravity, a bird flight. Killing squirrels, indeed!" She looked at us with as much disgust as on the first day, when we had failed to see ourselves in the mirror. It was not fair—Emma had asked the question, and the scorn was addressed to us all. But when had Miss Gray ever been fair?

So out we went, looking for hearts.

This was what we put into our potions. Into Melody's potion, she put all the plays of Shakespeare, with each mention of the word "heart" underlined in red, and each mention of the word "art" as well, even the art in "What art thou that usurp'st this time of night?"; *The Poetical Works of Keats* with each page cut into hearts; and a butterfly that she had found dead on her windowsill, a Red Admiral. With its wings outstretched, it looked like two hearts, one upside down. And we knew that Justina had been right: we were invisible that summer. Otherwise, Emma would have had to spend her pocket money on library fines. Emma put in the double yolk of an egg she had stolen from under the hens, which she insisted resembled a heart; chocolate bonbons that Callie had shaped into hearts; Cocoanut Kisses that we told her had nothing to do with hearts, but she said that she liked them; and hearts cut out of a Velvet Cake, all stolen from a Ladies' Tea that her mother was giving for the Missionary Society. Rose put in a heart-shaped locket that her mother had given her; her mother's rose perfume, which she said was the heart of the rose (the laboratory smelled of it for days); and water from the icebox that she had laboriously chipped into the shape of a heart. Mouse's potion contained a strange collection of nuts and seeds: acorns; beechnuts, butternuts, and black walnuts; the seeds of milkweed and thistle; locust pods; the cones of hemlock and cypress; and red hips from the wild roses that grew by Slocumb's Bluff. "Well," she said, "Miss Gray did say that the heart is the center. You can't get much more centery than seeds, can you?" Justina's collection was the strangest of all: when Miss Gray asked for her ingredients, she handed Miss Gray a mask shaped like a heart on which she had sewn, so that it was completely covered, the feathers of crows. "The crows gave them to me," she told us later, when we asked her where the feathers had come from, "once I explained what they were for. They seemed to know Miss Gray."

"Nicely done," said Miss Gray. "I think Justina's spell will be the strongest, since she has been the most focused among you, although one can't quite call this a potion, can one? But Emma's and Melody's potions will do quite well, and Mouse, I'll help you with yours."

"And mine?" asked Rose. If she had done something wrong, she wanted to know.

"Yours is complicated," said Miss Gray. "We'll have to wait and see."

∿

YEARS LATER, EMMA asked, "Rose, did you ever get your heart's desire?" They were walking in the garden of the house where Emma lived with her husband, the senator. Above them, the maples trees were beginning to turn red and gold. Whenever the wind shook the maple branches, leaves blew down around them.

"That's funny," said Rose, reminding herself not to think of her deadline. This was Emma, whom she hadn't seen in—how long? Her deadline could wait. "I don't think we ever told each other what we wished for. I guess what happened afterward drove it out of our heads."

"I suppose you wanted to fly," said Emma. "I remember—you were obsessed with flying, then."

Rose laughed. "I thought I was so good at keeping it secret!" She stopped and looked out over the lawn, where the shadows of the trees were lengthening. Soon, it would be time to dress for dinner. She worried, again, about her gray merino. Would it do for Rose's party? "No," she said, "I wished that my mother would love me. You remember what she was like, even at the end. What a strange thing to admit, after all these years."

"I wished that I could eat all I wanted and never get fat." Emma absentmindedly pulled a maple leaf from her hair, which was bobbed in the current fashion.

"Well, you got your wish, at least. There's no one in Washington as elegant as Mrs. Balfour." Rose looked at Emma, from her expensively waved hair to her expensively shod feet, in the new heels. "How do you like being a senator's wife?"

Emma let the leaf fall from her fingers. "Has the interview started already?" Rose laughed again, uncomfortably. Nothing is as uncomfortable, her editor had told her, as the truth. Emma continued, and to Rose her voice sounded bitter, almost accusatory, "So did she ever tell you that she loved you?"

How much easier it was, to answer questions instead of asking them. To pretend, for one afternoon, that she was here only as Emma's guest. "No, she never told me. But she did love me, I think, in her own way. It took me a long time to understand that. It wasn't a way I could have understood, as a child."

"Understanding—that's not much of a spell."

Emma sat on a bench beside the ornamental pond, where ornamental fish, red and gold, were darting beneath the fallen leaves. After a moment, Rose sat beside her. She looked at the patterns made by lichen on the ornamental urns, then at the statue of Melpomene, whose name on the pedestal was almost obscured by moss. She did not know how to respond.

"Have you heard from Melody?" asked Emma.

"Not since last spring," said Rose, grateful that Emma had broken the silence. "I don't think she'll ever come back. It's easier in Paris. She says, you know, there are no signs on the bathrooms. But I've brought you a copy of her latest. It's still in my suitcase. I meant to unpack it, but I must be losing my memory. You'll like it—one of the poems is about being a witch. I think that's what she asked for, to be a poet. It's still hard to imagine: Melody, the studious, the obedient one, in Paris cafés with artists and musicians, and girls who dance in beads! Drinking and—did you know? Smoking!"

Emma picked up a piece of gravel and tossed it into the pond, where it splashed like a fish. The sound was almost startling in the still afternoon. "It broke up the group, didn't it? When she left for college. I miss her."

Rose stared up at the leaves overhead, red and gold against the sky. "I think it was broken before that."

"We all paid a price, didn't we?" asked Emma. "Do you remember the advertisement? Reasonable rates. She never charged us, but I think we all paid a price. You—all those years taking care of your mother while she had cancer, when you could have been, I don't know, going to college, getting married, having a life of your own. Melody—she'll never come home. If she did, she wouldn't be a poet, just another colored woman who has to sit at the back of the theater. And me—"

Emma picked up another piece of gravel, then placed it on the bench beside her. "I can't gain weight, you know. No matter what. I've tried. Such a silly problem, but—I don't think James and I will ever have children."

"Oh, Emma!" said Rose. "I'm so sorry." What did her article matter? Emma had been her best friend, so long ago.

"Well, that's the way of the world," said Emma, her voice still bitter. Then suddenly, surprisingly, because this was Emma after all, she wiped her eyes, carefully so as not to smudge her mascara. "You gain and you lose, with every choice you make. That's the way it's always been. But you—" She turned to Rose and smiled, and suddenly she was the old Emma again. "All those years giving sponge baths and making invalid trays, when you barely stepped off the front porch, and now a reporter! Do you remember when we were reporters? Just before we were witches."

"I don't know if the society pages count," said Rose. "Although I suppose everyone has to start somewhere. If only we had stayed reporters! But come to think of it—I really am losing my memory—I have news for you. I've heard of Justina! A friend of mine, a real reporter, who was in Argentina covering the revolution—they're having another one this year—wrote me about an American woman who had married one of the revolutionaries, a man they call—why do revolutionaries always have these sorts of names?—The Mask. They call her *La Serenidad*, and there's a song about her that they play on the radio. He wrote it down for me, but I don't know Spanish."

"Now isn't that Justina all over?" said Emma, laughing. It was the first time, Rose realized, that she had heard her laugh all afternoon. After a pause, during which they sat in companionable silence, Emma continued, "Did you ever hear—"

"No," said Rose. "You?"

"No."

It grew dim under the maple trees, and the air grew chill. Emma drew her shawl about her shoulders, and Rose put her hands into her jacket pockets. They sat thinking together, as we had so long ago, when we were children—wondering what had happened to Mouse.

༄

EMMA HEARD THE news first, at breakfast. Her mother had just said, "Would you like some butter on your toast? Or maybe some jam? You look so nice and thin in that dress. Is it the one Aunt Otway brought from Raleigh?" when Callie came into the morning room and said, "Judge Beaufort, come quick! There's thieves in Ashton. They've gone and murdered Mrs. Balfour, and they'll murder us too, Lord have mercy on our souls!"

"What?" Emma's father rose from the breakfast table. "Who told you this?"

"Mrs. Balfour's Zelia. She stayed just to tell me, then ran on back to help. She's already called Dr. Bartlett, though she says he won't be able to do anything for Mrs. Balfour, poor woman. Blood all over her, Zelia told me, like she sprung a leak. May she rest in the lap of the Lord."

"That's enough. Tell Henry to get Mr. Caldwell and Reverend Hewes, and meet me there." Then he was out the door.

"You haven't finished your boiled egg," said Adeline Beaufort. "Emma? Emma, where are you?"

We watched the events at the Balfour house, the largest house in Ashton, whose white columns leaned precariously left and right, from the top of a tulip poplar, the three of us—Emma, Rose, and Melody. We had looked for Mouse in the cottage, but she was nowhere to be found.

"I heard it all from Coralie," said Melody. "Henry's her sweetheart—at least, one of them. He said the front door was open, and when they went in, they found Mrs. Balfour lying on the parlor floor, with a bullet through her heart. There was blood all over the carpet, and a whole pile of silver, teaspoons and other things, scattered on the floor beside her. They think she heard the thief, then came down with the pistol that General Balfour had used in the war and found him going through the silver. He must have taken it away from her and shot her with it."

"Gruesome," said Emma. "Look, there's the hearse driving up from Pickett's Funeral Parlor."

"And they found Justina in a corner of the parlor, barely breathing, with marks around her neck. They think she must have come down too, and he must have tried to strangle her and left her for dead." Not even our imaginations could picture the scene. Surely death was for people we did not know?

Emma's father came out, with Dr. Bartlett, Reverend Hewes, and Henry. We knew what they were carrying between them: Mrs. Balfour, draped in a black sheet, leaving the house where so many of her ancestors had died with more decorum.

"If he had the pistol, why didn't he just shoot Justina?" asked Rose. "It seems like a lot of trouble, strangling someone. Do you think they'll let us see her?"

"No," said Emma. "Only Zelia can see her. That's what Papa said—she's just too sick. But why don't we look—" and we knew what she was going to say. Why don't we look in the mirror?

The cottage was surrounded by men from the tobacco fields, who had been summoned to form a posse. "Stay away from here, girls," said Judge Beaufort. "That thief's been sleeping in our cottage—can you believe his nerve? We found a blanket and some food, even some books. We think it may be old Sitgreaves, the one with that idiot girl. He hasn't been seen for a while. But it looks like he slept here last night. This time, we'll send him to the prison in Charlotte, and that girl of his should have gone to the asylum long ago. I'll make sure of it, when I find her. But until we catch him, don't you go walking out by yourselves, do you hear?"

We looked at each other in consternation, because—where was Mouse?

"Miss Gray," said Rose. "Let's go talk to Miss Gray."

The roses had fallen from the La Reine and lay in a heap of pink petals on the grass. The garden seemed unusually still. Not even bees moved among the honeysuckle.

"Something's not right," said Emma.

"Nothing's right today," said Rose. "Who wants to knock?" No one volunteered, so she knocked with the brass frog, which was as polished as always. But no one answered. Instead, the door swung open. It had not been locked.

The Randolph house was empty. The sofa in the parlor, where we had eaten with a witch for the first time, the table in the laboratory where we had sat, learning our lessons, all were gone. Even the cats, which had only been partially there, were wholly absent.

"It was all here yesterday," said Melody. "She was going to show us how to make dreams in an eggshell."

"I found something," said Rose. It was a note, in correct Spencerian script, propped on the mantel. It said:

Dear Emma, Rose, and Melody,

Please stop the milk. Don't forget to practice, and
don't worry. Sophia and I will take care of each other.

Sincerely,
Emily Gray

We looked at each other, and finally Melody said what we were all
thinking—"How did she know?" Because it was evident: Miss Gray
had known what would happen.

We went to Mrs. Balfour's funeral. Even Melody sat in one of the
back pews of the Episcopal Church, beside Hannah. The organist
played "Lead, Kindly Light." We ignored the sermon and stared at
the back of Justina's head, in the Balfour pew close to the chancel, and
then at her face as she walked up the aisle behind the coffin. She was
paler than we had ever seen her, as though she had become a statue
of herself. In the churchyard, she watched her grandmother's coffin
being lowered into the ground, and when Reverend Hewes said "Dust
to dust," she opened her hand and dust fell down, into the grave, on top
of the coffin. Then she placed her hand on her mouth and shrieked.

We found her in the privet grove that had been planted around
the grave of Emmeline Balfour, Beloved Wife and Mother. We didn't
know what to say.

Justina looked at us with the still, pale face of a statue. She had
never looked so beautiful, so like a Balfour. "I shot her," she said.
"She tried to strangle me—she said she saw the devil in my eyes. But
I had Grandpa's gun, I'd been carrying it in the pocket of my robe for
weeks, and I shot her through the heart." Then she half sat and half
fell, at the same time, slowly, until she was sitting on the grass, leaning
against the gravestone.

"But the masked man——" said Rose.

"And the silver——" said Emma.

"That was Zelia," she said. She looked at her hands as though she did not know what to do with them. "Zelia scattered the silver before she went to get Dr. Hewes. She told me to lie still, and that there'd been a thief. But there was no thief—only me!"

We were silent, then Melody said, "She must have been going mad for a long time. You could have told us."

We heard the privet shake. "Don't you pester her no more," said Zelia. "Allons, ma fille. Your duty here is done." She helped Justina up and put a shawl around her shoulders, then led her away. But just before they left the privet grove, Zelia turned back to us and said, "And don't you forget to stop the milk!"

The next day, as we hid behind an overgrown lilac in the Caldwells' garden, Emma told us that Justina was gone. "To Italy, to find her father, I think. Papa saw her off on the train. Zelia was going with her."

Melody said, "I warned you about eating with witches. First Mouse and then Justina. It's as though they've disappeared off the face of the earth."

"Italy's not off the face of the earth," said Emma.

"It might as well be," said Rose. "And it's all her fault—Miss Gray's. I wish she'd never come to Ashton."

Eventually, when it looked like the thief who had killed Mrs. Balfour, whether or not it was old Sitgreaves, would never be found, we were allowed into the cottage again. The first thing we did was look into the mirror—it was the only mirror we could look in, all three of us, without arousing suspicion. "Show us Justina," we said, and we saw her on the deck of a ship, looking out over the Atlantic, with the wind blowing her hair like a golden flag. But when we said "Show us Mouse and Miss Gray," all we saw was a road through a forest of birches, with a low mist shifting and swirling beneath the light of a pale sun.

We practiced, at first. But Emma's mother decided it was time for her to come out into Ashton society, so she spent hours having dresses made and choosing cakes. Emma said that the latter made up, in chocolate, for the boredom of the former. And Melody said that she had to prepare for school, although she spent most of her time scribbling on bits of paper that she would not show us. Rose practiced the longest, and for the rest of that summer she could fly out of her bedroom window, which she did whenever she was sent to her room for punishment. But eventually we could no longer talk to birds, or turn gold into pebbles, or see the Battle of Waterloo in a mirror. We realized that we would never be witches. So the next summer, we became detectives.

ACKNOWLEDGMENTS

I would like to thank my classmates and instructors at the Odyssey writing workshop, who taught me that writing is a craft as well as an art—especially Jeanne Cavelos, without whose comments and advice I might never have written a publishable story. I would also like to thank my classmates and instructors at the Clarion writing workshop, who taught me to think of myself as a writer. I would particularly like to thank the following writers, who read one or more of these stories at some point in their composition and whose comments made them better than I could have by myself: Richard Butner, James Cambias, Ted Chiang, F. Brett Cox, L. Timmel Duchamp, Gavin Grant, Alexander Irvine, Alexander Jablokow, James Patrick Kelly, John Kessel, Ellen Kushner, Geoffrey Landis, Shariann Lewitt, Kelly Link, Maureen McHugh, Steven Popkes, Mary Rickert, Benjamin Rosenbaum, Christopher Rowe, Delia Sherman, Vandana Singh, David Smith, Sarah Smith, and Mary Turzillo. I am grateful to Luís Rodrigues, who turned a bunch of stories into a book, and Sean Wallace, who courageously published that book, as well as to Virginia Lee, who allowed us to use her gorgeous art on the cover. And I am particularly grateful to Terri Windling, for her encouragement over the years and for writing an introduction that makes me sound more interesting than I usually find myself. My thanks to them all. And finally, I would like to thank my husband Kendrick, who read these stories first and always commented on them candidly, and my daughter Ophelia, who inspires me every day.